MW01169649

The Writer's Romance

ELSA KURT

Copyright© 2018 Elsa Kurt
All Rights Reserved
ISBN-13: 978-1986477093

DEDICATION

To my husband, always.

CONTENTS

ACKNOWLEDGMENTS

First and foremost, my gratitude goes to the town of East Hampton, Connecticut, for being such a charming and perfect setting for my story. It was from the very first time we drove along Lake Pocotopaug that I knew I wanted a story based there. Thank you to Sheri Spalding, owner of the historical 95 Main building—once the site of Siebert's Opera House and place of my very first book signing event—for letting me include the location. I'd have been remiss had I not sent my characters to ECO coffee shop across the street and Po's Rice and Spice next door, so thanks for being such cool places. Similar thanks go to Angelico's Lakehouse. We've enjoyed our many visits there, where we did indeed see the legendary CT Blues Hall of Famer Jeff Pitchell on several occasions. Thank you to Jeff and Betsy Pitchell for allowing me to give Jeff a cameo. Lastly, thank you to my team of Beta readers who help me make a better story. Mary Ellen, Jen, and Carol…you guys rock.

Despite having plenty of 'visual inspiration,' The Writer's Romance is a work of fiction. Aside from the aforementioned, the characters are fictional and not based on any one specific person, but rather a composite of many. Any similarity between them and real persons, are coincidental.

ELSA KURT

PROLOGUE

Mitch watched Katharine dash from the stage but could do nothing to stop her. The hosts had drawn him into a conversation—none of which he could recall after—and he'd missed his chance to speak to her. This was supposed to have been the moment when they shook hands and let bygones be bygones, and yet Mitch was once again left ravaged in the wake of Hurricane Katharine. He said as much to Sam when he pulled up to the station's front entrance.

"So, how'd it go?" Sam asked as Mitch closed the passenger door.

"That woman—" he began, throwing his cap onto the floor mat at his feet.

"Uh-oh. Here we go."

Mitch ignored Sam's lament and launched into a thirty-minute diatribe of Everything Awful About Katharine Evans.

"Uh-huh. All I really hear is, you really, *really* like this chick."

Mitch opened his mouth, ready to rebuke the accusation, then sighed and laughed a little. "Yep. I suppose I do. She's smart, beautiful, in great shape, and turns out she's philanthropic, too. I mean, who'd have thought *that*?"

"Yeah, well—"

"But she's also hot-tempered, rude, and demanding. Don't you think so?"

"I kind of—"

"I mean, I guess I did provoke her a little bit. But we made up for it with that video. Right?"

Sam said nothing.

"I said, right, Sam? Why aren't you answering me, Sam?"

"Oh, are you done? Can I speak now?"

Mitch looked contrite. Yes, he'd gone on a tangent. Katharine Evans seemed to have this effect on him quite often. He let Sam speak. Halfway through, his mind wandered back to that confounding woman and what she might be doing right then…

2

ONE

TALL, DARK, & IRRITATING

Katharine Evans blinked slowly, her eyes wide and unfocused. Everything in her peripheral was fuzzy, but the window sill, where her gaze had transfixed, was sharp and clear. A deep scratch against the dark wood grain. A fine layer of dust. A thumbtack. *Why is there a thumbtack on the window sill?* The words 'window sill' began repeating slowly in her head, drawn out. A distant little voice in her head sang out, 'you're stalling.' Still, she didn't move. The house was quiet, the world outside her window equally so. It wouldn't last much longer. As if on cue, a loud *clack* echoed across the lake, bouncing off the houses in a quick staccato. Katharine jumped, then sat up straighter in her home office chair. *Focus, now. Ugh.* She looked at the computer screen. *Five hundred words, that's all I've written. I can barely sit still for five minutes, let alone the hours it's going to take to get this done.*

Katharine's editor expected *twenty* thousand. By tomorrow. The all-too-familiar fluttering of moth wings in her chest began, but Katharine quelled it with sound logic and reason. *Relax. You've got twelve pages of archived material. Send them some of that, if you must.*

At the rate she was going, she might have to do precisely that. The loud noise seemed to have worked as an alarm clock for not only Katharine but for Mother Nature's creatures as well. The chatty whistles of chickadees, the harsh squawk of a blue jay, and the caw of a crow in the trees had begun in earnest. She'd pushed open the curtains the moment she walked into the room, and now a gentle breeze trembled the edges of the thin, lacy material, carrying the scent of freshly cut grass and adding even more distraction for Katharine. No matter how many times she tore her eyes away, the view of the lake kept calling her attention from the keyboard and the blinking cursor on the screen. Outside the window, down and across her lovingly landscaped, rectangle yard, the early morning sunlight danced on the rippling currents. The blue sky gave the dark water a cobalt hue. Her mind drifted again. Twirling a long strand of caramel-colored hair between her thumb and fingertip, she leaned back against the chair's backrest and stared forlornly through the mesh screen. *Well, when you live year-*

round in a lakeside house, these are your distractions. Better than the city any day. Slowly, Katharine pulled her gaze away, but a glimpse of cherry red through the row of privacy bushes caught her eye. Her kayak. It was a perfect morning for a paddle around the lake. Hardly anyone would be out there on a weekday. Abruptly, Katharine forced herself to sit up straight and spoke aloud.

"No. Nope, not an option, kid. Katharine Evans, get back to work."

As a rule, Katharine avoided talking aloud to herself, but she needed a jolt to get focused. With a dramatic sigh, she looked around the sunny room, seeking the inspiration her storyboard wasn't offering. Her office was like another universe compared to the rest of her small bungalow. The other rooms were decorated in rich, warm earth tones, conveying a warm cabin-like atmosphere. This space was bright, with floral prints and lace accents. *Shabby chic.* That's what they called it. Whoever 'they' were. It wasn't really her style, but it *was* her book's main character's style. Chelsea Marin, teen 'it girl.' Now into book three of a series with no definite end in sight.

Not that Katharine was complaining, of course. Sure, young adult wasn't the genre she set out to write, but it *was* the one that brought in the money for her to live the way she liked. Alone. Secluded. Undisturbed. The doorbell rang. *Of course, the doorbell would ring right now.* Katharine ignored it. Then the knocking began. Incessantly. She stood with a scowl and tip-toed down the stairs and into the living room, so she could peek out the window.

These curtains were still drawn against the morning sun, so she pushed them aside enough to peek one eye out. A long-faced young man stood at the door and looked right at her. It was her handyman…whose name she'd forgotten immediately after he introduced himself on his first day working for her. Since he reminded her of Shaggy from Scooby-Doo, she'd taken to calling him that. Not to his face, of course. Shaggy smiled brightly with a lopsided grin and waved as if anything about her manner was welcoming. Katharine dropped the curtain back in place and jumped back.

"Hello? Uh, good morning," his voice cracked on 'morning.'

So fitting, he sounds like Shaggy, too.

"Go away. No one's home."

"Mrs. Evans? You— I know you're home. You just answered me."

Katharine swung her front door open so hard it blew back her hair.

"It's *Miss* Evans, and there is a sign—see it? Right there," She rapped a short, unpolished nail on the hotel style door hanger for emphasis.

"I—yes, I know. But you said if—"

"I said, if you had an emergency, you could knock. You're not bleeding, are you?"

"No, I—"

"No broken bones?"

"No, but—"

"But what? What could be so important, that you have to disturb me after I specifically said *not* to?"

"Well, uh, there's a guy here? I mean not here, but next door. He asked me to give you a message?"

Katharine blinked at the man-boy posing statements as questions at her. What the heck was his name again? *Think, Katharine. Brad? No. Brennan? No. Brandon*! *That's his name*. He'd been her handyman for the past six months, longer than anyone else had lasted. She supposed the least she could do was remember his name.

"Brandon. Do you recall what I said to you when I hired you?"

"Uh, yes." He held up a grass and dirt streaked hand and ticked off each rule as he went. "Do not disturb you unless I'm bleeding, broken, having a heart attack, or being murdered. Payment is in the mailbox. Text any questions or concerns."

Brandon nodded and smiled like he'd correctly recited the Gettysburg address. Katharine closed her eyes and pinched the thin cartilage at the bridge of her nose. After she'd counted to five in her head, she looked up again at Shaggy—*Brandon.*

"So, why. Are. You. Here? On my doorstep?"

"Oh, right! Well, the guy— the one next door— he said I should, um, give you a heads up? Or something like that."

Brandon frowned a little, perhaps trying to recall what '*the guy*' told him to say. Katharine's patience, what little there was to begin with, was at its end.

"Okay, listen. First, the only person next door is a crotchety old man—Vincent Genoma. Second, Genoma and I have spoken *once* in all six years that I've lived here. It was to agree on Arborvitae bushes as a divider between properties. *His* property is a blight, *mine* is private. We leave each other alone. That's the deal. There is no 'heads up' to give here."

"Oh, this guy—the one I talked to? He's not old. I mean, not old like that. He's older than me. Maybe like your age. Or old—"

"Brandon?"

"Right. Yeah, anyhow. He's the guy on T.V. You know, the one who fixes up houses for people? Cool, right?"

"The guy who what? I have no idea what you're talking about, Brandon. Do me a favor. Tell him to do whatever the heck he wants, so long as it doesn't affect me."

Brandon looked over his shoulder, then back at Katharine. His disheveled, strawberry blond hair fell over his eyes, and he shook it away. He shifted from one work boot-clad foot to the other and scratched the small, stubble-free circle on his chin. His mouth opened and closed, and his Adam's apple bobbed, but no sound came out. It seemed he had more to say but hadn't yet worked out what it was.

Katharine had all she could take, so with a terse smile, she stepped back into the safe confines of her home and began to close her door on the lanky man. She ignored Brandon's attempt to step forward, and the envelope he held up. The second before the door clicked shut, a loud motorized whine ripped through the quiet. Katharine whipped the door open again and sprang through the frame, nearly knocking Brandon over.

"What is that? What the *hell* is that?"

"That's what I was trying to warn you," he yelled over the noise. "He, uh, he's clearing the overgrowth on Mr. uh, Genoma's property. They're gonna fix up his house."

"Fix his house?"

Brandon shrugged and backed his way off Katharine's front porch, dropping the envelope as he did. "Sorry, Mrs.—I mean Miss Evans, I don't know anything more. You'll have to ask him, I guess."

Katharine grabbed the dirt-streaked paper from the porch, turned on her heel, and stomped back inside, slamming the door against Brandon's apologies. She ripped the seal open, muttering to herself the whole time. "*T.V.* guy. House *fixer-upper*. *Over*growth. Give me… a break." Then she quickly unfolded and read—or rather skimmed— the notice inside.

The date in the corner told her it had been hand-delivered several weeks ago and stated the intentions of DGTV to film an episode of one of their reality shows in the neighborhood. Why it was in the hands of her handyman, she had no idea. At the very end of the notice, it stated that—if she had a complaint to file— she had ten days to do so. *That* would have been two weeks ago. She was out of luck.

We'll see about that.

She pulled on her garden boots as she grumbled, not caring if she was still in her pajama shorts. Or that her off-the-shoulder t-shirt practically screamed 'I heart the eighties.' Then she threw her long hair in a quick, high pony-tail. A fast glance in the hall mirror told her she looked like she was a thirty-four-year-old going on fourteen, but she didn't care. There was no way she could work with that kind of racket going on.

"It's not even eight in the morning. This is not happening. Not today, damn it. No way, buddy. No way." She was out the door and stomping across her lawn in a flash, muttering and swearing the whole way. Brandon had busied himself at the lilac bushes, giving surreptitious side glances at her as she stormed past. He knew better than to say anything more. She was terrifying for such a tiny woman.

Katharine shoved her way through the deer-sized opening between the two yards. Once through to old man Genoma's side, she began to look for the source of the horrible noise. The front lawn—if that's what it could be called—halted her. It had at least a full summer's worth of tall, dry grass. Car skeletons and old tires littered the ground like a forgotten graveyard. A moss-covered birdbath leaned against a rusted metal ladder like two drunks in a bar. There was an ancient looking lawnmower at the edge of the cracked asphalt driveway where it had likely died on the spot. The house itself—once a charming bungalow like hers—was weather worn and sagging. A long strip of rusted aluminum gutter had pulled away from the roof and hung at a jaunty angle. One distressed, barn-red shutter dangled beside a cardboard blocked window. Like everything else, they were faded by sun and neglect.

Katharine shook her head in disbelief. She knew it was run down six years ago—when she and the old man had their one and only run in—but it had gotten much worse since. Like Katharine's house, Genoma's home was set way back from their narrow, winding road. Tall evergreens and thick bushes blocked all but the sudden opening of the driveway, which curved in a way that made it near impossible for a passerby to casually see in. To view more than a sliver of property, you would have to pull into the drive and follow the bend. It was precisely why Katharine had fallen in love with her own house the first time she looked at it with the realtor.

"Wow, Genoma. This is bad," she whispered.

The clamor of machinery had momentarily stopped, and male voices volleyed back and forth from the backyard. Katharine followed the sounds, taking cautious steps over and around the debris, thankful she'd worn her boots. There were several fresh, deep tire tracks in the trampled grass alongside the house, leading her into the back. Katharine stopped short at the sight that met her when she rounded the bend. A television crew, excavation machinery and a dozen or so of workboot and helmet-clad men milled about. A few had chainsaws, two had large video cameras, and others had clipboards. They were all taking orders and instruction from a man in an old baseball cap and faded blue jeans. He leaned casually against a large, mustard-yellow piece of equipment, gesturing at various points around the yard.

The moment Katharine's eyes alighted on the man in the baseball cap, she trudged over to him, determined to put a stop to the ruckus. She ignored the stares and a couple of low whistles aimed in her direction, keeping her eyes on the target. A voice in her head spoke unbidden.

Hello, Mr. Nice Jeans. She shook her head against it. *Nope.*

By the time she reached him, he'd already climbed back into the cab of the yellow beast and had started it up. It roared to life, setting her teeth on edge.

"Hey!" Katharine's voice broke as she called out. She didn't have the kind of voice meant for yelling. It had a rasp to it and was a little on the low side. It embarrassed her growing up with a voice like that. People always laughed a little and made comments like, 'what's a dainty thing like you doing with that voice?' As if she'd had a say in the matter. It was no surprise the man in the baseball cap could neither hear nor see her. She tried again, twice more. Katharine looked around. No one seemed to be paying the slightest bit of attention to her now. Frustrated, Katharine grabbed the first thing her eyes landed on—a filthy, deflated soccer ball—and whipped it at his leg. It whopped him on the side of the head. He threw his hand up in surprise and looked for the source of the projectile. When his eyes met hers, her heart did the cliched somersault. They were cornflower blue and seemed to look right inside her. *Cornflower blue? Wow, how lame. Some writer you are. Oh, my God, he's good looking. Stop staring, you dummy.*

Without taking his eyes away from Katharine, he turned off the machine, then turned in his seat to face her. The crew stood mostly silent but for a handful of guffaws and amused calls of, 'uh-oh, Mitch.' He shushed them with a wave of his hand. Still, his twinkling eyes stayed locked on Katharine's green ones.

"Did you just throw—a soccer ball at my head?" Instead of being angry, he looked amused. A smirk tugged at the corners of his mouth, causing the dimple in his cheek to deepen. His ridiculously swoon-worthy eyes crinkled at the edges. Katharine was momentarily dumbstruck.

Rugged. That's the word for Mr. Nice Jeans. Get ahold of yourself. He's the reason you're not working on your book right now, remember?

"I—no. Well, yes. I was aiming for your leg, though."

"Oh. I see. And…*why* were you aiming for my leg, may I ask?"

A short guy wearing his baseball cap backward and his well-worn Boston Red Sox t-shirt untucked came around from behind Katharine with a large camera perched on his shoulder. He turned his round lens in her face. He grinned and chomped his gum and rolled his hand at her. She stared at him. He yanked his head back, away from the eyepiece and mouthed, 'keep talking.'

"What? I—get that thing off me, will you?" To the man in the machine, "Can you tell him to get lost please?"

"Sam, buddy, back it up a bit, will ya?" He turned back to Katharine. "Okay, lady. We're on a time schedule here. What can I do for you, hmm? Do you want an autograph?"

"A—an autograph? *What*? No, I—"

"Yo, Eddie, get this lovely lady a promo cap," he called over her head.

"I don't want an autograph, I want you to stop this racket. *Now*."

"Stop? I don't—" He paused, and gave her a harder look, then he slapped his knee and wagged a finger at her, squinting a little. "Ohhh, you're the mean neighbor lady, aren't you?"

"Mean neighbor lady? Me? *Mean*? I beg your pardon!" Katharine was mortified. And furious. *Her*, mean? And did she actually say, 'I beg your pardon'?

"Are you the one next door? With the fortress of Arborvitaes? And No Trespassing signs every three feet?"

Katharine crossed her arms in front of her chest and cut her eyes away. Then she thrust her chin and arched her eyebrow at him. "So, it's 'mean' to appreciate privacy, now? Great. In that case, fine. Yes, I'm the mean neighbor lady, and I am trying to work over at my mean neighbor lady house, so if you could save the noise for, oh, I don't know... never? That'd be great, thanks."

From up on his steel perch, he looked at her in disbelief. Then he lifted his cap off his head and raked back his wavy dark hair. She could see it was peppered with grey, more so at the temples. Her favorite look. Distinguished.

Oh, my God, stop focusing on his looks.

"Let me get this straight, sweetheart. You want an entire construction and production company—ones which are not on *your* property—to stop labor because you're *trying to work*? Is that what you're saying to me?"

He climbed out of the cab and hopped down in two swift moves and strode towards her. The smirky grin hadn't left his lips, but his eyes took on a steely glint. She put her hands on her hips and widened her stance. Katharine was not going to be intimidated by this six-foot-tall, solid hunk of a man.

Ugh, you just thought of him as a 'hunk of a man.' Stop it, Katharine. You write teen romance, not live it.

When he stopped mere inches from her, Katharine had to crane her neck. It was impossible not to notice that he towered over her. He lowered his voice so only she could hear. Well, she and the steadily inching forward cameraman, that is.

"Lady, I don't know what it is *you're* working on, but what *I'm* working on is keeping a crew of thirty men in business. *I'm* working on a remodel that's going to change a young couple's life for the better. I'm working on making *my* living, too. So, I do apologize if that conflicts with your plans, but I'm afraid it's not on *my* list of priorities today. You had a chance weeks ago to lodge a complaint. No one did. Now, if there's nothing else I can do for you here, I'm going to have to ask you to leave.

Unless you'd like a hard hat and a chainsaw, that is?"

Katharine's hands dropped to her sides and balled into two small, tight fists. She set her full mouth in a hard line and slit her eyes up at him. "Well, if that wasn't the most backhanded apology I've ever heard! You know what? Thanks for nothing." Katharine began to walk away, then turned and marched back. "No, that's not true. Thanks for ruining my day and for likely causing me to lose my advance, too." His insipid expression infuriated her even more, but all she could think to say was, "Keep your stupid chainsaw and your ugly hardhat and have fun on your obnoxious excavator."

Katharine gave him a mirthless, tight smile. He took a step toward her, but she turned quickly— flicking her ponytail in his face—and stomped away, back towards the front of the house.

"You're welcome! Oh, and it's a bulldozer," he called after her.

She spun around as best she could in her garden boots and glared. "What?"

"It's a bulldozer. Not an excavator. In case you wanted to know. And my name's Mitch, by the way."

The smirk was back on his lips. Katharine threw her hands out and narrowed her eyes at him again, then shook her head.

"I don't care what it—or *you*—are called. Goodbye!" Katharine took several steps backward as she spoke. It was a poor choice considering the state of the yard. One moment Katharine was upright, and the next she was staring up at the blue sky from ground level, the wind knocked out of her. She'd stepped back into a deep rut, no doubt caused by the ginormous tires on the stupid machine. There was no way to save face. Now the only thing rivaling Katharine's outrage was mortification. Mitch strode over to her with an air of forbearance as if she'd fallen on purpose. She warded off the outstretched hand and righted herself with as much dignity as she could muster.

"Are you—"

"I'm *fine*, thank you." Katharine hissed through gritted teeth. She wasn't fine, her insides were jangled up and she'd barely gotten her breath back. Knowing full well she was covered in dirt, she held her head high and tramped away, ignoring the sharp pain in her diaphragm as best she could. This time she watched where she was walking. She also suspected that Mitch's eyes—and at least half the crews' eyes—were still on her. He confirmed her suspicion when he called out once more to her.

"Bye, now! Have a great day! Oh, hey…" His sharp call didn't garnish even a pause in her step. She refused to reply.

***

Mitch Ford bent down and retrieved a rectangular object from the rut where Katharine had fallen. He brushed the dirt off a pink phone case, which caused the screen to illuminate. "Katharine Evans, hmm? Okay, Ms. Evans, looks like I'll be seeing you again, won't I?"

TWO

FROM BAD TO WORSE

"Where is it? Where is my stupid phone?"

Katharine had been searching for the last hour, retracing her steps throughout the house from the time she awoke. She was also speaking aloud to herself again. She really needed to get a dog. It's easier to justify talking to a dog than yourself.

"I woke up, went to the bathroom. No, not there. Kitchen. Nope. Office. Not there. Shaggy—I mean *Brandon* showed up. I went next door..."

Her heart sank. Could she have dropped it in the jungle Genoma called a front yard? Or worse, in the *back*yard where that, *that man* was? It had been more than six hours since she'd gone over there and made a fool of herself. She couldn't go back now.

Although, the steady cacophony had recently stopped. Maybe they were all gone by now, and she could go search. She *was* ready for a break.

Somehow, despite the incessant drone of chainsaws and exca— *bulldozers,* she reminded herself— the loud shouts, and calls of testosterone overloaded men and slams of truck doors, she managed to squeeze out not quite half of the expected twenty-thousand-word count of the manuscript. Sure, it took a little help from some of the deleted text she kept on back up, but once she cleaned it up and rehomed it, it worked well enough for a first draft. She'd also cranked her headphones up, filling her head with the most current pop music—her 'mood music' for writing in the teen genre. Certainly not *her* taste, but it helped her churn out pages of age-appropriate vernacular for the young masses. Not the bare minimum of what she owed her editor, but she'd make sure she met her deadline in time. It probably wouldn't be her best work, but she had plenty of room and opportunity for improvement. *And* a solid track record for producing precisely what her publishing house was looking for. So far.

She'd intended on rewarding herself with a phone call to her brother, Nate. He'd be surprised to hear from her this early in the day. She could virtually hear his sweet voice in her mind, calling her his Kit-Kat. He was her Nate The Great, her big brother. He loved it when she called him that, *big brother*. Katharine's eyes stung with the threat of tears. She missed Nate. When he decided to move out on his own, Katharine was terrified for him.

While Down's Syndrome had hardly held him back from any goal he set, it was still a cruel world out there. Not everyone would treat him with the kindness and patience he deserved. It had been proven time and again over his forty years and her thirty-four. Bullies. Employers who took advantage of him. His health care providers. Jerks who found it funny to talk down to him.

Their mother, Alicia, was forty-five when she had Nate, their father, Nathanial, was fifty-five. He was their planned child, Katharine their surprise. They were late-in-life parents who doted on their two children. They did their very best in raising Nate and Katharine, but they weren't like modern-day late-in-life parents. Today, fifty is the new forty. Back then, fifty was, well, it was just fifty. They were kind, patient and gentle with Nate, but it was Katharine who took on many of the physical responsibilities. It never phased her that she was the younger sibling, doing what a parent or an older sibling would do. Nor did she ever think of Nate as being disabled in any way. No one could say otherwise in her presence. Nicky D'Amoti found out first hand. Katharine got into her first and only fist fight with him when she was nine. He was her age, but bigger. A lot bigger, but that didn't deter Katharine.

It was a crisp, fall afternoon and she and Nate had walked to the local park. Nate loved the swings most of all, and small Katharine was pushing the much larger Nate on one. Nicky was on the half court, tossing a basketball into the tattered net. Truth be told, Katharine knew he'd be there. She'd overheard him talking to his friends at school. Up until that day, she'd had something of a crush on Nicky D'Amoti, with his dark hair and coal black eyes. Not that she'd have ever told anyone. As Katharine had hoped, Nicky spotted them and came over, his basketball under one arm.

"Hi," said Katharine.

At first, Nicky said nothing. He merely watched Nate, his expression unreadable. Finally, he thrust his chin out and said, "What's *wrong* with him?"

Katharine had been asked this question before and was always able to respond with what her parents had taught her to say—there's nothing *wrong* with Nate. He's just different, that's all—and then everyone generally moved on. This time, though, her hackles rose. It wasn't the *question* that bothered her, it was the way it was asked. She stepped away from the swing, ignoring Nate's request of, 'again Kit-Kat, push me again' for the moment.

"What did you say?" she asked. She really did want to give Nicky a chance to correct himself. She wanted to keep liking him. But then he blew it.

"I *said*, what's *wrong* with him. Is he retarded, or something?"

Katharine closed the distance between them, her hands fisted at her sides. "What's wrong with *you*, jerkface?"

Nicky didn't get a chance to answer. As the word *jerkface* left her lips, so did her fist from her side. She punched Nicky D'Amoti square in the mouth, splitting his lip. His eyes widened in shock, his fingers touched his bleeding lip. Then his eyes narrowed, and he shoved Katharine so hard she fell backward onto the cold ground.

"Katharine," screamed Nate. He jumped off the swing and charged Nicky, plowing him down. They tangled and grunted in the dry leaves and dirt, and Katharine tried to pull them apart. Suddenly several more bodies were piling onto the trio. Nicky's friends had arrived and jumped in to help their buddy. They punched and kicked at Nate, who by then had curled up into a ball, crying. Katharine screamed and beat on their backs, legs, and anywhere she could.

"Get off him! Get OFF him! GET OFF HIM," she screamed, her voice raw.

They didn't stop until the bellowing voice of a man jogging by with his long-eared dog shouted out, "Hey! What's going on over there?"

The cowards sprang off Nate, knocking Katharine down once again. Then they scattered like roaches. Katharine scuttled on all fours to Nate—still curled up— and pet his head, tears streaming down her face. The man jogged over and knelt beside them.

"Hey, sweetie. Your nose is bleeding. Here." He handed her a tissue from his pocket, then helped Nate up. He checked him over, roughed up his hair a bit, and said, "You're okay, buddy. You're okay." And for the most part, they were. Nate had some bruises and a cut over his left eye. Katharine had no idea how she'd gotten the bloody nose, but it was numb, and her eyes kept watering. The man walked them home, letting Nate hold the basset hound's leash. It cheered him up considerably, and soon he'd stopped talking about the mean boys and instead asked all sorts of questions about the dog. When they reached the house, the man explained what he had seen to their parents.

"Nate, sweetheart, are you alright?" cried their mother.

"I'm okay, Mom. This is Romeo." Nate pointed to the dog, "Can we have a dog like him?"

Alicia cried and hugged both Katharine and Nate, and Nathanial took his car keys off the hook by the front door and left. Presumably to pay Nicky's parents a visit. Several hours later, he returned with a long-eared puppy and a shrug to his wife's questioning eyes. Katharine went up to her room and stayed there, not even coming out to see the puppy until everyone was sound asleep. Something had fractured inside her that autumn day, but it wasn't a bone.

It was the intangible *something* that allows us to trust and love. At the tender age of nine, Katharine Evans vowed she would never trust anyone besides Nate and her parents ever again. The only soul she told was the little puppy, whispering it in one of his long, silky ears that night as she curled up beside him in his doggy bed.

Life went on as usual afterward in the Evanses' home, but school was another story. The harassment began in earnest. Nate was in a school for kids with special needs, so Katharine took the brunt of it all. Every day was an ordeal, but she didn't like to worry her parents—they had enough to deal with— so she kept it bottled up. She was proud of the walls she'd built. Soon, she was like a glacier. Nothing touched her, no one moved her, except for Nate, of course.

When Katharine was twenty-two and Nate twenty-six, their father passed away. Their mother passed not long after. Nathanial and Alicia had financially planned for their children's inevitable future without them, and Katharine had promised them both she would always take care of Nate. She remembered thinking at her mother's funeral that it would be Katharine and Nate against the world from then on. Nate had other ideas.

While Katharine had turned away from humankind in general, Nate was the opposite. He loved everyone with abandon and openness. When people were cruel, he forgave them. When they misjudged his intellect, he educated them. Katharine was neither forgiving nor patient. No matter how often Nate told her not to get so disappointed by people—they didn't know any better—she found she couldn't help herself. Katharine had hung on to her nine-year-old self's sense of logic—no one can disappoint you if you don't let them in.

Katharine was so lost in her memories, that when the sound of the doorbell chimed, she jumped. Was it a coincidence that her last thought before the bell rang was 'let them in?' Could it have been a sign? Then she chased the silly notion away, reverting to her usual tendency toward annoyance. *Seriously? Twice in one day, someone's at my door. Great.*

This time, Katharine went to peer through the peephole, forgetting she'd rehung the 'do not disturb' sign over it so it would be impossible to miss. Clearly, that didn't work either. She cracked the door and peeked out through the opening. Whoever it was, was standing back, out of immediate view. She opened the door wider. Mud crusted work boots. Faded jeans. Powder blue button-down shirt, sleeves rolled to bare tanned, muscular arms. Tan neck…strong, square jaw, lips parted into a smile showing straight, white teeth. Those swoon-worthy blue eyes. *Him.* Her eyes dropped back down at his hands. One was wedged in his front pocket. The other held her phone.

"Hey, there. I think you dropped this? Earlier? Pretty sure none of the fellas have a pink phone case. And uh, you were the only woman around, so…"

"Rose-gold."

"I—what?"

"Rose-gold. The case. You called it pink."

Katharine stepped out onto the porch, closed the door behind her and crossed her arms in front of her chest. His presence on her porch disconcerted her. He made her skin feel hot and her heart…*flutter. Oh, come on. Heart flutters? A hunk of a man? This is ridiculous. Get him out of here. Quick, before you say something stupid.*

Mitch chuckled. "Rose…gold. Right. Anyhow, hope you don't mind my bringing it over to you. Your, uh, signs gave me pause for thought, I must say."

"Well, that is kind of the idea of No Trespassing signs, isn't it?" She meant it to sound teasing, light. Even to her own ears, it sounded brittle and discourteous. She was sorely out of practice in the banter department.

ELSA KURT

"Yeah. Well, anyhow, here's your phone. Sorry for…" Mitch glanced at the sign on the door, "disturbing you. Just trying to be a good Samaritan." He extended the phone. Katharine tore her eyes from his face long enough to take it. They'd both stepped forward at the same time, so when she grabbed it, her hand landed on his. He didn't pull away, nor did she. Their eyes locked. His eyes gleamed mischievously. Hers remained wary, guarded. The spell was broken by a shout from behind the bushes separating the two yards.

"Yo, Mitch! Calling it a day, man. See you tomorrow. Good luck with the mean lady! If you're lucky, she ain't home!"

Mitch yanked his hand from his pocket and tugged the visor of his cap to hide his eyes. It couldn't hide his smile, though. The smile infuriated Katharine all over again, and she whisked the phone and her hand away.

"Sorry 'bout that. Well, I'll be on my way. We'll, um, try to turn the volume down on the noisy machines tomorrow, Katharine."

He dared to wink when he said that. Then he turned away and started down the stairs. Katharine, the woman whose career was built on her ability to string sentences together, was speechless. As she gaped at him, he pivoted and pointed up at her phone.

"Oh, and Nate? He is one really cool dude. Tell him I enjoyed our conversation and his autographed hat is as good as in the mail!"

Nate? How did he…

Katharine looked down at her phone. Nate had called, and Mitch Whatever-His-Name-Was had answered. Now she understood how he knew her name.

"Hold it! You talked to my brother?" Her eyes narrowed. "About what?"

"Oh, you know. The weather. The Red Sox. My show. You."

"You talked to my brother? On my phone? About *me*?"

Mitch shrugged. "Among other things."

She refused to ask him what was said. She could only imagine. Nate was utterly unbeguiling and unfiltered, he'd answer any question asked of him with complete honesty. People took advantage of that all the time. If Mr. Big Shot T.V. Show guy thought he was slick, using a man with special needs like that, she would...

"Katharine? He's a sweetheart of a man. A pleasure to talk to. He thinks *you're* pretty special, too. Although he said—and I quote—he wishes you'd find a boyfriend and cut him some slack."

Before she could respond, her phone rang. It was Nate, again. She smiled at the picture that automatically came up anytime he called. It was them at the lake, standing waist deep in the water and making 'duck faces' for the camera. When she looked up again, Mitch was passing through the bushes and back to Genoma's yard. They'd still not properly introduced themselves to each other, and now had no reason to ever do so again. *Too bad.*

"Hey, Nate the Great! How you doin'?"

"Oh, crap. It's you." Nate's voice on the other end of the line was full of undisguised disappointment.

"Gee, thanks a lot. Um, who else would it be, buddy?"

"I was hoping my friend Mitch Ford had your phone still. I was going to tell him about our favorite fishing spot on Lake Pocotopaug. He said he likes fishing. I told him you like to go fishing, too."

"Oh, you did, huh? What else did you tell him, Nate?"

"I told him you're single and you write books for teenagers with hormones. And your favorite color is turquoise, and you hate roses."

"Wow, buddy. Thanks, I—"

"And your favorite actor is Cary Grant and you think most people suck. And that you couldn't tell time until you were eleven."

"Nate! I *could* tell time. Okay, fine—not on an analog clock. Why did you tell him so much about me?"

"Because he asked why you're so cranky. That's not the word he used though."

"Oh, really?"

Heat rose in Katharine's cheeks.

"Relax, Kit-Kat. I've heard swears before. And you can be a bit—"

"Alright, alright. I get it. Never mind your new friend Mitch Ford. What's new with you, hmm?"

Katharine and Nate talked for over an hour. He told her all about the latest fundraiser they'd done for their non-profit group—aptly called Nate's

Great Cause—and she detailed her most recent book for him. As their conversation came to an end, the familiar lump formed in her throat. Nate was only thirty miles away, but it may have well been five million. He didn't need her anymore. He was independent. Thriving. Maybe Nate *never* really needed her at all, and it was the other way around. *She* needed *him* as her buffer from the world.

"Katharine, don't start crying again. Everything is going to be okay. Isn't that what you always said to me?"

"Yes, yes. I know buddy. You're right. I'm fine, really. I love you Nate the Great.

"Love you, too, Kit-Kat."

They hung up with promises to talk the next day again. Katharine decided it was a perfect time for wine. The second her glass was poured, her phone chimed again. This time it was her dreaded publicist, on live chat, no less. With a quick sip and a sigh, she sat at the table and answered.

"Hey, Tori. To what do I owe this pleasure?"

"Oh, puh-lease, Katharine darling. I know you better than to think you view any call from me with pleasure."

Tori laughed at her own humor. Her hair filled most of the small frame.

"Love the new hairstyle, Tor."

"Mhmm. Goin' back to my roots, baby. Glad you like. Alright, you ready for some exciting news?"

Heavy dread filled Katharine's chest. Anything Tori found exciting would be an absolute trauma for Katharine.

"I suppose so…"

"Okay, drum roll, please!" Seeing there'd be none, she continued, no less enthused, "Girl, I got you on Connecticut Today with that cute little Steve what's his name and his pretty Marla something. And don't say no. You are contractually obligated to make these appearances. No ifs, ands, or buts. You hear?"

Katharine dropped her head onto the table.

"Oh, my word. Dramatic much? Relax, girl. It'll be over before you know it. Thursday, five a.m. sharp. Check your email for a press packet for the website. Books and promo will be on your doorstep tomorrow. Peace out, baby."

Tori ended the call while Katharine was in mid-shout.

"Next week? I'm not ready for that, Tori!"

Ooh, darn her!

Katharine's stomach began churning, and her wine lost all appeal. Live television. Answering questions about her books, her life, herself. In a week. "Noooooo," she called out into the empty room. Her voice bounced off the ceiling beams and around the house. It was a lonely sound. For the first time in a very long time, Katharine hated the solitude. *This has nothing to do with Mitch Ford. Oh, yeah? Then why was that your first thought? Shut up.* Now she was arguing with herself. Katharine really needed to get out more. Out of her head, *and* out of her house. And she knew right where to go.

***

Mitch left Katharine to her phone call and sprinted across the yard. Before he pushed through the narrow opening between Katharine and Genoma's yards, he turned back to look at her. She tucked a long, loose strand of golden-brown hair behind her ear and Mitch could see her smiling against the receiver.

My God, she's gorgeous when she smiles.

Mitch's heart swelled. The sensation caught him by surprise, and he began to smile. Then he shook his head. *Forget it, old man. She's got trouble written all over her.*

THREE

MEAN GIRLS GOOD

"Another round for my old friends, and my new ones, too!"

"Mitch, man, you're the best!"

"Yeah, sure. We'll see if you say that tomorrow morning at seven a.m."

Sam groaned into his beer glass. Then he perked up.

"Hey, what happened with the dragon lady next door?"

"Happened? Nothing happened. I brought her the phone."

Sam swiveled in his bar stool and turned his baseball cap backward. Mitch kept his eyes trained on the game on the television above the bar, knowing full well his ever-scruffy cameraman-slash-best friend was giving him *the look.*

"What, Samuel? Say it."

"You like her."

"Stop."

"Admit it. You like her."

"Nothing to admit. Drink your beer."

"Dude, you're not getting any younger. No offense."

"Funny how people say, 'no offense' immediately after saying something they know is offensive."

"You're deflecting, man. Come on. Just because Leanne was a crazy, ax-wielding, full on sociopath, it doesn't mean..."

"Thank you, Samuel. I get your point. Sociopaths, bad. Mean girls, good."

"Aww, stop it, Mitch. You said yourself—after you talked to her kid brother—there's more to her than meets the eye."

"Older brother."

"Huh? Sounded like you were talking to a kid. Whatever. Anyhow, all I'm saying is, you've been single a long time. Sparks flew between you and that chick. By the way, she looks great on tape."

"Did you just say 'chick?' That's so—wait, you saved that footage from today?"

"Yep. Cinematic gold. The fans will eat it up, bro."

"Don't you have to ask her permission to air it?" Mitch laughed. "Good luck with that."

"Ah, well, that's where you come in, my friend. Go on back over there tomorrow and turn on the old

Mitch Ford charm and she'll be eating out of your hand."

"She's not a horse, Sam. Geez."

"Nope, nope. You're totally right. That chick is a *fox*, man. Even looking like a girl in a WHAM video from the eighties, she was hot."

"WHAM, huh?"

Mitch let out a big hoot. The genuine kind that lit up his face and rolled like a wave, lifting everyone around him. The patrons closest by began smiling and chuckling too, even though they had no idea why. Crazy Leanne had told him once—much to his discomfort—he affected people that way everywhere he went. Folks wanted to be in on his joke and under his shoulder clap. He exuded charm and approachability the way sun radiated light and heat. Most importantly, it was sincere. It may have been the only genuinely nice thing she'd ever said to him.

The conversation got shelved, and the crowd filtered out to the tiki lounge outside. A local blues band would be playing soon. Jeff Pitchell and Texas Flood declared the large billboard sign on the door. The drinks were flowing, and the sky was full of stars. The only thing missing was a pretty woman on his arm.

Jesus, listen to yourself. Sam's getting to you.

Mitch shook his head, trying to clear the unbidden image of Katharine Evans from it. He looked around and startled at the sight by the bar. It was her.

"Hey, look, isn't that…"

Mitch was already walking towards the petite, long-haired beauty in a crimson sweater falling off one shoulder. He vaguely wondered if that was perhaps her signature look. He took in the admiring glances which fell her way, and her aloof manner. She looked straight ahead, making eye contact with no one. He was an astute people reader. Katharine was uncomfortable and out of place, and she was hiding it with an unapproachable air. A short young man with incredibly thick eyebrows sat beside her and tried to get her attention. She turned her head away, pretending not to hear him. That's when her eyes met Mitch's, then slid away. The bartender set down a shot of something clear in front of her, and she downed it swiftly. He could see her mouth 'another' to him.

To Mitch, it seemed like every human obstacle blocked his way. After an eternity, he was beside her. He tilted a raised eyebrow at her second empty shot glass. She shrugged.

"Do you usually party like this on a Monday night?"

She glanced down at his beer and said, "Do you?"

"Touché, madam. Touché."

Katharine exhaled a slow breath through her mouth. She rolled her shoulders and turned her head from side to side. Then she looked him in the eyes.

"Sorry, I—" she began.

He spoke at the same time. "You should—"

"What?"

"What?"

They *kept* speaking at the same time. Mitch tipped his hat to her. She smiled fleetingly then took a deep breath.

"I was going to say, I'm sorry for—"

Just then the band began to play, and Katharine's words were drowned out. She shrugged and grimaced. Mitch laughed and patted her hand, letting the touch linger. A blush rose in Katharine's cheeks in a way that Mitch found adorable.

The first licks of Johnny B. Good roared through the speakers, and a gaggle of women grabbed ahold of Mitch and pulled him to the dance floor. He raised an apologetic salute and obliged his fans.

Great, she probably thinks I'm a middle-aged Lothario.

Still, every time his eyes drifted to where she was, they held each other's gaze.

Coincidence. She's probably thinking I'm a buffoon.

At last, Mitch was able to escape the group of women and made his way to Katharine once again. He was too late, it would appear. The short guy had finally gotten her attention. From behind her, Mitch eavesdropped and watched the man touch her arm and ask if he could buy her a drink. Katharine shrugged, then said, "Sure. Vodka, seltzer, lime."

"Great, great. So, what's your name? You from around here? My name's Tony. I work construction. What do you do?"

"Whoa. Slow down, Tony. It's Katharine. Yes. What was the last question? Oh, I remember. I'm a writer."

"Oh, hey, no way! A writer, huh? You know, I've always wanted to write a book."

"You don't say?"

"What?"

"I said, you don't say!"

Mitch could hear the sarcasm in her tone, but judging by the look on Tony's face, he was oblivious. If only he could see her face as she feigned interest as Tony launching into a summarization of his book idea.

FOUR

COME DANCE WITH ME

Katharine was already tired from the effort of conversation and ready to go home. She'd made a mistake in coming out. This wasn't her thing... this *peopling*. Her drink arrived as she opened her mouth to give her apologies. It seemed a waste and very rude to not drink it, so she raised her glass to his with a smile.

I'll drink it fast and go. Thank God for Uber.

She'd lost sight of Mitch Ford, which was probably a good thing.

Mitch. Which. Mitch. Which.

The rhyme stuck in her head, and she giggled.

"What—what's so funny, Katharine?"

Short Tony had pronounced her name as 'Katrin.' This made her laugh even more. Tony, of course, wasn't in on the joke and his hesitant laugh illustrated the fact. Katharine didn't care. The music, with its steady driving beat, made her sway and nod her head. She couldn't remember the last time she'd danced. High school?

"Come on, Tony Baloney, come dance with me."

"Wait, I can't…okay."

Tony shuffle-stepped and clapped his hands out of time with the music while Katharine lost herself in the raucous wail of the guitar. Jeff Pitchell himself jumped out into the crowd and came straight toward Katharine. The last ounce of reserve melted away, and she danced with abandon. Another drink was pressed into her hand, and she took it with a whoop. Suddenly, Katharine Evans was having *fun*. With people. One song turned into four, two drinks became three. By the time the band took their break, Katharine was indisputably drunk.

She suddenly remembered poor Tony and looked around for him. She spotted him at the bar. Beside him was none other than Mitch Ford. They seemed to be in earnest conversation. Or at least, Mitch was, and Tony was silently bobbing his receded hair-line head with an awestruck stare. Katharine rolled her eyes and sauntered over to the two men.

"And, what do we have here, gentleman? Is the great Mitch Ford wowing you with his buckets of irresistible charm?"

"Katharine…"

Mitch said her name and it made her insides tumble. Or maybe it was the alcohol. She wasn't sure anymore.

"Mitch…"

She matched his serious tone, then laughed and pointed at him. Her depth perception was slightly off, and her finger poked his cheek. His dimple to be exact.

"Ooh, so serious, Mr. Ford. You have a dimple. A cute, little boy dimple. Right...*there*."

Her inside voice told her she was behaving like an obnoxious twit, yet she couldn't stop. Everything was so darn *funny*. Mitch's expression said otherwise, which made her giggle more.

"Uh, Kat-rin? It was really nice meeting you. I uh, had a great time. But, uh, I think it might be time your boyfriend takes you home. Unless..."

"I'll take it from here, Tony. Great meeting you, pal. That hat will be in the mail tomorrow. Send my love to your mother and thank her again for watching the show."

"Ooh, yeah, thanks for watching the show, pal," mimicked Katharine.

"Alright, Ms. Evans. That's enough from you, I think. What do you say we get you home, hmm?"

"Um, I say nope," she stretched the word a mile long, then added, "the band's goming, *coming* back on in a minute and I want to dance."

FIVE

DON'T BREAK THE SPELL

Katharine threw her arms up in the air, nearly smacking Mitch in the face, but his reflexes were quick. He jerked away, then looked around, scratching the back of his head. The band was a big draw, and the outside patio was filling rapidly. Mitch spotted the band's headliner, Jeff Pitchell. It gave him an idea.

"Katharine? Can you do me a big favor and stay right here? Right *here*, this spot, for one second?"

"Hokie Dokie, Pokie. I'm going to stay right here, just like Mr. Big Shot T.V. Show said. Yes, sir Mr.—"

"Okay, great. Hang on." Mitch weaved his way through the crowd amidst back claps and gasps of, 'that's Mitch Ford.' He politely acknowledged them, but all the while kept his eyes on the musician. Their eyes met, and recognition flashed in the singer's eyes.

"Hey, man, I know you! Me and the wife watch the Rebuilder all the time. So glad you could make it out to *my* show."

"Thank you, much appreciated. You guys put on a hell of a show, my friend."

"Thanks, man. Thanks a lot."

"Hey, can I ask you a quick favor?"

"Sure, sure. What's up?"

"Follow me and play along."

He shrugged and followed Mitch to the bar. Much to Mitch's surprise, Katharine had indeed stayed put. Only, she had a small fan club of her own surrounding her. *All men, what a shock.* Mitch gave a wry head shake.

"Excuse me, fellas. Uh, Katharine? I've brought a friend over to meet—"

"Oh, my God! Jeff *Pitchell*. I love you. I totally, totally *love* you!"

Jeff chuckled, "Well thanks, sweetheart. We love our fans, too."

"Yes," interrupted Mitch, "in fact, Jeff was just saying he'd like for you to sit up in the VIP section, up there on the balcony."

"I—what? Yes, yeah, right. Our, uh, VIP section is right up there, go make yourselves comfortable. Well, I've got to get back out there. Nice meeting you both."

"Thanks, buddy. I owe you one," Mitch said in his ear.

"No worries, man. Get that girl some coffee, pronto."

Mitch turned back to Katharine. She was swaying to music only she could hear, her fingertips steepled below her chin and her eyes closed. That strange sensation tugged at his chest again, and he was momentarily frozen. A small smile pulled at the corners of his mouth. *I could fall for this woman. Easily.*

Katharine, as if sensing his stare, opened her eyes and gazed softly into his. It was as if she was seeing inside of his soul. *Don't be ridiculous, man. She's a drunk woman in a bar. A mean dragon lady when she's not that. Get a grip.* Mitch grabbed her hand and pulled her through the crowd a little less gently than he'd intended. From behind him, her giggles bubbled, and her husky voice strained over the crowd.

"'Scuse us. Pardon us. VIP, people. VIP coming through."

At the staircase to the balcony stood an imposing bouncer with a neck tattoo. His too-small short-sleeved shirt clung to the contours of his exceptionally muscled torso, and he stared stonily over their heads, only dropping his gaze to them when they were directly in front of him.

"Sorry, no balcony access tonight," he looked around Mitch at Katharine, "too many drunks. Not safe."

"I appreciate that. I really do. Any chance you could be persuaded to let us go up there? I promise I'll keep an eye on her."

Mitch gave him his best, '*hey, c'mon, buddy*' smile, tilting his head to the side and spreading his arms out, palms up.

"Sorry, no... wait. Aren't you Mitch Ford? From the Rebuilder show?"

"Guilty as charged," said Mitch.

"Aw, yeah, cool. I heard you were in town doing a show. The house on Hawk Nest Road, right? There's a neighbor everyone says is gonna be a real—"

"Right! Yes, well. So, about that balcony?"

The hulking man's eyes darted around, then he unlatched the rope and motioned them up.

"If anyone asks, I gotta say you snuck up there, okay?"

"Understood, my friend, understood. Katharine? *Katharine*."

Katharine had begun swaying again, a plastic cup held high in her hand. At least this time it was to actual music, and not only what was playing in her head. Mitch took her elbow and guided her up the narrow steps.

"I've *got* it, geesh," she said and swatted his hand away.

Halfway up the staircase, the toe of Katharine's high heel shoe caught on the lip of the step. She'd have gone face first had Mitch not grabbed her around her waist and held her steady. When she turned to push off him, she listed too far, almost taking them both for a tumble down the stairs, yet she still managed to save her drink. Thanks to his many years in construction—which included balancing on scaffolds while holding planks of wood, siding or roofing—Mitch was lean and muscular and had quick reflexes. He countered their off-kilter tilt and pulled her against him as he fell against the wall.

"Oh," sighed Katharine against his neck.

"Are you alright, Katharine?" *She smells like honey and citrus. How nice.*

His lips were against the crown of her head, breathing in her scent. Her hand was splayed over his heart, and he was afraid she could feel it racing. She pulled back enough to look up into his concerned face. He watched her eyes fall to his mouth and wondered what it would feel like to kiss her. He leaned in. She tilted her chin up.

"Hey! Everything alright up there?"

The spell was broken. Mitch set Katharine straight, keeping a firm hand on her elbow, and called behind him to the anxious bouncer.

"All good, thank you!"

SIX

WELL THAT DIDN'T GO AS PLANNED

The near-kiss had sobered Katharine, but not nearly enough. Everything was sharp and blurry at the same time. Everything except for Mitch Ford. He stood out against the dark night in his faded blue denim and crisp white button-down shirt. His light blue eyes studied her with wariness and…something else.

"Let's get you sitting down, shall we?"

Abashed and still unsteady, she accepted his help into a well-weathered resin chair. He pulled a matching chair opposite hers and sat beside her. For a while, they said nothing and looked up at the stars and listened to the band. The sound was different up there on the roof, it rolled like waves over the side of the building and bounced off the bricks, but it was still nice. Katharine tilted her head back to see the sky better, but when she did, everything began to spin wildly, and her stomach roiled. She sat up straight, a panicked look on her face.

There is no way I am throwing up in front of this guy.

Mitch leaned forward, half standing and ready to assist her.

"Katharine, take a few deep breaths. Don't close your eyes, though. That'll make it worse. That a girl. Slow. Inhale. Exhale."

Katharine did as she was told, and soon the feeling passed.

"I'm so embarrassed. I don't—I'm not a drinker. I—this isn't, like, a thing I do."

"I figured as much. Care to share what made this night…special?"

"Oh, I don't know. Just…"

Katharine threw her hands up and shrugged. Thankfully, Mitch's sympathetic smile told her he seemed to understand.

"It's okay, Katharine. No need to explain. Everyone needs to … go on a bender once in a while."

She smiled shyly at him, he grinned back. Something exciting was happening there on the rooftop of Angelico's Lakehouse. But where would it lead? Where *could* it lead? Mitch Ford traveled the country. Katharine Evans was a homebody, practically a recluse. What could they ever have in common? They each took turns watching the other's profile under the glow of twinkling lights strung over the balcony railing. Mitch reached for her hand, and she let him enfold hers in its warm grip.

I hope nothing breaks this spell, they both thought.

"Mitch! Mitch! You up there? Hey, there you are- oh! Hey, uh, Mrs. Um, Miss, uh…"

It was Sam.

"Evans. Katharine Evans."

"Right, from next door to the build! Oh! I guess he asked you, then, right?"

"Asked me what?" Katharine turned to Mitch, a question in her eyes. She caught him making a cutting motion across his neck.

"Uh, oh," heaved Sam.

"Mitch? What's he talking about? Asked me *what*?"

Mitch put his face in his hands and rubbed it briskly. Whatever he was about to say, Sam beat him to it.

"The tape. Today's footage? You know, from when you stormed over, all mad hatter-like and threw that soccer ball at Mitch, then he ripped you a new one, and then you took a header into the dirt… oh, man, it's hysterical."

"You want to use the … footage of me? From— is *that* what this was all about? Oh, my God. I am so stupid. I thought you—wow, and to think I—. You were trying to butter me up. All so I'd agree to let you use an embarrassing video of me for ratings on your stupid show. I am an *idiot*! Screw you, Mitch Ford. And your show."

Katharine stood, kicking back the lightweight chair hard enough to topple it. Then, without thinking, she dumped the remains of her plastic cup on his head. She set it back on the table and brushed past the slack-jawed Sam. At the bottom of the stairs, she had to tap the bouncer's shoulder several times before he noticed her. Upon seeing her angry expression, he became a protective bear.

"That guy do something to upset you?"

"Yeah, he's a big jerk!"

Mitch's heavy footsteps followed Katharine down the stairs. He called her name, with Sam echoing him from behind. The bouncer let Katharine through but blocked Mitch and Sam from leaving.

"Katharine! Katharine, come on."

"Leave the lady alone, Mr. Big Shot."

"Oh, great, now she's got you calling me that, too? Katharine, please listen to me," he called over the big man's shoulder.

But Katharine had already made her way inside, irately pounding out a call to Uber, and exiting the front doors. She didn't care if Mitch was left to pacify the stone-faced bouncer. *See if an autographed hat will cut it this time around, jerk.*

SEVEN

UNINTENDED PLANS

The next morning greeted Katharine with a pounding headache and a dry mouth. The sunlight that had seemed so appealing yesterday, today was like shards of glass stabbing her eyes. She'd never bothered to change out of her clothes from last night. One crimson high heel was still wedged on her foot and tangled in her sheets. The other hung precariously from the curtain. She must've kicked it off with a bit too much vehemence.

She rose slowly, taking gingerly steps towards the bathroom and dreading her reflection in the mirror. Even if she looked only *half* as bad as she felt, it was going to be unsightly. One glance told her she was right. She was a mess. And she still had to write. Coffee was about to be her best friend for the day. And bacon. Definitely bacon, too. She tried not to replay the events of the night before, but like a bad dream, the memories kept hitting her in waves. The shots, the music, Mitch Ford.

Mitch Ford. That sneaky, underhanded, self-serving jerk.

He didn't *like* her, he was *using* her. Use her embarrassment for his show. Well, he had another thing coming. There was no way she'd agree to that kind of humiliation. Even as she fumed, she pictured the moment in the stairwell. Her lips so close to his throat, breathing in his clean, outdoors scent. It was a woodsy, fresh blend that drifted from his skin and intoxicated her even more than the alcohol had. Added to that, was the flecks of grey at his temples, and his gorgeous cerulean eyes. But then there was the way he deceived her. He'd conned her and made her feel like a fool, and…

Stop it. Better yet, use it for writing. Use him as Chelsea's antagonist. Perfect.

It may not be the kind of revenge he'd ever see or know about, but *Katharine* would know. That would be good enough for her. Her coffee pot gurgled and thumped out the last drops of black gold into the carafe and Katharine took her steaming cup up to her sunny office. The first sip did wonders in clearing some of the cobwebs from her fuzzy brain. Before long, fresh plot ideas sprang to mind, and the familiar rush of excitement in knowing her characters were about to come to life again flowed through her.

It never ceased to amaze her that a story originally written solely for her brother's eyes, evolved into a publishing contract. All thanks to

Nate, too. She'd had one book professionally printed and given it to him as a birthday gift on his thirtieth birthday. He'd taken that book everywhere with him, showing anyone who'd look at the inscription in the dedication. One of the people he pushed the book on happened to be Wes Thompson Taylor, the head of W. T. Taylor Publishing. He called her personally the very next day. Now, she was on her third book for him, more tentatively expected in the future.

For as much as she'd *not* intended on writing young adult fiction, the series had been a catharsis for Katharine. Growing up with elderly parents and having a sibling with special needs had isolated her. It made her … different. Apart. Other. It wasn't Katharine's imagination, either. Adults treated her one of two ways. They either looked at her with cloying pity and poured saccharine sweet sympathy over her, or they never even noticed her existence. There was no in-between. Her peers were another story altogether. There were bullies of all varieties— pranksters, physical attackers, and loud-whisperers. Then there were the ones who didn't know what to say or how to act, so they simply stayed away from the Evans kids. Back then, there weren't the educational tools and awareness they have now. Katharine and Nate had to deal with it all on their own. The upside, she learned how to throw a mean right hook. The downside, she was a loner.

From it all, Katharine had a wealth of stories. Except now she got to re-imagine them all and give them the outcomes she'd wished for. In Katharine's protagonist— Chelsea Marin— she found the voice to say and do all the things she'd wished *she'd* said and done when she and Nate were growing up.

Of course, it was only natural she gave Chelsea a sister with Downs-Syndrome, who she named Carli. Like Nate, she suffered bullying and unkindness from their peers. But unlike *Katharine*, Chelsea had the courage and power to protect Carli and others with special needs from the cruelties of the world.

The underlying theme of Katharine's books was always about perseverance, empowerment, compassion, and ultimately, educating young people about the positives of differences. Through Carli, Katharine was able to put out the message that 'different is good.' Her publicist called it an 'easy hook,' but for Katharine, it was so much deeper than that. It was her do-over.

She shook away those ruminations and began developing a storyline for the Mitch-like character, jotting down quick notes on paper. Katharine imagined him as a newcomer to Chelsea's small town of Palm Haven. She grudgingly gave him good looks and charm, but then became stuck on what his fatal flaw would be. Maybe he smelled bad? No, too basic. Katharine tapped her pen against her chin. Mitch was tall, with blue eyes. So, his character would be as well. Next, his name. Rich Lord? Too obvious. At last, she compromised and went with Maxwell Lord. Once that was settled, she listed his faults.

Too... handsome. Too charming. Too tall. Too... no, stop that.

Even after he'd humiliated and embarrassed her, all she could think of was his good qualities. How was she ever going to make him a bad guy if all she could do was swoon over him? Katharine realized the best way for her to develop her Mitch Ford/Maxwell Lord character was to just start writing and let it create itself. She set the pen down, pushed the paper aside and cracked her knuckles.

The moment her fingertips touched the keyboard, a sound like a buzz saw roared through her windows. Only, it wasn't *like* a buzz saw, it *was* a buzz saw.

"No. No, no *no*! Not today! Not *now*."

Katharine dropped her head in her hands. This could not be happening. She stood and crossed the room in long, angry strides and threw the window sash up.

"Shut UP!"

Katharine couldn't even hear herself over the din. She curled her fingers around the frame and slammed the window shut again. Then she yanked down the blinds and swept the curtain closed. All that managed to do was darken the room. It was no use. Next, she cued up her playlist. Pop music infused with rap, precisely right for writing teen drama. And making her headache return. Nothing was helping. Out the window closer to her desk, the one which overlooked the lake, Katharine spied the cherry red tip of her kayak poking out from the edge of the blooming hydrangea bushes. It had been waiting patiently for her since last week. She took one last glance at the laptop, then the far window facing Genoma's backyard.

"Kayaking it is."

Twenty minutes later, she was dragging the fiberglass kayak to the launch beside her rickety dock. Once in and shoved off the sandy shore, she paddled fast, intending to get as far from the noise of Mitch Ford and his crew as possible. For added measure, she plugged her headphones into her ears and let Claude Debussy's Clair de Lune flood her brain.

The lean muscles in her arms pumped rhythmically with each long pull, and before long she was following the curve of the shoreline. The tension knots in her shoulders eased, and her scowl became a blissful grin. The gentle plinks of the piano keys twinkled through her headphones. The morning sun sparkled and danced on the undulating surface. The air smelled of sunshine, water, and pine. As she passed Sears Park, the unmistakable whiff of suntan lotion drifted out on the breeze. When she glided past Angelico's Lakehouse, she averted her eyes in embarrassment, and a surge of renewed anger pushed against her breast.

The question was, who was Katharine most angry *at*? Mitch Ford for leading her to think he was interested in her? Or herself, for *being* misled? And for getting drunk. And embarrassing herself. Numerous times.

Ugh. You're a fool, Evans. This is why you don't 'do' social.

She'd begun paddling harder, grunting with the unnecessary exertion. A fine sheen of sweat coated her body, and though the workout exhilarated her, she lifted her paddle from the water and let it rest on the kayak. *Breathe. Relax.*

Katharine focused on the music in her ears, the gentle bounce of the kayak above the water, the warm late summer sun cresting the tree line. Turning the small vessel around and squinting, she could barely make out her tiny dock. *Home.* Buying the once run-down, chocolate brown bungalow was the best thing she'd ever done. She loved her little life on that pretty lake, that quaint town. Sure, she didn't know a single neighbor or belong to any community organizations. Yes, she only shopped at odd times, shunned small talk, and avoided eye contact whenever out. She didn't mean any offense to anyone, she liked her solitude.

The night before was the perfect example of why. She tried socializing, and she got drunk, made a fool of herself, and passed out fully clothed. That's why. *But you did have fun, admit it.*

She sighed. It was true. Up until she realized she was being played for a fool, she had been having fun. The music, the dancing, the starry sky and twinkling string lights. The smell of Mitch Ford's cologne…

Stop.

"Watch yourself, lady!"

The sharp bellow broke through the peaceful melody emanating from the headphones. Katharine startled, and she pulled an earbud loose. She looked around for the source of the warning call. She didn't have to look far. A pontoon boat loomed before her, it sunburnt occupant stared down at her with a mixture of annoyance and concern. His chubby, sunscreen streaked, ginger-haired twins blinked down at her as well.

"Sorry, sorry."

Katharine had drifted close enough to push off with her hand, which she did along with her apology.

"No problem. Say, are you the one who owns the house next to Mr. Genoma's property? You're the writer, right?"

Katharine cringed internally.

"Guilty as charged. I am she. The writer."

Even to her own ears, she sounded pretentious. Not like a native. Not like a normal person.

"Ye-ahh. Uh. Right. I'm Jim. These are my boys, Joey and Jeremy. We—my wife, Janie and me— we live on the other side of you. The McNamara's? My wife brought you a casserole when you moved in. Cookies at Christmas. Every Christmas, actually. I think your doorbell is busted, or something. You never answer your door."

Katharine's face had gone pink, and she stammered, "Oh, wow. I—it must be. I, uh, it's nice to meet you, Jim. Sorry, I, um, get really caught up in writing, so..."

She trailed off, not really knowing what more she could add. She already looked like a total jerk. Katharine had indeed heard the ring of the doorbell each time. And each time she deliberately waited until the woman rounded the corner before opening her door wide enough to pull the tray through. A handwritten note always accompanied the plates, 'Season's Greetings from your neighbors, the McNamara's! Jim, Janie, Joey, and Jeremy xo'. Or,

'Happy Easter! From, The McNamara's xo!' Or… well, insert any and every holiday. Cookies, cakes, pies, you name it. Clearly, Janie McNamara liked to bake.

Katharine had never once acknowledged the trays, or them when they waved from their minivan as they passed her by. Now, it was coming back to bite her in the rear. Jim McNamara's sardonic expression told her he believed she was an anti-social, rude, snob of a woman who probably believed she was better than everyone else. In fact, she could easily imagine him relaying the story of this meeting.

"Oh sure," he'd say, *"I finally met her, Miss I'm Too Important to Talk to the Peasants. She's not all that. Skinny little bird of a thing. Couldn't even put one sentence together. Beats me how she writes a whole book!"*

They'd all laugh and nod in agreement. Not only would she be called the mean neighbor lady, but now they'd add unintelligible snob, too. Suddenly, Katharine found herself wanting the McNamara's to like her. Before she knew what she was doing, she called out to him.

"Hey, I—I'm having a small get-together at my place this Saturday. Maybe you guys could join us? It's a—an end of summer… thing."

What the heck are you saying? You don't have any friends. Not one. Oh, well, surely, he'll say they have plans already.

"Well, that's really nice of you. We'd love to, right boys?"

The boys stared from Katharine to their father.

Katharine, perhaps a little too brightly, exclaimed, "Great! That is so great! So, uh, Saturday? Um, one o'clock? See you then?"

"Sure, sounds good. I'll have Janie whip up one of her famous appetizers."

Katharine was already paddling away, back towards the safety of home. She raised a hand in a quick wave but didn't turn back. She didn't need to look to know they were staring at her with surprised, confused expressions. It was the exact mirror of her own face. Mentally, she went down a list of people she knew to invite.

Nate… and well, just Nate.

Who could she get to show up at such short notice? Maybe she could beg random strangers at Angelico's. The bouncer there seemed to like her well enough. She could ask Tori to take the drive from New York, she supposed. Other than that, there was no one. Katharine had hardly expanded her circle past acquaintanceship with anyone. For the second time in two days, Katharine was regretting her extreme introverted ways.

Lost in her panicked ruminations, Katharine glided up to her launch. Once there, she hopped into the chilly water and pulled the kayak out. As she back-stepped, her wet-shoe lost its grip on the packed dirt and Katharine fell hard on her bottom. Swearing, and trying to not let go of the boat, she attempted to stand. From behind her, a hand grasped her elbow and steadied her, while another grasped the kayak's rope. She looked up over her shoulder, once again startled. It was *him*. Mitch Ford.

"Are you always this off-balance, or…"

"Or, what are you doing here? You can't walk onto someone's property and sneak up on them, you know. I think they call it stalking or something."

Katharine yanked her elbow from his grasp and promptly lost her balance again. This time, she steadied herself, blowing loose strands of hair off her forehead. Mitch smirked down at her, his eyebrow arched. The reflection of the sparkling water danced in his eyes and Katharine's insides dipped. She hated that he made her so...unhinged. But she kind of liked it, too. Not that she'd ever admit it.

"Actually, Katharine, I came to apologize for last night. It was all one big misunder—"

"Oh, I think it was all perfectly clear, Mr. Ford. Now, if you'd kindly go away, I have work to do. And I'd appreciate it if you'd get back to *your* job, too. The sooner you people are done over there, the sooner I can get my life back to normal."

Mitch pulled off his hat and ran a callused hand through his hair, then put his hands on his hips.

"You know, lady, you are a real pain in the butt. I come over here to apologize—and by the way, you could try the same—and you berate me. I don't—"

"Me? *Apologize*? For what? Believing you were a decent human being? For not wanting to have embarrassing videos of me on your stupid show? Or for thinking I had a right to live in peace and *quiet* on the peaceful, *quiet* lake house *I* own? You have a lot of..."

"Oh, don't you even say *I* have a lot of nerve! *You* have a lot of nerve! My show, by the way, has helped *hundreds* of people rebuild their lives. I contribute to society, sweetheart. What is it you do, again? Oh, I know, you hide in your cute little house and write teen romance books. Geez, get over yourself."

Katharine was so angry that if she had anything handy, she'd throw it at him. Before she could refute his pompous, erroneous claim about her books, he added,

"And yes, you should apologize. Thanks to your dramatics, your bouncer friend threw me out of the restaurant. Literally."

If Katharine weren't so livid, she'd have doubled over laughing at the image of Mitch Ford being manhandled out of Angelico's. Well, she did laugh out loud, but it came out more like a derisive snort. They circled each other in a small arc, like boxers in a ring.

"Serves you right," she shrugged. "Maybe the next time you try and manipulate someone, or take advantage of them, you'll think twice."

"Take advantage? Take *advantage*," Mitch stepped close to Katharine, so close she could smell his undeniably sexy, outdoors scent. He brought his face close to hers, close enough that she could see the adorable scar above his right eyebrow and smell minty gum on his breath. When his lips just about touched her ear, he whispered two words.

"You…wish."

Katharine's pulse quickened at his nearness, and her body swayed slightly toward him as if on its own accord. Catching herself, she leaped back and scowled menacingly at Mitch. She was going to wipe the arrogant smirk off his face if it was the last thing she ever did. This time she *did* grab the first item handy. Her oar. She swung it wide in front of her, pointing the paddle at his mid-section. Mitch jumped back, his eyes widening in surprise.

***

"Are you crazy, lady?"

"Yes, and you're going to get this thing across your face if you don't get off my property."

She jabbed it at him for emphasis and Mitch stumbled back. He wasn't sure whether he should laugh or yank that oar from her tiny hand.

She's out of her mind! But man, is she cute when she's angry.

Mitch was so busy backing up and staring at the way the sunlight caught Katharine's hair, that he didn't notice the change in her expression, or hear what she said next.

"I said, you're walking the wrong…"

A loud splash interrupted her. Mitch found himself waist deep in the lake, a bewildered expression on his face. For a moment, Katharine stared in shock. Then, she dropped the oar and covered her mouth with one hand. It was no use, laughter bubbled out from behind her hand. But she wasn't the only one laughing. They both turned towards the sounds. It was coming from the bushes separating the Genoma's yard from hers.

There stood the entire Rebuilder crew, doubled over laughing and pointing. Sam was there, too—with his camera wedged securely between his shoulder and head, no less. He gave a huge smile and a 'thumbs up' signal to Mitch. Katharine's laughter died on her lips and her eyes slanted as she looked from one to the other.

"Are you *kidding* me right now? *Another* play for the cameras? You are unbelievable."

She kicked the oar out of her way and stomped back to her house, not giving Mitch a second glance.

"Katharine, wait! I had *nothing* to do with that! I didn't know they followed me, I swear. Come *on*."

It was no use. Before he could utter another word, her back door slammed loud enough to reverberate across the lake. Mitch looked around. Everyone had gone back to the work site.

"A little help here," he called to no one.

EIGHT

NOT ANOTHER SHOWDOWN

Thursday morning arrived all too quickly for Katharine. Her sense of dread about the upcoming interview hadn't subsided in the least. In fact, it had bloomed into full-fledged heart palpitations and hives. Thankfully, none of them were on her face, and the one on her neck was beginning to subside. She'd arrived at five a.m. at the studio where they taped the show. Though she'd seen the Connecticut Today show several times, she'd never realized it was taped in a *town*. She'd assumed it would've been in one of the more prominent cities, like Hartford or New Haven. *Hmm, learn something new every day.*

A pretty but stern make-up artist named Katya brushed powder across her temples and brow. Katharine closed her eyes and tried to calm herself.

"Hey, girl! Now, don't you look—what's that on your neck," said Tori from the doorway.

Katharine jumped, knocking the brush from Katya's hand. It bounced off her black silk blouse before falling to the floor. A cream-colored bloom of powder burst across her top and dotted her matching black pants.

"Tori! You scared the heck out of me!" To the make-up artist, she said, "Sorry, Katya." Then Katharine looked down at her clothes. "Oh, no, my blouse!"

"Is okay, I fix," declared Katya confidently.

"You can fix *that*?" Tori pointed to the large splotch of powder on Katharine's shirt.

"No, I not can fix this. *This* I fix."

She waved her hand in front of Katharine's face. Then the corners of her mouth pulled down in a frown. She squinted at Katharine for a moment before nodding and shrugging. "You stay still, yes?"

"I was still until this one scared the—"

"Oh, now, I told you I'd come down and give you some moral support, girl. Didn't I?"

"No, Tori, actually, you didn't. But thank you. I'm so nervous, I could throw up."

"Hey, no throwing up in our dressing room, lady! Knock, knock! Mind if I come in and say hello?"

It was Steve Hurley himself. He was adorable on T.V., even more so in person. Katharine wasn't good with people in general, and she was even worse with celebrity, even a local one. She supposed the only exception to the rule was Mitch

Ford. But then, she wasn't doing so well with him either, was she?

"No, I mean, yes. Please come on. In, I mean. Please come in."

"Whoa, okay. Someone here is a wee bit anxious, hmm?"

The utterly charming Steve Hurley looked from Katharine to Tori and back again. He took both of her hands in his and compelled her to look into his eyes.

"Now, Katharine, sweetie. There is nothing to be nervous about. I promise. We are going to have a blast! Just a bunch of friends, chit-chatting about your books and Mitch Ford's hit television show, right?"

"Right. Wait, what?"

Katharine looked from Steve to Tori with saucer-wide, panicky eyes.

"Alrighty, I'm off to beautify my mug. See you out there!"

Steve was out the door before she could ask him what he meant. She had a feeling Tori knew. "Tori? Did you know anything about this?"

"About what?" Tori had become extremely interested in her cuticles and wouldn't look up at Katharine.

"About *what*? Um, about Mitch Ford, that's what."

"Oh, that. Yes, well... funny story. You know my friend, Justin? No, wait, I suppose you wouldn't since you never show up to any party I've ever invited you to. Anyhow, my friend Justin is Mitch Ford's publicist. And *he* told *me* Mitch is working on the house next door to yours. Small world, right? So, I was like, 'Hey Justin, why don't you see if you could get your guy on the show with my girl, here,' and he was like, 'you know what, that's a great idea, Tori,' so, I was like—"

"Okay, okay. I get it. What else?"

"What, '*what else*'?"

"I can tell you're not telling me something, Tori. What. *Else*?" Katharine's knuckles turned white as she gripped the armrests and her shoulders had bunched up almost to her ears. Katya pushed them down.

"Okay, don't get mad. Promise me you won't get mad?"

Katharine dropped her face into her hands, much to the intense irritation of Katya, who was watching and listening as if they were a tennis match. She roughly tilted Katharine's head back up and re-powdered her. Katharine was resigned to let her paint her face like a clown at this point. Things were only about to get worse, she was sure. Something told her the whole state would be laughing at her by the end of the morning. Tori continued, her words coming out in machine gun bursts.

"You see, when Justin called Mitch, his camera guy answered his phone. There was some kind of loud ruckus goin' on or something. They were at a bar, I think. Anyhow, the camera guy told Justin that he was arguing with some lady who lived next door to their build, and they had some great footage of the two of them goin' at it. So, I put two and two together. Me and Justin coordinated everything, and voila, here we are!"

Katharine was speechless. Jaw-dropped, wide-eyed, blatantly dumb-struck. If she weren't living it, she'd have said it was the plot of a made-for-television movie. A stout woman wearing a headset poked her head in the doorway. "Five minutes till go time, Miss Evans."

In horror, Katharine looked down at her ruined blouse. "Tori! I can't go out there like this. What do I do?"

"Calm yourself, woman. Here," Tori lifted her paisley scarf over her head and draped it over Katharine's. "See, no one will ever know you got yourself a big ole blob of powder on you."

Sure, they'll be too busy laughing at me making a fool of myself. She'd convinced herself that Mitch had brought the video of Katharine yelling like a banshee at Mitch, being sent away like a spoiled brat, then last but not least, her stumble and fall in the muddy rut. It would be the perfect revenge for him to embarrass her yet again, this time publicly.

"Time to head out, Miss Evans."

Well, this is it. My moment of doom awaits.

"Oh, now stop acting like you're walking the plank, girl. It'll be over before you know it. Remember, plug The Chelsea Marin Chronicles One and Two. Hype the release date for Three and give Steve and Marla this."

Tori pressed a gift basket filled with Chronicles Swag. T-shirts, mugs, signed books and more.

"I have to walk out with this? What if I trip?"

"She *can* be a bit clumsy," a deep voice called out from behind Katharine.

Mitch Ford. Perfect.

"Look who's talking," she spat out.

"Well, hello there, *handsome*." Tori, the traitor, batted her eyes at Mitch and fluffed her hair. Katharine glared at her, but it went unnoticed.

"Hello yourself. I'm…"

"Mitch Ford, this is Tori Brown, my publicist. Tori, Mitch Ford, stalker star of Builder."

"It's Rebuilder, thank you. And you wish I stalked you. A pleasure to meet you, Tori. Justin told me to say hello if I saw you today."

Katharine ignored their pleasantries and cut in before Tori could respond.

"Did you know about this yesterday?"

Mitch smiled apologetically at Tori and turned a cool, condescending tone to Katharine.

"Why, yes, Katharine. I did indeed know about today. I'd have told you about it, but you were busy trying to stab me with an oar if I recall correctly."

"You do not recall correctly," Katharine hissed up into his face. Or at least tried to. The oversized basket was between them, the bow at the top in her way.

"Oh, so now you weren't jabbing me with the end of your oar?" He turned to Tori, whose mouth was agape, "I have witnesses, too, you know. Do *you* know she's, she's… *crazy*?" He turned and leaned over the basket and hissed the word 'crazy' into Katharine's face.

Good. Glad I'm not the only one flustered here.

"Okay, you two? Take a chill. I cannot *even* be having this kind of nonsense. You hear?"

Both Katharine and Mitch turned their backs to each other, refusing to look at Tori.

"I said, do...you...hear? Mitch Ford, do not make me get on my phone to Justin. Katharine, do not test me, girl."

Although Tori had been born and raised in a small town by the name of Winterset in Iowa, her ten years in New York had loaned her a stone cold, I-will-hurt-you, edge to her tone when it was necessary. It was useful, to say the least.

In unison, they both muttered, "Yes, Tori."

"Good. Now wait for your cues, then get out there and be charming, funny, and *likable*."

Duly chastised, but no less amiable towards each other, they waited side by side. Tori, standing guard behind them, observed the side glances they gave each other with an amused grin that dropped the moment Katharine caught her.

From out on the stage, Marla Madison, the co-host of the show, started Katharine's introduction.

"... local writer of the wildly popular Chelsea Marin Chronicles—kids just love these books, by the way..."

"As do I Marla, as do I..."

"So, you're saying you read teen fiction, Steve?"

They bantered back and forth until their producer gave them a signal to keep moving.

Marla continued, "What do you say we bring her out here, guys?"

Applause, cheers.

Here goes nothing.

70

"Come on out, Katharine Evans!"

Katharine managed to make it on stage without tripping or knocking anything over. She sat on the loveseat across from the hosts, who graciously encouraged the audience to clap.

"Look at you, you little thing, you! Isn't she adorable, Marla."

"Steve, don't embarrass her. But you are, Katharine, I have to say. I assumed you'd be, I don't know, taller."

"It's fine, I hear it all the time. Not that I'm adorable, I mean. That I'm short and, well—." The hosts blinked and smiled at her. "Thank you for having me on the show. This is, uh, for you guys."

"Stop it! How sweet is this? Ooh, look at all the goodies," Steve said.

They bantered again, Katharine sat with a frozen smile on her face and shooting her eyes off-stage at Tori, pointedly not looking at Mitch. Tori mouthed something, but Katharine couldn't make it out. Suddenly, Steve was repeating her name.

"So, Katharine. Tell us about your books. You have this character, Chelsea. She…"

Steve saved her some of the descriptive work, likely sensing her nervousness. However, when he mentioned her Carli character, Katharine's reserve dropped.

"Oh, yes! Carli is Chelsea's kid sister, and she has Down's Syndrome. She's my favorite character, I must admit. Everything Chelsea does is for and because of Carli. They have an extraordinary relationship that I hope conveys through the stories—"

"And a little birdie told me Carli is actually based on—"

"Oh, yes, my brother Nate. He's amazing. Smart, funny, talented. He's the whole reason why I wrote the Chelsea Marin Chronicles in the first place."

Tears stung and brightened Katharine's eyes. Marla reached across the coffee table and squeezed her hand. Steve filled the moment with talking about Katharine and Nate's charitable foundation.

"That is *such* a feel-good story, Katharine," Steve turned to the camera, "and it gets even better folks. Every book sold donates a portion of the proceeds to Nate's Great Cause, a non-profit group that advocates for people with Down's Syndrome. Tell us a little about what kinds of things your organization does, Katharine."

She needed no further coaxing to talk about Nate's Great Cause, making sure to clarify that Nate himself was CEO, and she was merely an advisor to him. She chanced a glance off stage again to gauge Tori's approval, but her eyes met Mitch's. He looked chagrined and... something else. Something that made her insides do that strange slip and dip again.

"...changing topics a bit, Katharine. Katharine?"

Katharine startled at her name, "Yes! Sorry, Steve."

"You have a little real-life chronicle going on in your backyard, don't you?"

"In my what... oh. Right. *That*."

"That's right, Steve," Marla interjected. "Katharine has the one and only Mitch Ford filming right next door! Hey, ladies in the audience, isn't that *exciting*?"

Cheers and less than lady-like hoots and whoops burst from the crowd. Katharine groaned quietly.

"What do you say we bring him out, hmm?"

Louder applause, cheers.

"Mitch Ford, come out here!"

Mitch emerged from the wings as if he were born on television. Waving to the crowd, pointing and winking here, then there. Patting his heart and nodding humbly. They ate it up. Women were actually yelling his name. Katharine, forgetting she might be on camera, rolled her eyes. She wouldn't know until much later, but that eye roll, paired with Mitch's entrance, became a viral 'gif' within an hour. It was dubbed, 'Mitch Ford's Biggest Fan, NOT.' Steve Hurley observed it all with mirth.

"Well, well, well, Mr. Ford. You are popular with the ladies, aren't you?"

"Oh, stop. Please, call me Mitch." Then he half turned to acknowledge Katharine with a cool, "Hello, Miss Evans."

"Hello, Mr. Ford."

"Please, sit," said Steve.

Mitch glanced at the empty spot on the loveseat beside Katharine, then eyed her warily.

"Yes, right there. Beside Katharine. Don't worry, she won't bite." Steve put a hand up beside his mouth, and stage-whispered, "Or maybe she will?"

Twittering laughter from the audience. Mitch turned and sat down. The seat was slightly lower than he'd anticipated, so when his bottom landed on the cushion, it sprung Katharine up comically. At least, the audience found it amusing. Katharine seethed internally, but a thin smile remained plastered to her lips. For as petite as she was, Mitch was giant. He encroached her personal space with his long legs and jutting elbows.

"You're on my—"

"Can you just—"

"If you could try—"

The two of them shifted and muttered at each other, oblivious of the camera, the audience, *and* of the show's hosts staring at them in amusement. She tugged the hem of her blouse out from under his thigh. He squirmed and drew in his elbows. They were two people doing everything in their power to not have any physical contact in a spot which might as well have been a telephone booth.

"Ahem," Steve voiced theatrically, "we heard there's been some…shall we say, sparks between you two." Then, playing to the audience, he leaned forward, nodded at them, and said, "What do *you* all think?" Loud applause answered him. He sat back as if he were a lawyer in a courtroom resting his case.

Marla took over the interrogation. "Steve, doesn't this sound like it could be a great story for a romance novel?"

"Oooh, it does, Marla. Hmm, now what would you call it," said Steve.

"I know," said Marla, 'The Writer's Romance'! Doesn't that sound like a fun read?"

"I like it, Marla. Or—I know—maybe, 'Love on Lake Pocotopaug.' It had a ring to it, no? Either of you care to comment?" Marla and Steve blinked and smiled at them.

"No." They answered in unison. Once again, Steve nodded knowingly at the audience. Someone shouted out, 'I think it's puppy love,' and the audience erupted yet again.

This has gotten completely out of hand.

Mitch must've thought so as well. He attempted to redirect the freight train onto safer topics. "Ah, so, I'd love to tell you a little bit about the rebuild we're doing right now for the show."

"The one next door to Miss Evans, right?"

"Y-yes. That's right. The grandchildren of one Vincent Genoma contacted us some time ago about fixing up their grandfather's house as a ninetieth birthday present. He'd served in World War II, was a devoted husband and father, adored his grandkids... just an all-around great guy who'd fallen on hard times after his wife passed away."

Katharine bit her lip in dismay at how little she knew of the old man next door. Then she realized he'd been referring to him in the past tense. She interrupted.

"I'm sorry, wait. Is Mr. Genoma—"

"He passed away last March, Katharine. You... didn't know?"

"I—no I guess..."

"So, Katharine, your longtime next-door neighbor passed away a year ago, and you didn't even know it? Wow, that's—"

"I've only lived there six years, so..." Katharine trailed off. All eyes were on her like she'd stolen candy from a child. Mitch cleared his throat, then continued.

"Anyhow, we followed up with the family after discovering Mr. Genoma's passing and learned the grandson who'd originally emailed us had also fallen on some hard times. He'd followed his grandfather's footsteps into the military. Around the same time he messaged us, he deployed. While overseas, his caravan was ambushed, and he was severely injured."

Gasps and sympathetic moans rippled like a wave through the audience. Marla put her hand to her heart and shook her head as she asked, "And then what happened, Mitch?"

"Well, we knew we couldn't let an American hero down after all that. So, we got a crew together and headed down to see what could get done for this wonderful family."

"Wow, that is fantastic, Mitch. You're going to give them a brand-new start, right in their beloved grandfather's home. I can't imagine a better ending to a story."

"Wooo, that was some emotional stuff right there, wasn't it," asked Marla of the audience. The audience concurred.

"What do you say we lighten things up a little bit, hmm?" The audience clapped and cheered on cue, ready for some levity.

"We have something here— brought to us by your cameraman, Mitch—and I think you're all going to get a kick out of it. But first, a commercial break!"

Oh, no. He didn't. Of course, he did. It was like being on a roller coaster. In the dark. Jolts and twists, ups and stomach-flipping downs. All of which she couldn't see coming. A moment ago, her eyes had softened on Mitch Ford's face as he spoke about helping the young man and his family. There was genuine passion in his voice, a need to help that came through in his every utterance. Then, the bombshell… the '*something your cameraman brought.*' It could be only one thing. Or several, she supposed. Perhaps a montage of everything she'd said in anger. Both of her falls. Heck, maybe he even got her drunken fiasco at Angelico's on tape.

Katharine mentally plotted a series of possible scenarios in which she could escape the impending mortification. A bomb scare. Spontaneous combustion. A tornado. Maybe a sinkhole would open underneath the set. Or…

"Katharine, stop ignoring me. I am trying to tell you not—"

"What?" Katharine snapped at Mitch.

He slapped his hands on his lap and shook his head. "You know what, never mind."

"What could you possibly have to say to me? Is it 'haha, gotcha good'? Or maybe, 'prepare to have your life ruined'?

"No," he said with a slow, deliberate tone, "I am try*ing* to *tell* you that: You. Don't. Have. To—"

"Wow, chauvinistic much? Tell me, do you speak to all women like they're children?"

"Only when they *act* like one!"

Katharine fumed. If she were a cartoon character, steam would be shooting out from her ears. Mitch

glowered back at her from only a nose width's
away. Meanwhile, Katya and her assistant
attempted to refresh their makeup. She looked from
one to the other and rolled her eyes.

"Hey, lof-birds, how about you give me a chill
for a minute? Or, would you like to do the kissing
now?"

Katharine and Mitch jumped back as if bitten.
She flushed, and he scowled. Katya chuckled and
set to work.

"There, *mach* better. Except, you, stop with the
red face. And you, big man. Stop with the face
lines, you scrunch up, my makeup look like cake."

From the corner of the set, another voice called
out a countdown.

"Live in five, four, three, two…"

The set cleared but for the hosts, Katharine, and
Mitch. The man doing the countdown pointed at
Steve and Marla, and they resumed their banter.

"Alright, welcome back! So, if you're just tuning
in, we are sitting with the author of the popular
Chelsea Marin Chronicle books, Katharine Evans
and the star of the hit show, The Rebuilder, Mitch
Ford and I've gotta tell you, folks… there is some
chem-is-*tree* going on here!"

"Oh, why Marla, I never knew you felt—"

"Steve! You stop that. No, I'm talking about
these two over here."

The audience gives an adolescent chorus of,
'*woooooo.*'

"What? Wait, no—he and I, we, he's not—"
Katharine stammered and looked at Mitch to set
them straight.

"Yeah, no—I mean, she's— I'm—" He was no better.

Steve and Marla gave one another exaggerated wide-eyed, raised eyebrows, knowing grins. Then they turned to the audience, who unsurprisingly hooted and laughed.

"Well, then," exclaimed Steve after the laughs had died down, "Mitch, it seems like this isn't the first time Katharine's gotten you a little…*flustered*, shall we say? Tell us about this little clip your cameraman gave us, hmm?"

Here it comes. Katharine sank back in her seat, trying to make herself as small as possible and hoping the cushions would swallow her up. Her body went numb as she forced herself to listen to Mitch 'set the scene.'

"Well, I had spotted Katharine coming in from the lake on her kayak and decided to pop on over to discuss some…details. About the build, you see. And well, how about we go ahead and show the clip?"

Behind them, a screen glided up, and the lights dimmed. An image of the show's logo—a silhouette of a man in hardhat—filled the screen and the theme music played. Then, Mitch was on camera in his trademark faded jeans and baseball cap, walking towards the camera.

"From time to time," spoke onscreen Mitch, "we—or I, as it happens— get a little carried away and well, mishaps happen. Unfortunately for me, my trusty cameraman, Sam, is always around to catch it when I do. Take a look at my latest…misfortune."

The image of Mitch's sardonic expression faded and was replaced by one of Katharine and Mitch by the lake. It was shot from behind Katharine, putting Mitch in full view. It began with Katharine saying, '*I said, you're going the wrong...*' Then the camera zoomed in on Mitch's face. His eyes bulged, his mouth gaped with an 'O.' Then the camera panned back enough to show his arms flailing. The studio audience gasped as he fell into the water, then their laughter filled the studio. Sam had zoomed in again for a close-up of Mitch's bewildered face, then pulled back enough to show Katharine in partial profile, pointing and laughing at him. Then the clip faded out.

Katharine slowly turned to look at Mitch, her brows drawn close together, her head tilted. This was the video he chose to share? *His* embarrassing moment? She had completely misjudged him. Everyone laughed around them, but they sounded far off, muted. Mitch was staring at Katharine with a calm, placid expression. A slight smile touched his lips, and his eyes were soft on her. Her cheeks burned and her throat constricticted. Katharine looked down at her hands so he wouldn't see how flustered she'd become. Though she couldn't meet his gaze, it bore a hole in her downturned head.

Somehow, they got through the rest of their segment. The moment Katharine said her thank you's and goodbyes to the two hosts, she bolted from the stage to the semi-safety of Tori. She had too many conflicting feelings racing through her mind, and she needed time to think.

Before Tori could say a word, Katharine blurted, "Can we get out of here, please?"

"Sure, sure, honey. Hey, you did…great."

Katharine shot her a suspicious side glance.

"Really, I mean it. It wasn't bad at all. But you have *got* to fill me in on Mr. Fine Faded Jeans, okay?"

"Yes, fine. But not now. I just want to get out of here."

They were nearly out the door when Katya caught up to them. "There you are. You, take this. Is my business card. You do appearance, I do making up, *da*?"

"Da., uh, yes. Yeah, sure, that would be great. Thank you, Katya," said Katharine.

"Yeah, yeah. Do like Katya say, and go on date with sexy hammer man."

Before Katharine could respond, Katya turned and walked away.

"Sexy hammer man, huh? Has kind of a ring to it, doesn't it?"

"Tori, please. Don't."

"Alright, alright. Geesh, touchy."

NINE

THAT WOMAN

Mitch watched Katharine dash from the stage but could do nothing to stop her. The hosts had drawn him into a conversation—none of which he could recall after—and he'd missed his chance to speak to her. This was supposed to have been the moment when they shook hands and let bygones be bygones, and yet Mitch was once against left ravaged in the wake of Hurricane Katharine. He said as much to Sam when he pulled up to the station's front entrance.

"So, how'd it go?" Sam asked as Mitch closed the passenger door.

"That woman—" he began, throwing his cap onto the floor mat at his feet.

"Uh-oh. Here we go."

Mitch ignored Sam's lament and launched into a thirty-minute diatribe of Everything Awful About Katharine Evans.

"Uh-huh. All I really hear is, you really, *really* like this chick."

Mitch started to rebuke the accusation, then sighed and laughed a little. "Yep. I suppose I do. She's smart, beautiful, in great shape, and turns out she's philanthropic, too. I mean, who'd have thought *that*?"

"Yeah, well—"

"But she's also hot-tempered, rude, and demanding. Don't you think so?"

"I kind of—"

"I mean, I guess I did provoke her a little bit. But we made up for it with the video. Right?" Sam said nothing. "I said, right, Sam? Why aren't you answering me, Sam?"

"Oh, are you done? Can I speak now?"

Mitch looked contrite. Yes, he'd gone on a tangent. Katharine Evans seemed to have that effect on him quite often. He let Sam speak, although he couldn't stop his mind from wandering back to that confounding woman and what she might be doing.

***

While Mitch seethed and stewed about Katharine, she was doing much the same with Tori as they crossed the parking lot to their cars. Tori—much like Sam had done—shrugged. She was unfazed by Katharine's foul mood. She'd worked with her for the past three years, as well as plenty of other over-sensitive creative types. They sometimes needed to be handled with kid gloves, and different times required a firm hand and a good shove. Tori was adept at all that and more. It also so happened she genuinely liked Katharine Evans. Something not very many people could say. Mostly because they never got a chance to know her, though.

"I'm not touchy," Katharine pouted, then calmed. "Okay, fine. Maybe a little bit, sorry. How about I treat you to lunch? There's a great Thai place near my house."

"Ah, what a surprise. You, picking a spot close to home? I'm teasing you, that sounds great. I'll follow you there."

Less than thirty minutes later Katharine pulled into the parking lot of Po's Rice and Spice, trailed by Tori. When they climbed out of their respective cars, Tori's expression was dubious as she read the sign.

"Po's Rice and Spice, huh?"

"Yup, best Lemongrass Chicken ever."

"Wow, Katharine Evans goes *out* to eat?"

"No, silly. I get take out. This is the first time I've ever dined in." They walked through the door. "Ooh, it's so pretty," said Katharine.

"See what happens when you get out of your bubble occasionally?"

Katharine looked around the bright, contemporary Asian décor and smiled. It was the first real smile Tori had seen on her that day. They were seated at a corner table, overlooking the quaint, historic street. The waitress set two menus before them.

"Can I offer you a beverage? Glass of wine, perhaps?"

"A bottle," they both said simultaneously.

The two women laughed as the waitress disappeared. Tori was dying to broach the subject of Mitch Ford, as well as the viral gif, *and* the next appearance she'd booked for Katharine, but realized all might be best addressed *after* she'd had some wine. No one hated book promoting appearances more than Katharine seemed to. Once the glasses were poured and lunches ordered, Tori toed her way into the easiest of the three topics.

"So, Katharine, my love…"

"Oh, no. Anytime you call me, 'Katharine, my love' it's never good."

"Now, now. Settle down. Drink your wine. There you go. Let's discuss your next appearance, shall we?"

Katharine groaned and nodded into her wine glass.

"That a girl. We—are you ready for it—we are going to put you on…. *wait for it*… The Up All-Night Show!"

Katharine blinked at Tori as if she had two heads.

"Stop that. I *know* you've heard of the Up All Night Show."

"I—yes, of course, I've *heard* of it. I just can't fathom why you'd think it's a good idea to put *me* on it. Can't we keep doing the little bookstores and author conventions? I've gotten used to those, you know."

"Katharine, it's going to be fun! A great opportunity, too. So, don't flake out on me now."

"Tori, you saw today's fiasco. I looked like a deer in headlights. I could barely get a sentence out."

"Now, that's not true, Katharine. When you spoke about Nate and the foundation? Oh, my word, they were eating out of your hand. Plus, the camera loves you. A lot. Speaking of that... we may want to work a little bit on—how shall I say—your poker face."

"My... poker face?"

"Yes. You have a, uh, well, transparency to your feelings. An *expressive* face, you could say."

Katharine blanched visibly, proving Tori's point. Tori averted her eyes and fidgeted with her earring.

"What, Tori. What are you not telling me?"

"I think, maybe, it's best if I show you. But first, let me remind you—any publicity is good publicity, right?"

Tori eked out a nervous laugh as she slid her cell phone across the table to Katharine. Katharine's brow squished together, then her eyes went wide with dismay.

"Wh—what is this...oh, my God. You're kidding me? Is this—can other people *see* this?"

"Oh, honey, yes. Yes, they can, and they have. Twenty-five thousand times and counting. Don't worry, it'll get replaced by something else in a hot minute. You'll see."

Katharine couldn't take her eyes off the small screen. More specifically, she couldn't stop looking in horror at her close-up eye roll on repeat.

"I can't—this is…"

"Katharine! Stop looking at it. Let it go, girl. At least more people will know who you are now, right?"

"Uh, yeah, they'll know me as the awful woman who rolls her eyes at the man America loves, and who laughs at him when he falls. Ugh, that is just like him, too. He tried to play it off as, like, 'hey I'm Mr. Self-Deprecating. Oh, look at me, I'm so charming and affable and cute. Aww, shucks, I'm a good ole boy—"

"Uh, Katharine?"

Tori had dropped her chin and cocked her eyebrow at Katharine. Katharine's mouth opened, then snapped shut again. She sat back and crossed her arms over her chest and looked away, her small jaw thrust out with a defiant air. Tori waited.

"What?"

"Cute, huh? He is more than cute, he's, like, on the fast track to becoming a national treasure. And he is sweet on you, girl."

"*Sweet*? On *me*? Um, no, definitely not. He is trying to ruin my life. He's Enemy Number One. *That's* who he is. And to think—he nearly had me fooled for a minute, there. I almost believed he was trying to protect me from embarrassment. This is all some kind of set up, or a publicity stunt, or—"

"Okay, Katharine, maybe you could try to include *me* in this monologue you're having, and we can turn it into a conversation. You know, that thing people do with one another? How about you tell me what's really going on here, hmm?"

Katharine closed her eyes and took a deep breath, then exhaled slowly. After downing her wine and refilling the glass, she told Tori almost the entire story. When she finally finished, Tori sat back and let out a low whistle. She appraised her reclusive client with a new eye.

"Katharine Evans, you are just a cute little volcano, ready to erupt, aren't you?"

"I am not," she muttered with a petulant tone.

The waitress arrived with their check and Katharine reached for it.

"Oh, no. This one is on me, girl. When you come out to my neck of the woods next week, you can treat. Deal?"

"Deal."

Tori paid their tab and as they walked to the door, she said, "Good. Now, why don't we do a little shopping before I head back to the city?"

Katharine hesitated, but Tori laughed and gave her arm a tug. The duo strolled arm in arm out of the restaurant and onto the side street. Next to Po's was one of the many old historical buildings that stood in close formation along the winding street.

"What's going on here?" Its wide front steps and oversized display windows caught Tori's eye.

"Oh, well, according to the local paper it's been recently bought and newly renovated. I think a boutique and maybe an art gallery are going in? I'm not sure if they've filled the leases yet."

"Oh, Katharine. We really need to get you out into your community. Look, I bet that's the owner over there."

Tori smirked to herself. She knew it was pure torture for Katharine to get out and 'people' as she called it, but she was on a mission. *I am going to get this girl out in the land of the living, even if it kills me.* She glanced at Katharine, shuffling reluctantly behind her. *Or I kill her.*

TEN

CROWD CONTROL

Katharine sighed for the millionth time that day. Tori had a knack for conversing with anyone, anywhere, about anything. It was what made her such a good publicist. By the time Katharine caught up with her and the blonde woman at the front of the building, Tori had the whole story of the place.

"Katharine, this is Sheri. Sheri, Katharine." To Katharine, Tori said, "Did you know this was once an opera house?"

"Ah, nope. No idea," Katharine smiled politely.

"That's right," said the woman. "Siebert's Opera House, it was. Now it's going to be a mix of retail and residential, so if you know of anyone looking to rent or lease, come see me."

"Hmm, you know what?" said Tori, "I think I have a couple ideas. Let me have your number, Sheri, and I'll get back to you."

They said their goodbyes to Sheri and strolled on. Katharine couldn't imagine what ideas Tori might have about the space, but then again, she really didn't know much about Tori at all. The realization filled her with chagrin. In all the time they'd known each other, had Katharine *ever* asked her anything about her personal life? She knew the answer, of course.

"Tori? Am I the most self-involved person you've ever met?"

"You? Nah, you're like, eight on the list."

Katharine threw her head back and yelled at the mid-day, late summer sky. "I am an awful human being!"

"Oh, stop. You're no worse than anyone else trying to get by in the world. We're *all* self-involved, honey. Just to different degrees. At least you live, like, an authentic life. You stay true to you. That's a good thing."

"Yeah, well, I'm starting to realize maybe I've been a bit *too* true to myself. I'm getting tired of...me. Does that make any sense?"

"Yeah, sure. I get it. Too much of anything isn't good. Listen, I think the book tour will be good for you. You branch out, get out of your shell..."

"Wait. Book *tour*? You didn't mention a book tour." Katharine wasn't sure if it was heartburn rising in her throat, or panic. Perhaps it was both.

"Katharine, did you not read the email I sent you?"

Katharine had to think. No, she only half-read it. The half that talked about the Connecticut Today segment. The more she thought about it, she vaguely recalled a bunch of dates below the body of the message.

"No, yeah. Right, I know, I know." She didn't sound convincing, even to her own ears.

"Go back and read it, Katharine. Twelve dates, all New England. Four of them are in the city so you can crash at my place. Unless all your weird people-phobias won't let you cohabitate with others or something."

Katharine swatted Tori's arm playfully and thanked her for the offer. Then her face lit up with a sudden idea. "Oh, my God. Tori! Say you can come to my house this Saturday? Please? I'm throwing a—a party and well, I need actual guests to show up. Please say yes, please?"

"Oh, my Lord, somebody catch me, I'm about to faint! Katharine Evans is having a party? And you are asking me to come? As a... *friend*?"

Tori pretended to fan herself with her hand. Katharine ignored her and explained how her impromptu party came about. When she finished, Tori shook her head at her in disbelief.

"So, you've lived next door to these people for six years, and you never spoke to them? Not even once?"

"I think I might have called out over the bushes once. Okay, maybe 'called out' isn't exactly the right word. It was more like... shouted. About their cat."

Tori's infamous arched brow was enough to pull a full confession. "Alright, so I may have yelled over the bushes that if their cat…*did his business* in my garden one more time, I would call Animal Control on them for animal neglect."

"Wow, Katharine. You really know how to make an impression, don't you? Clearly, you need some help turning your image around. Lucky for you, you have a professional in your corner."

"So, does that mean you'll come?"

"Yes, I will come to your sad little soiree. Can I bring a date?"

"Of course! The more bodies, the better."

"Okay, but remember you said that, you hear?"

Katharine was too relieved and grateful to question her. Continuing their stroll, Katharine instead asked Tori about her life and background. Though she looked surprised by this new and improved Katharine Evans, Tori seemed happy to oblige. After they walked Main Street, they returned to Po's parking lot and said their farewells.

"Well, thanks again for being there today. And for talking me off the ledge. And…"

"Oh, enough with the thank you's, girl. We are all good. I'll see you Saturday, *and* I'll bring my famous shrimp dip."

"Perfect. Thank—right, you know. Oh, and here's your scarf back. You were a lifesaver, you know."

Katharine gave Tori an awkward hug. *Well, look at me, Katharine Evans, hugger of people. Another first. I'll be Up All-Night Show ready in no time. Yeah, right.*

Katharine climbed into her sweltering hot car, cursing the black leather seats. She rolled all the windows down, cranked the air conditioning and pulled out of Po's with one last wave to Tori. On her short drive home, Katharine replayed the day's events. From the powder staining her blouse to the moment she locked eyes—and horns—with Mitch Ford, to the horrible interview. Lastly, to the embarrassing 'viral gif.'

What a day.

But was it really *all* so bad? She had begun to nurture her first friendship aside from her brother. She got the word out about Nate's foundation. She got to see Mitch Ford in his faded denim again. Katharine's foot pressed her brake a little too hard on the unbidden image of Mitch. *Oh, no you don't, Katharine Evans. You stop thinking about him right now. He is a creep. A creep with bottomless blue eyes and a sexy voice and...*

The loud blast of a car horn behind her jolted her from the images turning her insides mushy. The stoplight had turned green, yet she'd sat there staring into space. Mooning over a guy she half wanted to strangle. She waved her hand in the rearview mirror and said '*sorry*' as if they could hear her. As she wove her way along the twisting side streets—once again thankful for her small size of her chocolate brown, white-striped Mini Cooper—Katharine vowed not to give Mitch Ford another thought. But when she pulled onto her narrow road, she had no choice but to acknowledge the existence of the man hell-bent on ruining her life.

That might be a bit of an exaggeration, hmm?
She pursed her lips against the tiny voice of reason
attempting to wiggle its way into her consciousness.
One look at her ordinarily quiet street was enough
to convince her he was indeed trying to ruin her life.
Along one side of the road, for as far as she could
see, news vans and rubber-neckers impeded her
way. A uniformed police officer directed traffic. It
was a full ten minutes before she could get close
enough to ask through her rolled down window
what the holdup was. As if she couldn't guess.

"Sorry, ma'am. Do you live on this… oh, hey!
You're the lady from this morning's Connecticut
Today show! My wife said it was the best laugh of
her day."

"Well. That is… great. I'm so glad. Now, can I
please get to my house?"

"What? Oh, yeah, sure. The show really amped
up the interest in the area, so it's gonna be a bit
hairy out here until Mitch Ford is done taping.
Makes it worse that this is a dead-end street, you
know? Lots of gawkers and news crews who want
an exclusive. But I bet you get all the inside track,
don't you?"

The police officer grinned and winked
knowingly. Then—seeing Katharine's murderous
expression—waved her on her way. Several
carloads of gawkers with their cell phones
congested the street. Men and women with too-
perfect hair and makeup leaned against their vans
drinking coffee and looking bored. Until they
caught sight of Katharine, that is. Her window was

still rolled down, and her name was being called out by several unfamiliar voices.

"Hey, isn't that the Evans woman?"

"Yeah, hey, it is! Get a camera on her, quick."

In an instant, Katharine's little brown Mini Cooper had a swarm of cameras surrounding it. Men with stiff side parts and women with shellacked helmet hair thrust microphones through her window and in her face.

"Katharine, are you and Mitch Ford dating?"

"Miss Evans, do you really hate Mitch Ford or is that an act?"

"Hey, Mrs. Evans, do you plan on—"

"It's *Miss* Evans," she shouted over them, "and get out of my way!"

Katharine honked her horn several times for emphasis. No one moved. Then, over the din, the sharp whine of a bullhorn sounded, followed by the unmistakable rumble of Mitch Ford's authoritative voice.

"Alright, folks! The show's this way! How about you let the lady through. That's right, can't be upsetting the natives, now can we?"

He chuckled, and they all followed suit, like adoring minions. He took slow steps backward, and they followed. Katharine muttered under her breath, "Thanks, Pied Piper," and moved past the row of backs as the clamored for Mitch's attention. He had them rapt, Katharine quickly forgotten. Their eyes met over the crowd, and Mitch tipped his hat as she passed. Katharine turned away, but not before shooting him a loathsome glare. He laughed into the bullhorn.

A moment later, Katharine pulled into her long driveway. The safety of her little bungalow—tucked into its curtain of bushes and trees—beckoned her, and she sighed. She had more than fulfilled her 'peopling' quota for the day. She climbed wearily from her car and headed straight for the protection of home. Relief coursed through her as she cleared the porch steps—no reporters had tried to follow her. A self-satisfied grin spread across Katharine's face. Then, a woman's voice called out from behind her. Katharine steeled herself for the onslaught of invasive reporter questions.

Does anyone pay attention to No Trespassing signs anymore? I'll teach her.

"No trespassing," Katharine whipped around and yelled. "Didn't I make it clear I'm *not* taking any questions? I'm going to give you until the count of three to get off my property, then I'm going to run you off it myself!"

"Oh! I—it's me, Janie. Your neighbor? From…next door? You, um, invited us to a party at your house this weekend? I'm checking if you needed any help? Or, maybe I'll just come back…"

"Janie!" Katharine palm smacked her forehead. "I'm sorry, no, please. I thought you were one of those reporters and… never mind. Uh, come in."

Ugh, why did I invite her in? I have no idea what to say to this woman. 'Hi, sorry I ate six years' worth of cookies and never said thank you? Janie followed Katharine inside like a skittish kitten, her purse clutched to her chest. Once inside, her shoulders dropped, and her eyes grew round as she took in the interior of Katharine's small house.

Katharine looked around, too, trying to see it through Janie's eyes. The front door opened onto a small, four by six-inch, vintage and slightly threadbare rug. Straight ahead, there was the staircase leading upstairs. It was walled on the left, with a white banister on the right. To the left of the foyer, a pale-yellow half wall. On it, a row of hooks fashioned from antique keys. A windbreaker hung on one, a floral print umbrella and a set of keys dangled from another. Her garden boots leaned against each other on a little blue rug. Over the ledge, a view of the small dining area. Rectangle farmhouse table, four mismatched chairs at each side, and a mason jar of blue hydrangeas. Beyond that lie her sunny kitchen. A butcher-block island took up the center of the wide room. Suspended above it, an antique looking wrought iron pot and pan rack with copper cookware gleaming from each hook. In the center of the island sat a milk pitcher with more of those deep blue hydrangea blooms. A lone chair was pulled out from underneath the lip of the island, a coffee mug set before it. Copper accents mingled with rustic wood throughout the tidy space.

To the right of the foyer, her living room. The fireplace was trimmed in flagstone and flanked by two built-in bookcases holding rows of books, framed photographs, and a few potted plants. Between the fireplace and a well-worn caramel colored leather sofa sat a hand-carved teakwood oriental blanket chest, made in the early 1800's. It was one of Katharine's few valued possessions, found at a steal in an antique store several years before. It was a warm, cozy room, inviting and charming with its earthy tones and plush area rug over the wide-plank floorboards. Katharine always smiled a little at the sight of it.

"Oh! Well, this isn't what I expected."

Katharine blinked at her, unsure how to react. When she'd bought the small house, it had been boxy and compartmentalized, outdated and drab. To Katharine, it was claustrophobic, but she could see the potential when she closed her eyes. So, with the help of a very patient and tolerant contractor, she set about knocking down walls, restoring the wood beams in the ceiling, and creating a space which embodied all the things she loved— old libraries, farmhouses, cottages, and cabins. She also knocked down the wall separating two of the three upstairs bedrooms. One large master bedroom and an office were all she foresaw herself ever needing. The end result was the cozy, warm, yet bright living space she'd hoped for. Katharine cocked her head at Janie.

"What were you expecting?"

"I—well, to be honest? I imagined you'd have, like, all white…everything. And famous art, like Picasso or something, on the walls. Sleek stainless-steel appliances and a ritzy fireplace, and…" Janie blushed, "Sorry, I guess I may have given it too much thought. I swear, I'm not, like, a stalker or anything!"

Katharine laughed, taking mercy on the woman. She had a pretty, all-American, girl-next-door look. Long strawberry blonde hair swept into a neat ponytail, big blue eyes, Barbie-esque height, and ultra-friendly air. She was literally the complete opposite of Katharine. The realization caused Katharine to smile at her.

"No, I'm the one who's sorry. I'm afraid I'm a little on the reclusive side. It's nothing personal at all, I'm just…"

"Anti-social?" Janie nodded and scrunched her nose, wincing a bit as she said the words. No doubt worried that Katharine still might bite her head off at any moment, but still wanting to be helpful.

"Yeah, something like that. Anyhow, can I offer you a drink? Coffee, tea…?"

"You got any wine?"

Katharine blinked in surprise.

"Uh, why yes, actually, I do. Red or white?"

"Oh, anything will do. Jim and the boys have been driving me crazy. It is the *worst* having them all home! Summer vacation cannot end soon enough, I tell you."

Katharine poured them their wine and smirked. She remembered her and Nate's summer vacations well. They drove their parents insane. Her smile faded as a darker memory seeped into her mind. Summer camp was not an option for Nate and Katharine, thanks to bullies. So, they spent their summers home with their parents, too. Suddenly, she remembered she had company. *Small talk, must make small talk.*

"No camp for the boys?"

"Ha! Have you *met* those two terrors? There isn't a camp in the state that'll take the McNamara boys. Not for lack of trying, mind you. Last year, they got kicked out of two camps. *Two*. This year, I told Jim, I said, 'Babe, I am not having it. No way. You change your shift, I don't care how you do it, but you are helping me with these two this summer.' I won that battle, thank you very much." She raised her wine glass and clinked it against Katharine's.

I like this woman. Could I be making a second friend? In one day? Miracle, an absolute miracle.

"So, your husband does shift work? What exactly does he do?"

Now it was Janie's turn to slow blink at Katharine. "He's a... State Trooper. There's a cruiser parked in our driveway, like, every single day." She wagged her thumb in the direction of her house as she spoke. "It says, 'K-9 UNIT on the side."

These are statements, but each one ends with an upward inflection. Katharine perks up at the last statement-that-sounded-like-a-question.

"You have a dog?"

Janie set her hands on the table, with her fingers spread as if bracing for an earthquake. "Oh, my. You really don't get out much at all, do you?" She smiled to lessen the harshness of her rhetorical question.

Katharine shrugged and put *her* hands out, skyward. "Arrest me, guilty as charged. Oh, wait! No pun intended." She giggled at her own accidental joke and was surprised when Janie joined in. She shook her head and rolled her eyes as she did, but Janie laughed nonetheless. When she stopped, she answered Katharine's question.

"Yes," she sighed. "We have a German Shepherd named Dax. Jim and Dax jog past your house practically every day. Two summers ago, he got out and ended up on your front porch. Jim came up your driveway searching for him and found the two of you on your porch swing reading a book. Well, you were reading, Dax was sleeping. Does this ring *any* bells?"

Katharine's brow drew together for a moment, then she thumped her forehead with her palm.

"That was your husband! Oh, wow, that was *your* dog? He was so sweet. I kind of hoped no one would come for him."

"Dax, *sweet*? I wish the guys at the barracks could hear you say that! No one except for us can get close to Dax, he's too aggressive. They almost retired him from the program for it, but they're giving him one more year. Anyhow, I'm impressed that Little Miss Recluse here won the favor of big bad K-9 Dax."

"Well, I guess one mean old dog can recognize a kindred spirit, right?"

"Oh, stop! You're not old … *or* mean! In fact, you are way sweeter than you seemed on…"

Janie slapped her hand over her mouth, and her eyes went saucer-wide.

"You saw this morning's show." Katharine stated flatly, "Great, now the whole world thinks I'm horrible." Then she dropped her head on the table with a groan. Janie tentatively patted her shoulder.

"There, there, now. It—it's not so bad, sweetie. As of this morning, only three networks picked up the story. Although I suppose by now, it's spread like wildfire…"

"Not helping, Janie," Katharine's voice came out muffled against the crook of her arm.

"Right. Sorry. Well, it'll all blow over. That gif will be replaced…"

"You saw that, too? Oh, man."

"Darn me and my big mouth. Honestly, all the girls at the gym could talk about this morning was Mitch Ford's blue eyes. And the way his jeans fit. The ones at the coffee shop? Same! All day long, it's been 'Mitch Ford *this*' and 'Mitch Ford *that*.' It got so even Jim had enough of listening to me!"

Janie laughed at her attempted humor, Katharine did not. Although, she did start to feel a little bit better. Until she caught Janie avoiding eye contact. "You're just sparing my feelings, aren't you? Tell me the truth. What's everyone saying?"

"Honey, are you sure you want to hear it? I mean, don't they say it's better for celebrities to not read stories about them?"

"Well, yes they do. But *I'm* not a celebrity. I'm a relatively small-time author no one would ever even recognize on the street."

"Oh, honey. They will now. It's not only the gif that's gone viral, it's the whole fireworks between you and Mitch Ford that's got everyone talking. They've dubbed you two, 'KatMitch.' You know, like 'Brangelina' and KimYe. No? You've never heard of—never mind. Anyhow, what I'm saying, is that you two are a *thing*."

"B—but, we're *not* a thing. There is no 'thing' going on. He's a jerk, hell-bent on making *me* look like the jerk."

"Mhmm."

"No. Not, 'mhmm.' Really!"

"Okay, well, if you say so. But, between me, you, and this bottle of wine, I know I'd—"

Janie's cell phone buzzed. She pulled it from her purse with a heavy sigh and rolled her eyes as she read the message.

"Ah, well, there's the 'Ji' to my 'Jimne.' Apparently, Jeremy has flushed Joey's goldfish down the toilet, alive. Now, Joey has Jeremy's Yugimon cards and my crème brule torch. So, on that note, I'm out. See you Saturday?"

"You're so calm. How are you so calm right now?" Katharine was agitated *for* her, but Janie looked nonplussed.

"Please, honey, you think this was my *first* glass of wine today? Kidding, I'm kidding." Then she put her hand up to the side of her mouth and stage-whispered, "I'm not kidding."

They laughed, and Katharine walked her to the door with wishes of good luck. Janie, in her yoga pants and her form-fitting, racerback tank top, strolled down the driveway as if in absolutely no hurry at all. Her long ponytail swished with each step. She'd already pulled her phone out and was composedly telling whoever was on the other line that when she got home, there was going to be a reckoning and they all had better run. She used the same tone of voice one would use when saying, 'I made you this nice apple pie, and there's ice cream to go with it. Hope you like it'. Katharine was impressed. And exhausted.

A glance at the clock above the stove told her it was five o'clock. Too late for a nap, too early for bed. Too buzzed to write. *What to do, what to do.* Katharine had not looked at her phone since leaving the television studio that morning. Now she eyed her purse as if it held a ticking bomb instead of a cell phone. She went so far as to make a full arc around the chair on which it hung as if it were a venomous snake dangling over the backrest instead of an innocuous pocketbook.

You're ridiculous. Get the phone and see what's going on in the internet world. The moment she reached inside and looked at her illuminated screen with all its icon notifications glaring at her in red circles, she would have to acknowledge the day's events indeed did transpire and weren't just a bad dream. *Ugh. Stop being such a chicken and read them already.*

Her inner voice was right. Time to put on her big girl pants and face the music. Or backlash, in this case. Maybe she was exaggerating. The world had probably already moved on from... *KatMitch,* or whatever the heck Janie called it. Surely, there were more exciting things to focus in on than a woman who wrote books for teens and guy on a reality network television show. How well known *was* this show, anyhow? She realized she had no idea. Television was never really her thing, she was a book girl.

I guess there's an easy way to find out. If I could stop being a coward and look him up. There were also nine missed calls. She groaned as she scrolled through the call log. Most were from Tori, and the rest from Nate. As much as she hoped to talk to Nate, her gut told her she'd better deal with whatever Tori had to throw her way. It would no doubt have something to do with all those red alerts on her phone since Tori was the one who'd installed and co-managed the accounts. Which in Katharine's case, that meant *fully* managed on her behalf since she had no interest in social media. Or savvy. Just as Ari decided to place the call, the phone buzzed in her hand. It was Tori, for the seventh time. She took a deep breath and answered.

"Hello, Tori. Long time no talk," she exhaled.

"Katharine! Where have you been? Did you turn your phone off again? Girl, it's been crazy. Look at your social media!"

"Whoa, slow down, Tori. Um, hi, first of all. Let's see, hmm. I've been home, drinking wine with my new friend and neighbor, Janie. No, my phone was *not* off… it was on vibrate. What was the last thing? Oh, stupid social media. No, I haven't looked yet."

"Oh, my God. I cannot *even* with you. Katharine, the world is infatuated with KatMitch! They want more, and they want it now. The Up All-Night Show has requested we move your appearance to next week. Actually, they were shooting for sooner, but Justin said Mitch was booked solid, so—"

"Wait, what? Did you say, Mitch? You mean they want us to appear *together*? No. Nope, absolutely not. I'm not doing it, Tori."

"Kat—" Tori softened her sharp tone, "*Katharine*. Sweetheart. This is what we call momentum. Exposure. Opportunity. Success. Don't you want to be a successful— and by successful— I mean *paid* author? What is wrong with you, girl?"

Katharine became petulant, knowing her argument was contrary to all Tori had spelled out for her. "He's a jerk. I don't want to be stuck on the same stage as him again. He's going to embarrass me and make me look bad, *again*. And I *do* make money. So, there."

"Do you even hear yourself right now? Are you twelve? Did we just go back to junior high school?" Under her breath, Tori muttered, "Honestly, I do not get paid enough for this nonsense."

"I don't—"

"Uh-uh," Tori stopped her in her tracks, "First, I don't know why you're so hard on that fine-lookin' man. After all, he did only show the clip of him falling in the water. It's not like you made him fall in, right?"

Katharine didn't respond.

"Katharine Evans, please tell me you did not make the man fall into the pond."

So, Katharine may have left out a few details about her encounters with Mitch over the past week.

"Well, I didn't *make* him. And anyhow, he shouldn't have been on my property."

Tori heaved an exasperated sigh and muttered under her breath again. Katharine could pick out words like, '*out of her mind*' and '*so help me God.*' It made her smirk a little, the picture in her mind of Tori pacing back and forth. She envisioned Tori shaking her fist at the ceiling, a look of utter vexation contorting her normally placid face. After a pause, she composed herself enough to deal with 'the talent.'

"Start from the beginning, Katharine. Something tells me you left out a few details over our lunch.

Now it was Katharine's turn to sigh and behave put upon. "I told you...*most* of what happened. Fine, I may have left out the part where I threw a soccer ball at him. I mean, I was aiming for his leg, but, well, never mind. Oh, and I poured my drink over his head, but there was only a little bit left in the cup. And I got him thrown out of a bar, so he claimed. Oh, and I may have sort of, kind of threatened to beat him with my kayak paddle. But it was his own fault!"

"I'm sorry. Am I to understand you verbally and physically assaulted Mitch Ford, not once, but on several occasions?"

"Yeah, but—"

"Uh-uh. Hold up. Now, *you* are mad *he* might 'make you look bad'? Katharine, *you* are making you look bad! Tell me this is not on tape."

Katharine said nothing.

"Oh, my Lord. Of course, it's on tape. Here's what we are going to do. You, Miss Katharine who-can't-control-her-temper, are going to stay *off* your social media accounts. I, Miss Tori who-is-going-to-try-and-fix-your-mess, am going to do a full social media takeover."

"Well, technically, you already run my—"

"Shh. No talking. Here's what else you are going to do. You are going to go over to that house and apologize to Mitch Ford for your inexcusable behavior. Then, you are going to invite him to your little party. Then, you are going to turn your little self right back around and get back to your house. Got it?"

"But I don't *want* to apologize. You didn't see his smug face—"

"Mhmm."

"Or how he laughed when *I* fell—"

"Mhmm."

"Or the way he—he just gives me that look of his—"

"You done yet?"

"Yes. I suppose."

"Good, now prepare your apology. I am going to work out your new appearance schedule. Goodnight Katharine."

Before Katharine could protest, the call disconnected. She looked at the receiver and stuck her tongue out at it. It was further proof that Mitch Ford had caused her to devolve into one of the pre-teens she wrote for and about.

Great.

ELEVEN

PUSHED TOO FAR

The moment the news and tabloid's cameras were out of earshot, Mitch's genial smile dropped. He handed the bullhorn to Sam, who was walking beside him back to the backyard. Sam eyed him with curiosity. He'd never seen his boss slash best friend so wound up. Usually, Mitch really was as affable as his public persona conveyed, which Sam supposed made it less a *persona* and more his personality. Before he could say a word, Mitch launched into what could only be described as a tirade.

"I mean, really! Did you see her? Rude, right? Help a girl out, and she doesn't even give a wave. That's three times now, by the way. Three times, I've gone out of my way to help that woman. Well, no more Mr. Nice Guy. Tomorrow, I want all hands-on deck. Every chainsaw, every hammer, every—"

"Uh, I get it, Mitch. Sure, we can do that. But—"

"Good. That'll show her. Tell *me* I can't make noise. Who does she even think she is? *Writer*. I mean, it's children's books, not War and Peace. Am I right?"

"Sorry, are you looking for a response, or letting off steam? They're young adult books, by the way. Just saying."

"Young ad—and yes, I want a response. Never mind, I don't."

Sam shrugged and let Mitch ramble and mutter for the rest of their walk. By the time they'd reached the backyard and the rest of the crew, he'd exhausted himself. Or purged, was more like it. Enough so that he could address the rest of the team. He thanked them all for their hard work, outlined the plan for the next day, and dismissed everyone for the afternoon. Sam decided the boss-man could use a friendly ear and a cold beer.

"Alright, buddy, what do you say we check out that Thai place we saw on the way back here this morning?"

"I don't know. I'm not the best company right now, am I? That woman has—" Mitch paused and rubbed his face briskly, then said, "You know what? Let's go grab a bite. Po's something or other, wasn't it?"

They hopped in Sam's rental Jeep and took the short ride into town.

"Cute town, isn't it?"

Sam agreed. He'd known Mitch long enough to know when an idea was brewing in that head of his, so he waited quietly.

"You know," he began a little too casually, "this is just the kind of little town I could see myself settling down in. A home base, of sorts."

"Settle down? You? Here?"

Sam was more than mildly surprised. Mitch Ford had never, *ever* talked about setting roots down in any of the locations they'd worked. And they'd been to some incredible places. Of course, he had a suspicion as to what—or rather who—was piquing his interest. He also knew not to voice his suspicion.

"Well, yeah, you know. A man needs a place to lay his hat, call home. I'm forty-two, Sam. Been on the road a long time now."

"You're preachin' to the choir, buddy. I've been telling you this for the past couple years now if you've forgotten. Funny how all the sudden, you're ready to 'settle down.' Any particular reason for that? *Here*, that is. Settling down in *this* place?"

"What's that supposed to mean? No, I merely like…the town. The lake is appealing. The people are lovely. Well, *most* of the people, that is."

Sam didn't need to ask who he was referring to. It was as plain as the once broken nose on his face. He could see it was going to be a long night. They found Po's Rice and Spice easily and parked, unknowingly of course, in the same spot Katharine had parked that afternoon. Inside, they were greeted like old friends and given a corner table. The young waitress blushed and giggled, and the other diners slid surreptitious glances in Mitch's direction. He smiled and nodded at them all, taking it in stride as if it was completely normal to be gawked at and whispered about. Sam admired this about Mitch.

Sam also appreciated his friend's lack of ego. Over their eight years together—first as a regular construction company, then on to a public access show, and now a syndicated program that actually makes a difference in people's lives—he'd witnessed firsthand Mitch's genuine compassion and generosity. He loved connecting with people as much as he loved building. In short, Mitch was as good as a guy anyone could ever meet. Which made it so hard to figure out why Katharine Evans had such an adverse reaction to him. Something Mitch Ford was obviously struggling to understand as well.

"I just want to know, Sam. Am I crazy, or is that woman confounding?"

"Well, I think she—"

"Confounding! One minute she's throwing a soccer ball at me, then next, she almost kissed me. You didn't know *that*, did you? It's true, though. She did. I mean, she nearly did."

"Was that before or after she poured a drink over your head?" Sam's tone was wry, but he was surprised about the near kiss. That was the first he'd heard of it. *Now that would've been camera gold. Too bad.*

"Hilarious, Samuel. Alright, enough about her. Let's talk shop. How's the editing coming along?"

"Well, about that, Mitch. Bill is pushing for some good, candid stuff." This was what Sam had really been wanting—and dreading—talking to

Mitch about. "See, the footage of you and Katharine is the best thing we have, and I think we need to use it. I know you said you don't want me to, but—"

"No, you know what? Use it. Go ahead. I'm not going to protect Katharine Evans anymore. She is not my problem."

Sam raised his eyebrows.

"I mean it. Do it."

Sam knew that expression on Mitch's face. It was the one that spoke of finality, authority, and no room for questions. So, it was settled. There was just one last thing he needed to bring to Mitch's attention, and he dreaded it.

"So, uh, Mitch. There's just one more thing. I'm guessing you haven't looked at your social media yet?"

Mitch eyed Sam warily while he pulled his phone from his pocket. He looked down at the screen, tapped an icon, and began scrolling. Sam watched as a vein in his temple became more prominent and his jaw clenched and unclenched rhythmically. At one point, he muttered, "KatMitch? Ridiculous," and shook his head. At last, he powered off the phone and replaced it in his pocket. "This needs to be nipped, Samuel."

Sam nodded in agreement, although he hadn't the slightest idea how to make that happen. Fortunately, it seemed to satisfy him well enough and they finished their meal without another word on the topic. Mitch moved on to work related topics as if he'd never even seen the media frenzy over him and Katharine. Sam knew him well enough to understand that he was seething inside but wanted to keep up appearances. So, he played along until it was time to call it a night.

Once he'd dropped Mitch back at the bed and breakfast they were staying at, Sam met with his production team to finish the final edits, create the teaser, and send it to the studio for release. What would once take days could now be done in hours, thanks to the great digital age. He sure hoped Mitch knew what he was doing. Once it was sent out, it was a done deal, no take backs.

Sam sent the guys off to catch some sleep before they started all over again in the morning. He stayed on a bit longer. He had some last-second edits he needed to do, and Sam needed to be alone to do them. That way, he'd be the only one to blame for the inevitable fallout. After an hour or so, the last edit done, he stared at the screen with his hand over his mouth, fingertips drumming his beard-stubbled cheek. His other hand hovered over the laptop's mousepad, the white arrow poised on the 'send' tab. If he sent the full file, it would likely seal the coffin on his friend's chances with the writer. If he *didn't* send it, he was risking the show *and* his job. His palms began to sweat as he debated.

From beside the computer, his phone rang loudly, causing him to startle. His finger hit the tab, and the file sent. *Well, that's that. Now we wait.* He answered the call distractedly. "Yes, Bill. I just sent it to you. Yes, good stuff, sir. Thank you. Bye, sir."

TWELVE

IT'S NOT ME, IT'S YOU

After Sam's Jeep had pulled away from the bed and breakfast, and Mitch had navigated through the handful of curious guests, he shut his suite door with a heavy thud. For a moment, he closed his eyes and leaned against it. Then he yanked his hat off and threw it across the room like it was a frisbee.

What is wrong with me? No, what's wrong with her, *that crazy woman?* Mitch's eyes fell on the laptop on the small desk in the corner of the room. He usually reviewed Sam's files before they were sent out for production, but it was way too soon to expect them. What harm could it do to look at what this Katharine Evans was about? After all, they were now the 'trending couple to watch' according to social media. Even as he told himself not to do it, he lifted the cover and typed her name into the search browser. Within seconds, Katharine's entire public information was his for the perusing. Had she done the same, he wondered?

Immediately after her Wikipedia page, were several tabloid headlines linking the two of them. He rolled his eyes and ignored those for the moment, at least. He had to see what her books were about.

'Chelsea Marin Chronicles,' huh?

Despite his sneer, he read on. Mitch's sardonic smile slipped as his eyes scanned the text on the screen. A new appreciation for Katharine replaced the scorn. Her books had an actual message, and a great one at that. He recalled bits of what Katharine had said in her interview on Connecticut Today. Hadn't she mentioned a non-profit foundation? On impulse, he downloaded her first book. In minutes, he was quickly reading Katharine's story. She'd titled it, The Power Within. In it, her young heroine discovers her inner strength. The crux of the story is when she's given a choice to punish the bullies who had tormented her younger sister—who not-so-coincidentally had Down's Syndrome—or to use them to guide them toward making better decisions.

Mitch was impressed. Sure, it was written in a youthful vernacular, but it only showed she really took the time to understand her audience. He set the laptop aside. The first twinges of regret niggled at his brain. *I shouldn't have given Sam the green light to submit the tapes.* He checked the time, then his email icon. Sam still hadn't sent him a copy of the recordings. Maybe he'd called it a night, too. Mitch would give it a bit longer, take a shower, then call Sam to tell him he'd changed his mind after all.

Once in the bathroom, he looked at the jets in the tub and decided a good soak would do his aching back wonders. Two hours later, he awoke in the tepid bubbling water. *Whoops. Guess I was more tired than I thought.*

With a towel wrapped around his waist, he walk-ran, dripping on the hardwood floor, to his phone. Still no message from Sam. Mitch frowned, then shrugged. They'd been going full steam since they'd arrived in town so he wouldn't have been surprised if Sam decided to leave it for the morning. He plugged the phone into the charger, set it on the desk, and threw on a pair of sweatpants. Then he climbed back into the four-poster bed to see what else he could learn about Katharine Evans.

This time, he found her social media page. "Oh, Miss Evans. There is no way you're doing the posting and commenting on here. Way too nice for the dragon lady."

He shook his finger at Katharine's profile picture. It was a professionally posed 'candid' shot with a backdrop of the lake. The edge of a dock and part of a huge hydrangea bush framed the photo. She was smiling, but the smile didn't reach her eyes, and her arms were crossed in front of her chest. Mitch supposed it was the publicist, Toni, who set up not only the photo shoot but also her social media accounts. Grudgingly, he admitted to himself he could understand Katharine's disinterest in the medium. It was time-consuming, intrusive, and yet so *disconnected*. People became brave behind the anonymity of a keyboard and said whatever they wanted. He'd seen some of the boldest propositions, *and* some of the harshest criticisms hurled his way by people he'd never met. Yet somehow, they all deemed it acceptable to be inappropriate or cruel. So, yes, while it could be tiresome, it was also a necessary evil.

The fans of The Rebuilder Show were what kept it growing, so it was his duty to respond and engage with them whenever possible and let Justin take over only when he was too busy. One look at Katharine's awkward stance and barely smiling face were enough to cause Mitch to doubt that Katharine had the social skills to finesse such interactions. He frowned at his uncharitable and smug thoughts. *Why am I letting her get to me like this?* He'd told Sam to nip the whole nonsense in the bud, but even he realized it was next to impossible to stop a freight train in its tracks. They would just have to wait it out.

Mitch looked over at his phone and considered calling Justin. The clock on the nightstand read eleven-twenty. A lousy time to call for something non-urgent. Not that it stopped anyone from calling *him* at all hours. His phone rang. Mitch heaved a sigh and set the laptop on the bed. He crossed the room, unplugged the phone from the charger, and read the caller ID. He threw his hand in the air. *Of course, it's Justin. Why am I surprised?*

"Hey, kid. I was just thinking of calling you."

"Mitch, my man. That so? Everything alright, I hope?"

"Yes, fine, fine. It's about this… KatMitch madness. I—"

"We are on the same wavelength, dude! It is utter madness, bro! We have got to get ahead of it, dominate it and move it along."

"Right, exactly. Wait—move it along? You mean end it, right?"

"End it? Bro, are you crazy? That video was clutch, buddy. We need to amp it up, man. Listen, listen. So, right now, we've got classic romantic tension. Like, I'm talking Moonlighting chemistry. So, we run with it. Full steam, like a—"

"Moonlighting?"

"Dude. Come on, man. Moonlighting. Classic comedy from the eighties? Bruce Willis? Nothin'? Okay, never mind. Trust me on this. Tori agrees."

Ah, yes. He'd forgotten Justin's strange obsession with vintage television shows. He once sat through a thirty-minute dissertation as to why The Golden Girls was in Justin's 'Top Ten All-Time Greatest Shows' list. Mitch's head was spinning. This was *not* what he'd intended, but all he could do in between Justin's SoCal speak was stammer one-word questions.

"Tori?"

"Yeah, you know, Katharine's publicist. She'll handle the bombie, I got you, bro. It'll be all good. Just, uh, let me deal with the soc stuff."

Mitch dropped his chin against his chest in defeat and confusion. "I'm sorry, but what in God's name are you saying?"

Justin huffed into the phone. Then he slowed his speech as if talking to a child. "Right. Okay, bro. *Tori* is going to do *Katharine's* social media. *I* will do *yours*. All *you two* need to do is keep the chemistry hot. We need to get you two together again, in front of the cameras. The Up All-Night show is one thing, but we need something more…intimate, too."

"Yeah, well, good luck with that, kid. I have no interest in poking that bear again, and I'm sure she feels the same way." Mitch paced the floor, went over to the French door that opened onto a small balcony and stepped out into the warm night. The moment he did camera flashes blinded him, and he raised his hand to shield his eyes. Calls from the yard one floor down disturbed the quiet. His regret was instant. He back stepped into the room and shut the door. Then he yanked the blinds closed. All while Justin yapped on. Suddenly, his words seeped in.

"Hold it! What did you just say?"

"I said, we'll have your guy, Sam, at Katharine's party with you, but like, stealth, you know."

"Who said I'm going to a party at Katharine Evans? I am *not* going to a party over there. That woman will probably set me on fire."

"Well, it *would* make great ratings—"

"Justin!"

"Kidding, I'm joshin' you, bro. All I know is she's supposed to invite you. Don't worry, I'll be there, too. My girl Tori is bringing me as her plus one, bro. Alright, I gotta cruise. You have any questions, you hit me up."

"Wait, I have several—"

Justin had already hung up. Mitch stared at his phone, then slammed it down on the desk. He had a sneaking suspicion this build was going to be a big train wreck for his personal life. One he was powerless to stop unless he was willing to disappoint an innocent family, which he wasn't. No, Mitch Ford was about to sink deeper into the catastrophe called Katharine Evans whether he liked it or not. Resigned, he climbed back into bed. When he grabbed the laptop to close it, the screen lit up. It was Katharine's round, sea-green eyes staring back at him, her lips with a faint smile and her hair cascading over her shoulder. He recognized it to be her back-cover photo for her books. He must have clicked on the picture when he set the computer down on the bed. Despite himself, Mitch grinned at the surprisingly innocent face on the screen. *Well, at least she's a beautiful catastrophe.*

THIRTEEN

SOCIAL MEDIA SKILLS

"Hello? Anybody home?"

Katharine's eyes popped open at the sound of the chipper, melodic voice coming from her front porch. She was on her back deck, soaking in the sun and drinking her coffee... and pretending not to hear the noises coming from Genoma's backyard. It took her a moment, but she recognized the voice to be Janie's. To her utter surprise, she realized she was pleased to hear it.

"I'm in back!"

When Janie came around the corner, bearing a tray of muffins in her hands, Katharine raised her coffee mug and pointed to it.

"I'd love some, thanks. Brought you some muffins. Oh, my, it *is* noisy over there, isn't it?"

"Yep, welcome to my misery. Have a seat, I'll grab you a cup."

When Katharine returned, two steaming mugs of coffee in hand, Janie gave her a big smile. Too big. It was a smile Katharine would learn early in their friendship to mean 'I have something to tell you, but I'm afraid to.' She handed her new friend her cup and sat across from her.

"So," Katharine said, "what brings you over?"

"Oh, you know," she shrugged, "checking to see how you're doing with… everything."

Janie's long pauses caused Katharine to set her mug down on the patio table, lean forward in her seat, and study her face. The over-bright smile came back again, then she took a sip of coffee and slid her eyes away.

"Janie? Is there something you want to tell me?"

"Oh, doesn't the lake look especially beautiful this morning?"

"Spill it," said Katharine.

Janie rapidly tapped the side of the mug with one bubblegum-pink painted fingernail. Then, squinching one eye closed, she took a big breath and laid out her confession. "I maybe, kind of, totally mentioned your party this morning while I was at the gym."

Katharine stared at her, waiting for the other shoe to drop. Undoubtedly, there was still more. She tilted her head down and raised an eyebrow.

Janie continued, "You know that saying, 'the more, the merrier?' Well, I somehow sort of said you'd love more people to come. I mean it was only Trish and Gina. Oh, and Kathy. But then Gina told Jeff, and Jeff told Ned, and Ned is married to Trish's sister, so—"

"Stop. How about you tell me how many people are now coming to my small, intimate party?"

"Um, okay. So, if I had to guess? Twenty. Twenty-five, tops. I think."

Katharine fell back against the thick cushion of her chair and blinked at Janie. She wasn't sure whether she should laugh or cry. "Janie, I've never, *ever* thrown a party before. This is going to be a disaster."

Janie put on what Katharine could only describe as her 'mom face' and spoke in its accompaniment, her mom voice. "Okay, now, sweetie, it's *not* going to be a disaster. It's going to be fun! Have you gotten all your shopping done?" Katharine shook her head. Janie's smile slipped, then resurfaced. "Not a problem. Have you made a list yet?" Upon seeing Katharine's blank stare, she continued, nonplussed. "All right, that's fine, totally fine. Still not a problem. How about we do that right now? Me and you?"

She sent a dazed Katharine inside for pen and paper, then on her return, began dictating everything Katharine would need for the next day. The list was long and overwhelming. Fortunately, Janie took pity on her and offered to go shopping with her.

"There now, that isn't so bad, is it?"

"Oh, no, not at all." Katharine's tone dripped with sarcasm. What had she gotten herself into?

More than thirty people—strangers, no less—would be invading her home in less than twenty-four hours. She would know exactly three people: her brother, Tori, and Janie. At least there'd be no racket from next door going on. Then Katharine remembered—she still had to invite *him*. Janie, with her uncanny timing, spoke the dreaded name.

"Now, about Mitch Ford. There's a rumor he's going to be here, so that means—"

"Don't remind me. I still have to go over there and invite the oaf. Can't I simply *not* invite him?"

Another stab of anxiety pierced her. It grew as she watched Janie's face redden and her fingernail drum her coffee mug again. Katharine curled her hands around the wicker arms of her chair and pushed back against the cushion as if bracing for a crash.

"Well," Janie began, "it's kind of all over social media, honey. It made tabloid news, too. Haven't you looked?"

She had not. Not since Tori had all but banned her from using her own platform and she'd willingly obliged. Katharine bolted inside and grabbed her phone from the charger in the kitchen. She paced back and forth as it powered on, biting her nail. After waiting an eternity, she tapped her social media icon. The screen filled with images and links to articles speculating about the 'swirling rumors of a budding relationship' between her and Mitch Ford.

"Seriously? Don't people have anything better to do?"

Janie shrugged and opened her mouth to speak, but Katharine railed on.

"I mean, I met this guy, what? Barely a week ago? Suddenly now we're a 'budding relationship?' It's absurd! I can tell you: I don't care how good looking he is, I have zero interest in that smug, self-centered, arrogant—"

"Katharine—"

"—fake humble, chauvinistic—" Katharine paused and blinked at Janie, who was looking not at her, but over her shoulder. "He's behind me, isn't he?"

Janie put her head in her hand and nodded. Katharine turned slowly and tried to hide her mortification with a defiant glare. A sharp, preemptive rebuke was ready on her lips, but instead of anger on his face, he wore a boyish grin. He spread his hands out and tilted his head at her. "Aww, you think I'm good-looking? Why shucks, ma'am."

Katharine's cheeks were on fire. She ignored his attempt at disarming humor and thrust her phone in his face. He jerked his head back and squinted at the screen, then bobbed his head in understanding. "Ah, yes. That. It just so happens, that is why I came over. Katharine, I swear, I had nothing to do with it. We *both* have our publicists to thank."

Janie was watching them—mostly him— with rapt attention. They both turned to her at the same time, and she jumped like she'd been stung.

"Hello, I'm Janie. My husband, Jim, and I live on the other side of Katharine. We love your show, Mr. Ford."

Katharine mouthed 'traitor' at her.

Mitch said, "Why, thank you, Janie. You're too kind. Please, call me Mitch. Mr. Ford is my father."

Katharine rolled her eyes at him and stepped away, her face glued to her screen once again. "Listen to this: 'Mitch Ford to attend swanky summer bash at the home of his new girlfriend, writer, Katharine Evan.' It's Evans, with an 's' you idiots."

"It's really better if you don't read any—"

"Swanky? Who even uses the word 'swanky'?"

Janie slowly stood up and edged her way around Katharine as if she were a poisonous snake.

"Okay, Katharine? Sweetie? I'm gonna head on out and let you two... sort things. You come over when you're ready to hit the grocery store, alright?"

Katharine hardly looked up from her phone as she muttered her goodbye to Janie.

Mitch was much more gracious. "It was lovely meeting you, Janie. I look forward to meeting the rest of the family at the... you know."

He jerked his head in Katharine's direction. They both looked at her nervously. It was needless, she wasn't paying attention to either of them. She was too busy scrolling and swearing under her breath. Janie left them, throwing several glances back at the pair before she rounded the corner. Mitch waved her off, then returned his attention to Katharine.

"Katharine? *Katharine.*"

"What? Oh, God, you're still here? You know, when I get ahold of Tori, I swear, I'm going to—"

"Could you, perhaps, give the floor to someone else for one moment? Me, specifically."

Katharine shrugged and set down the phone. She crossed her arms over her chest and lifted her eyebrows at him.

"Thank you. Now, listen. This is not all bad, you know. Think of it as free press for your books. Have you even looked at your sales records since this all started up? I'll bet there's a spike. How about your charity organization? Guarantee there's a jump in donations there, too. Speaking of that, will my buddy Nate be here tomorrow?"

The moment Mitch mentioned Nate, Katharine smiled. *It is kind of sweet that he asked about Nate. Nate hasn't stopped talking about Mitch, either.* The grin faltered when she looked at Mitch. Her shoulders dropped, and she uncrossed her arms and considered him, a new expression on her face than the usual sour ones he'd probably grown accustomed to.

"Nate seemed to be quite taken with you. And yes, he'll be here tomorrow." After a pause, she said, "Obviously, you're invited."

"Great."

They smiled at one another for a moment, until it became awkward. Mitch rubbed the back of his neck and chuckled. Katharine tucked her hair behind her ear. Several times. Mitch found it endearing. They spoke at the same time.

"Would you like a cup—"

"Well, I guess I'll be—"

"Sorry, what," they both asked.

Mitch tipped his cap, "Ladies first."

Katharine smiled. "Would you like a cup of coffee? I suppose we should at least get to know each other a bit since we're the new 'it' couple."

"Yes, I suppose so, hmm? I'd love a cup of coffee, Katharine," he said with a slowly spreading smile.

She went inside with the sound of him saying her name reverberating in her brain, and Mitch sat down at her patio table. From her kitchen window, she could see him squirming in the plush, floral print cushioned chair. He resembled a bear at a child's tea party. When she came out, he tried to look natural.

Katharine made no attempt to hide her grin. "Well, look at the big, burly man in the pretty chair. The tabloids would love this. Maybe I should take a picture and send it to them myself?"

"I'd prefer not, Ms. Evans, thank you."

***

He accepted the outstretched mug with mock chagrin. He was secure in his manhood, and it wouldn't have been the end of the world to have his photograph taken in the flowery, girly chair, but still. Katharine positioned her chair beside his so they both could look out over the lake. At first, they sat quietly, gazing at the calm water. The sun climbed lazily over the trees and cicadas had already begun their crescendo buzz. It was going to be another hot day. By noon, the guys would be irritable and slow next door, thanks to the heat.

Mitch's gaze traveled the span of her yard. Variegated, elephant, and blue Hosta plants alternated with orange daylilies all around the perimeter. Creeping phlox in several shades of blue blanketed a stone border in some spots, and crimson carpet roses spilled over others. Several lilac bushes—well past bloom—intertwined, and a lone wisteria tree drooped over a bird bath. Birdfeeders and gourd birdhouses took residence on one side of the yard, while hummingbird feeders populated the other side. Below her kitchen window, two raised garden beds worked overtime to confine their inhabitants. One bragged a row of ripe fruit-laden tomato plants, cucumber vines that wove through and over an A-frame trellis, vibrant green bean bushes, a line of green cabbage, another of red, and lastly—that he could see—large squash plants. The other raised bed was host to all kinds of lettuces and herbs.

Mitch's eyes move from the garden boxes back to the opening of the lake. Two sizeable blue hydrangea bushes stood sentry on either side of her dock and kayak access. This is where Katharine's profile picture was taken. Everything about Katharine's nature-loving backyard was quaint and near perfect. All but for one very noticeable distraction. The sound of hammers, saws, and men shouting to one another carried through the bushes with jarring regularity. It disturbed the serenity of the haven Katharine had created for herself with deliberate care. Abashed, he turned his eyes on Katharine, who was watching the birds at their feeders.

"I'm sorry, Katharine. I see why you're so protective of your privacy now. This—back here— it's beautiful. You've got your own little paradise, and we're disturbing it. We've got a couple more weeks, barring any delays, then we'll be out of your hair, and your life can go back to normal."

Katharine sighed and shook her head. "No, *I'm* sorry. I mean, yes, the noise and disruption are awful, but what you're doing? It's pretty amazing. I've never so much as waved to Mr. Genoma, and here you are—a complete stranger—rebuilding his home for his war veteran grandson."

"Well, you know, makes great publicity and ratings for the show."

Katharine turned warmly toward Mitch and put her hand on his arm. "No, I don't believe that. It's not about publicity… *or* ratings for you, is it?" She didn't wait for Mitch to respond. "I knew it the moment I heard you speak on that show. You do it because you care."

Mitch squirmed again in his seat. People patted him on the back and told him how great he was practically every day, but he never got used to it. He never enjoyed it. Mitch did what he did because he could. He'd been blessed with the ability, then the means to change and better the lives of people less fortunate than him. It was how he was raised, to be a good human. Do good, be good. Simple as that.

"Eh, I'm not so bad for a—what did you call me? Self-centered, arrogant, fake—"

Now it was Katharine's turn to squirm. Mitch wasn't about to let her off the hook, at least not right away. But then she turned those big green eyes of hers on him, and all the sarcasm died on his lips. She looked genuinely mortified. Her small hand was still warm on his arm. He placed his over hers and leaned toward Katharine.

"I'm teasing you, Katharine. Don't worry, I've got thick skin."

She shifted closer. "I don't think your fake anything. I think you might be the most genuine person I've met in a long time."

They inched closer. Mitch could smell the intoxicating scent of her shampoo again. He took his hand off hers and reached up to her face. The lock of hair she'd been fastidiously tucking had come free again, and he tucked it for her. Katharine smiled shyly against his rough palm. All Mitch could think about was kissing her.

"Hey! Here they are! KatMitch, look over here!"

Mitch and Katharine jumped away from each other and searched for the source of the commotion. Camera's flashed, and several people burst through the bushes from Genoma's side.

***

One moment Mitch Ford's lips were inches from hers, and the next, pandemonium. Katharine's pitter-pattering heart shifted into thunderous pounding as she jumped up from her seat. Her shock and confusion became an unbridled outrage. Only part of her brain registered Mitch beside her, saying 'let me handle this' while the other part told her to become a raging shrew. She chose to heed to the latter, which would end up being unfortunate.

"This is private property! Get off my grass, you idiots!"

Katharine started marching toward the crowd, who were taking even more pictures as they laughed and pointed. Mitch grabbed her arm to stop her, but she swung free, yelling all the while. No one was leaving, they were just stepping back into the bushes and trampling her flowers. She looked around for something to throw and spied the hose instead. Katharine's eyes lit up with evil glee. *I'll show them.*

She'd be lying if she said she didn't hear Mitch warning her not to do it. He was right, of course, but Katharine didn't care. She was furious these people had the audacity to not only trespass onto her property, but to proceed to take pictures and film her while doing it. If this was what fame was like, she wanted no part of it. She grabbed the nozzle, adjusted it to 'power wash' mode, aimed and squeezed. As expected, the crowd scattered and ran back through the bushes. Once they were all gone, she released the trigger and set the hose down with a self-congratulatory cheer. From behind her, Mitch cleared his throat. Katharine spun around, expecting a high-five. Instead, she found herself on the receiving end of a stern, disapproving, and decidedly displeased Mitch Ford stare.

"What? Oh, come on, they deserved it."

"Yes, that may be very true. However, now we are once again fodder for their stories. That right there, is what Sam would call—"

"Cinematic gold!" Sam himself walked out from around the side of the house, camera perched on his shoulder like a giant parrot. Katharine looked from one to the other in disbelief.

"Again? You did this to me *again*? Get out of here."

"Katharine, this isn't—"

"Just go, Mitch. Please."

Her anger was only overshadowed by hurt. *This is what happens when you let your guard down, Katharine.*

Katharine's voice shook. She was dangerously close to crying, and she needed Mitch and his sidekick to leave her alone. Mitch took a step toward her, and she put her hand up and looked away.

"Don't worry. I'll play my part tomorrow, my half of KatMitch. I'll even play along for as long as your crew is here. But after that? I hope I never see you again, Mitch."

She passed them and went inside the house, shutting the door and blinds behind her.

FOURTEEN

LIFE OF THE PARTY

One hour before the party, Mitch stood in the lobby of the bed and breakfast with Justin. For the third time, he announced, "I don't think I should go to the party, Justin."

"Mitch, bro. It'll be fine, chill. Tori said Katharine was, like, totally dope with it. Here, take these." Justin handed him a bouquet of wildflowers.

"Gee, you shouldn't have," said Mitch.

"Dude, they're for your little bombie, man! It'll go over killer for the press, bro."

Mitch's right eye twitched with every utterance of surfer jargon that drawled from Justin's mouth. He anticipated a full day of that, along with God knew how many strangers. Not to mention spending the day with a woman who hated him.

Katharine. It pained him to even think her name. If she'd turned her anger on him, it would've been better than the look of betrayal and hurt in her beautiful eyes. He was the kind of man who lived by the 'do no harm' motto, and yet his presence in Katharine's life brought nothing *but* harm to her. He wanted to fix the damage—that was his thing, after all—and yet he was baffled as to how. Ending the build was out of the question. Finishing it sooner than scheduled, impossible. There was the party, which held possibilities he supposed.

Think big, old man. Their Up All-Night Show appearance. Maybe he could do something, like a grand gesture, to make her see he wasn't the guy she imagined he was. But what? What could he say or do to knock down the barrier between them? Maybe he could get some intel from her friends, Janie and Tori.

"Dude? You spacin' out on me, or what?"

Mitch pressed his palms against his eyes and heaved a big breath.

"No, Justin, I am not 'spacin' out' on you. I was thinking."

"Right, right. Cool, man. Okay, so you and Katharine gotta, like, keep the tension going for the cameras. You think you can do that?"

"Oh, I don't think that'll be a problem."

"Excellent, bro. Alrighty, let's cruise."

Mitch followed Justin out to the big SUV waiting outside the bed and breakfast. Sam was already inside, his camera trained on Mitch the moment they opened the door. Beside him sat an attractive blonde with glossy lips and beauty pageant hair.

"Hi, Mitch. I'm Lacy Taylor for Hey Hollywood. I'll be tagging along to interview you and Katharine today."

Lacy smiled brightly at Mitch. He blinked at her, then at Sam. Sam pulled his face away from the camera and shrugged at Mitch as he mouthed '*sorry.*'

"Hey Hollywood, huh? Little far from home, aren't you?"

"Oh, you're so funny, Mitch," said Lacy. No one laughed but her. She recovered quickly and pulled out her notes.

"So, Mitch. Tell me what brought you out to Connecticut."

Mitch swallowed a sigh and launched into his well-rehearsed and oft-repeated explanation. Lacy Taylor feigned interest and took a few notes. Every time Mitch paused to take a breath, she leaned forward with another question hovering. Mitch deliberately drew out his story, knowing full well the direction she was heading.

"So, then we rounded up the crew and took the road trip out here to beautiful East Hampton, and—"

"And met Katharine Evans," Lacy interjected.

"Ah, yes. As well as many of the wonderful local—"

"Tell me about your first meeting with Katharine. Is it true she threw a brick at you?"

"A brick? I—no, of course not. It was a soccer ball, and she was merely trying—"

"So, she *did* try to cause you physical harm, then? Did you two have a prior relationship? Is *that* why she threw a brick at you?"

"Again, it was not a brick. No, we'd never met before that day."

"Ah, I see. So, a woman you've never met before assaulted you because…?"

This was getting out of hand. Lacy Taylor was trying to twist everything up and make it something it wasn't. He didn't know what Lacy's angle was, but he *did* know he didn't like it. Not one bit.

"Listen, Lacy, sweetheart. You've got this all wrong. Katharine Evans is a very nice woman who merely wants to live a quiet life and write her books and be left alone. I simply want to finish our build next door and let her—let her go."

Silence filled the car. Mitch turned abruptly in his seat and faced front. He rested his elbow on the window frame of the car door and rubbed his stubbled chin with his hand. *What is wrong with me?*

He bit down on his knuckle and ignored the awkward silence in the car. He knew they were all exchanging weighted glances, but Mitch didn't care. His brain was wrapped around Katharine. Her eyes, her smile. Her frown and the faint chicken pox scar on her cheek. The smell of her honey and clementine hair. The sound of her slightly husky voice. Her little chin when it jutted at him in anger.

I've fallen for her. And I have to let her go. The SUV turned onto Katharine's street. Cars and trucks lined one side, making for a precarious passage on the narrow road. A mixture of guests and gawkers, no doubt. She was probably beside herself with the stress of it all. His heart clenched at the mental image of her being alone in a sea of people. Poor Katharine. The least he could do is keep the press out.

As Sam climbed out of the SUV, Mitch grabbed his arm and whispered in his ear, "Get rid of the reporter, Sam."

Sam looked from Mitch to Lacy—who was primping her hair in the tinted car window—then back to Mitch again. He opened his mouth, but then saw that Mitch's face was stony. Whatever he'd been about to say died on his lips and he nodded. "You got it, buddy.

Mitch nodded curtly and strode across Katharine's yard as if walking the plank. He noted the line of paparazzi along the street—their shouts and camera flashes—and shook his head. As bothersome as he found their intrusion, he could only imagine how *she* was handling it all.

***

"Wow, Katharine, you are way calmer than I expected you to be."

Janie was right, Katharine *was* calm… on the outside, that is. Inside, she had a storm brewing. Mitch would be coming, and that filled her with… confusion. Nate would be there, and that filled her with joy. Then, there were all the strangers invading her space. *That* gave her anxiety. Thankfully, Janie had stepped up to the plate and came out swinging for Katharine. She'd hustled them through the grocery store with expert level finesse, introducing Katharine to this person and that, then managing to move them along. Katharine marveled at how she handled this without offending anyone or coming across as rude.

Back at Katharine's, Janie had helped unload everything and even prepped all the dishes for the party. When Katharine apologized for keeping her away from her husband and kids, Janie had laughed. A lot. It was then Katharine realized maybe she was helping Janie as much as Janie was helping her. So, she let her take over and merely followed orders. Despite the minimal efforts on her part, Katharine still had butterflies.

"Calm? No. This is my quiet panic face."

"Oh. Well, in that case, you'll make a great mom one day. That's literally my face all day, every day. Let's go outside and grab a drink."

They walked out onto the patio, then crossed the yard to the makeshift bar— a long folding table with a white tablecloth and faux grass table skirt.

Katharine chuckled. "A tiki bar, huh?"

"Yep. Borrowed it from Angelico's. The bouncer is dating my sister," Janie shrugged.

"Not the guy with the neck tattoo, by any chance?" Katharine asked.

"That's the one."

Janie winked. There was no need for Katharine to ask if Janie knew about her *eventful* evening there. She poured them each a tall glass of wine and clinked her glass against Katharine's.

Katharine kept glancing at her watch. "Nate should be here any minute," she said.

In less than an hour, the first guests would be arriving. Neighbors and locals, likely. Then, Mitch and Sam, she guessed. Tori would show up fashionably late and larger than life. All Katharine had to do was hang in there. They were walking back onto the patio when a familiar voice called out from inside.

"Hello, anybody home?"

"Nate! It's my brother," said Katharine to Janie. "Out back, Nate!"

A moment later, Nate walked out onto the deck. Katharine ran to him and tackled him in a tight hug.

"Uh, Katharine? You are choking me. Geez."

"Sorry, I'm just so happy to see my big brother. Oh, hi. Who is this?"

A young woman stood shyly in the doorway. She had long brown hair, a sweet smile, and almond shaped brown eyes like Nate.

"Katharine, this is Alyssa. My girlfriend. Alyssa, this is my sister, Katharine. That's Katharine's friend over there. I don't know her name because Katharine hasn't introduced us."

"Right, sorry! It's nice to meet you, Alyssa. This is my friend and neighbor, Janie."

They all said their hellos, then Katharine tucked her arm through Nate's and walked him into the house. Once inside, she faced him with a mischievous grin, taking in his new look. Nate had always worn his hair a little on the long side and had a penchant for classic rock band t-shirts. On this day, he wore a polo shirt and khaki pants, and his newly trimmed hair was parted on the side. Katharine even smelled cologne on him.

"Look at you, big brother. Haircut, spiffy clothes. You clean up nice, you know. Now, how come you didn't tell me you had a girlfriend, Nate?"

"Thanks, sis. How come you didn't tell me you had a friend, Katharine?"

"Touché, brother dear. She's very pretty. How did you meet?"

"She is a volunteer at the charity. Guess what? She loves Journey!"

"Oh, well, then. That settles it—she's a keeper."

Katharine's heart was bursting with happiness for Nate. When they were kids, Katharine overheard a teacher say to their parents that 'they should prepare themselves for the impossibility of Nate ever having a normal life.' Their parents had walked away from the conversation broken-hearted and defeated, but not Katharine. She was livid. How dare she say that? Her brother had every right and reason to live a full, happy life. Just because it wasn't exactly like what everyone else had, didn't mean it was no less fulfilling. In fact, Nate had accomplished more and lived more fully than any of the 'normal' people she'd ever met. *Including me.*

It really hit Katharine. It was time to start living outside her small bubble. For the first time, Katharine acknowledged yes, she *wanted* success. She desired her books to sell and her name to be known. Not for her own ego, but for what it could do for Nate, their charity, and his life. Hers, too. If it meant playing along with the charade of KatMitch, then she would do it. But it begged the question: was it *really* a charade?

Katharine had replayed the events from the past week. From the moment her eyes landed on Mitch Ford for the first time, there was an undeniable, instant attraction to him. Even when she threw things at him. Which was often. *Why* did she always want to throw things at him? *Because he's infuriating, that's why. Oh, be honest. At least with yourself.*

If she *were* to be honest with herself, she'd admit she was afraid to care. To feel. To love. More than any of that, though, she was scared to be hurt. And Mitch Ford was precisely what a heartbreak looked like. A man with his rugged, masculine good looks, baritone voice that caused her bones to vibrate, along with that natural charm of his...well, she might as well get in line. *Ugh, and don't forget the whole 'he's a famous television guy' thing, too. Mitch Ford is—*

"Katharine? Are you listening to me? I said, when is Mitch Ford going to be here?"

"What? Oh, uh, soon. Any time now, I guess."

The doorbell rang, followed immediately by Tori's voice calling out. "Hello, I'm here! Let the party begin!"

"Hey, Tori. You're earlier than I expected! Where's Justin?"

Tori rolled her eyes and waved her hand in the air. "He is Mitch Ford's problem right now. I could not listen to the boy call me 'dude' one more time. Anyhow, we have things to go over, Miss Thang."

"Things? What things?"

"Hang on. Hey, Nate! How's it going?"

"Hi, Tori. I'm good. I have a girlfriend. Her name is Alyssa. She's outside, you should come and meet her."

"I will, right after I give your sister here a little pep talk."

"Good luck. You know how she is."

Katharine scoffed, "I'm standing right here, you know."

Nate shook his head and wagged his thumb at Katharine, then went out to the backyard without a second glance.

"Can you believe him?" Katharine asked.

"Hmm. It's you I can't believe, Katharine Evans. How about you explain the novella length text you sent me at one o'clock in the morning? One minute you're telling me you might be falling for Mitch. The next sentence you say you hate him. Then you want him here today, and then you don't. You got a fever or something?"

Tori pressed her wrist against Katharine's forehead for emphasis. Katharine gently slapped her away with a laugh.

"I'm fine. I'm—not fine. I just—I don't know what's wrong with me, Tori."

"I know what's wrong with her," interjected Janie from the doorway, "she's in l-o-v-e and doesn't want to admit it."

"Mhmm," agreed Tori. "Honey, I saw it from the second you two started sparring in the wings of the Connecticut Today show. Hell, the whole world could see it. Why do you think this all caught fire? People love *love*. Especially this kind—where it's all tense and dramatic. It's like watching a real, live soap opera."

"Oh, I agree," said Janie as she poured a glass of wine for Tori. "Okay, so, Katharine, I hope you don't mind, but I kind of took over your hostess duties. You, uh, have about a dozen or so guests out there so you might want to pop on out and say hey, okay?"

"Oh! Crap, I totally forgot. I'll go out there now." In the doorway, she paused. "Wait. What do I say to them?"

Janie pressed a hand to her cheek. Tori dipped her chin down and looked at Katharine from under her drawn brows. They responded in sync.

"Go say hello!"

"Right. I can do that."

She turned and went to greet her guests, but not before sticking her tongue out at her two new friends. The first people she welcomed were Jim and his two boys. She managed to successfully make small talk and was thus encouraged to make the rounds. She was feeling rather proud of herself—laughing, chatting… *people-ing* like a regular person, until an excited hush fell over the yard. Murmurs and stares, all in the direction of the French doors which led out onto the patio. Taking up nearly the entire frame was none other than Mitch Ford. His eyes swept the expanse of the crowd, nodding, pointing and waving to random guests. *God, does his every entrance have to look like he's walking on stage to accept an award?*

Katharine stood dead center of the yard. The couple who had been in front of her stepped aside, and Mitch's gaze fell on Katharine. Like the Red Sea, the crowd parted, and Mitch strode casually toward Katharine. Their eyes were locked on each other, but Katharine could feel the stares from everyone around them. The whispers and twitters were barely audible over the sound of rushing air in her ears. He looked exceptionally handsome in his trademark faded jeans and a crisp, beige, button-down shirt. The top two buttons were open, exposing the hint of chest hair and suntanned skin. The only thing missing was his trademark ballcap. His salt and pepper hair was tousled boyishly. Katharine imagined running her fingers through it, smoothing the errant locks. She blinked hard at the vision, then dropped her gaze to see he clutched a bouquet of wildflowers in his big, bearpaw hand.

"Hello, Katharine."

He said it low, softly, and her breath caught in her throat at the sound of her name coming from his lips once again. *Every time, without fail. Be cool, Katharine.*

"Mitch," she nodded. "Thanks for coming."

"Thank you for the invitation."

That they both knew was forced.

"Are those…"

"Oh, yes. Flowers. For you, the hostess."

Mitch extended the bouquet hastily. At the same moment, Katharine stepped forward to give him a polite thank-you hug. She instead got a bunch of flowers in her face. Those around them saw, and small laughs burst across the yard. Katharine jerked back, startled and embarrassed. The whole moment was turning into a comedy sketch. An angry bee darted out from one of the daisies and zigged and zagged at Katharine's face. She jumped back, forgetting the glass of red wine in her hand. The crimson liquid sloshed up and out of the glass… and all over Mitch's shirt. Gasps hissed all around, but Katharine was still focused on the bee.

"For Christ's sake, it's just a little bee, Katharine! Calm down."

Mitch's arms were outstretched, a ruby bloom across his shirt, and his eyes wide full of indignation and incredulity.

"No, I will not calm down. I'm allergic, Mr. Sensitivity."

"Mr.—I—you dumped a gallon of wine on me, and I'm insensitive? And stop jumping around, you're going to get—"

"Ow," Katharine cried out.

"Stung," said Mitch.

Katharine clapped her hand over her mouth. The bee had stung her upper lip. Her eyes watered as waves of pain radiated from the sting. Another collective gasp moved through the group of bystanders.

"It thung me."

Katharine's tongue had already started to swell, and her throat became scratchy and tight. Her eyes went saucer wide as she looked at Mitch. His expression of annoyance turned quickly to concern, and he grabbed ahold of her arm.

"Okay, you're going to be fine. Where's your epinephrine pen, sweetheart?"

"Ith—"

Katharine's eyes fluttered, and her knees buckled. Mitch swept her off the ground into his well-muscled arms. She let her head loll against his chest. The fear drifted away, and one realization remained. *It's okay. Mitch has me.* Then everything went dark.

***

This woman is going to be the end of me. Mitch charged through the house with Katharine in his arms, cognizant of the cell phone cameras trained on them. Inside the kitchen, he found Tori, Janie, a man Mitch recognized as Nate, and a woman he hadn't yet met.

"Where does Katharine keep her epinephrine pen?"

The women looked at him blankly, but Nate sprang into action. "She should have one in her purse. I'll look." A few seconds later, "Nope, not in here. She knows better than that!"

"Upstairs, in her bathroom maybe," Mitch asked.

"Yes!"

"I've got her, you get some ice for the swelling," Mitch ordered.

With a wan, lethargic Katharine still in his arms, he charged up the stairs two at a time. He found her bedroom and gently set her on the bed, then raced to her bathroom medicine cabinet. Sleep aids, vitamins, bandages…

"Ah ha! Here it is." Mitch uncapped the pen and knelt on the floor beside Katharine. Luckily, she was wearing shorts, and they'd be spared any later embarrassment.

"Katharine, sweetheart. You're going to be fine in one," he gave her the shot, "minute."

Still kneeling beside her, Mitch smoothed her hair from her face. Her eyes were closed, her bee-stung lip puffy and red.

"You look like Sleeping Beauty," he said.

"Yeah, well, she acts like Grumpy," called a voice from behind him.

It was Tori, followed by Nate, Janie and the woman he didn't know.

"Here's the ice, Mitch," said Nate.

"Is she going to be okay," asked Janie.

"Yes, I think she's going to be fine. Does anyone, by any chance, have an extra shirt I could borrow?"

"In the wardrobe, spare bedroom. Nate, you know where." It was Katharine, her voice husky and low.

"Hey, you," Mitch smiled down at her, "you gave us quite a scare."

"Yeah, Katharine, I didn't even know you were allergic to bees," said Tori.

Tori's tone was accusing, and even a bit hurt. It was like no one really knew Katharine at all. It made Mitch feel sad for her. Why was she so cut off from the world? He needed to know more about her, and he was determined to find out. But right then, he needed these people to do damage control downstairs.

"Alright, folks. Katharine's got a yard full of people, all wondering what on earth is going on.

How about you start putting the word out that all is well, and Miss Evans will be out momentarily?"

"Already on it. Justin is out there putting the spin on. I'll go help him," said Tori.

"And I'll start putting the food out," said Janie.

"Mitch, that's my brother Nate and his girlfriend, Alyssa. Aren't they the sweetest?"

"Yes, thank you for the introductions, Katharine," Mitch chuckled down at her. "Nate, Alyssa, so nice to meet you both. You, uh, mind grabbing me that shirt, buddy?"

"Sure, come on Alyssa. Let's leave the lovebirds alone."

"Nate," Katharine warned.

Mitch chuckled and gave Katharine a side glance to see how mad she was. She was smiling, too.

"So, you don't hate me?"

Katharine fell back against the pillow and sighed. "I didn't hate you, Mitch. I—I don't know what comes over me when you're around. Honestly? I think my problem is I really—"

"Here you go, Mitch. It was my Dad's. You're about the same size as he was. Maybe a little bigger."

Nate, with Alyssa trailing behind him, returned holding out a light blue chambray shirt.

"I told him the color would be perfect for you, Mr. Ford. It matches your eyes."

"Why thank you, Alyssa. You both are very kind."

Alyssa blushed, and Nate scoffed. "Come on, Alyssa. Quick before Mitch Ford steals my girl."

Nate took a reluctant Alyssa by the hand and pulled her away, back to the party. Chuckling, Mitch tossed the clean shirt on the edge of Katharine's bed and began unbuttoning his stained one. He'd be glad to finally get the ruined garment off and…

"Oh—"

***

Mitch Ford was in her bedroom, unbuttoning his shirt, while Katharine was lying in her bed. The impropriety hit her like a brick, so she jumped up and made for the door. Only, Mitch, in his awkward effort to let her pass, stepped to his left as she shuffled to her right. They both moved again. Then, a third time. On their last awkward shuffle, Mitch placed his warm, broad hands-on Katharine's bared shoulders and looked down at her with a placating grin. Clearly, he intended to move her in one direction while he moved in the opposite, but the physical jolt of his hands on her skin froze them both.

She looked up into his impossibly blue eyes and found herself speechless. His thumb caressed her skin, sending a shockwave through her body. Katharine stepped in closer. His shirt was open, his bare chest exposed. Mitch's eyes softened, and he tipped his head down to meet hers.

"Well, what do we have here? Hey, bro… *and* chica. Tori told me where I could find you two."

Mitch's jaw tightened, and he exhaled through his nose hard enough to flutter Katharine's hair. He dropped his hands from her shoulders. She stepped back guiltily, her skin tingling from where his work-rough hands had just rested.

"You found us, Justin. As you can see, I'm getting changed."

"And I was—he—"

"No worries, man. Whatever. Would've been better if the cameras had caught it, but they got some killer vid from the yard, dude."

Mitch rubbed his face briskly and ran his hands through his hair. "Great, just *great*. How much did they get?"

"Oh, man, like, *everything*! Katharine throwing her drink at you, Katharine getting stung by that bee. You, carrying her away like Tarzan. It was stellar, bro. Primo for prime-time."

Mitch swung around to face Katharine, "Katharine—"

"It's okay, Mitch. I know. It's not your fault. It's mine. I'm no good at any of this. I'm like a walking disaster around you. Just—let's go and get this over with. The sooner we do, the sooner we all can get back to our own lives."

The reality of everything—the disparity in their universes and experiences—set in again and the rosy possibilities Katharine had foolishly let herself envision evaporated like a puff of smoke. She stepped around Mitch and passed Justin. She paused in the doorway, and said softly, "Oh, and thank you, Mitch."

He frowned. "For what?"

Katharine gave a short laugh. He was such an all-around great guy that saving a woman's life was all in a day's work for him. What on earth made her think she deserved a man like him?

"For not letting me die from anaphylactic shock, silly. And…" she shrugged and looked away, "for lots of things."

She took the stairs carefully, still feeling woozy. Only, she wasn't sure it was from the toxins in her system or the pain in her heart. Even though Katharine had never been in love before, she recognized the sensation easily enough. *Heartache.* She needed to get through the rest of the day, then the Up All-Night Show. Oh, and then whatever other public appearances Tori had lined up. *And let's not forget the next couple of weeks where the man of your dreams is literally next door.*

FIFTEEN

UP ALL NIGHT

Four days later, Katharine stared into the dressing room mirror, a dour look on her face. Tori had accompanied her for the taping of the Up All-Night Show and was giving Katharine her version of a pep talk.

"On the upside, Katharine, the publishing company gave you an extension on the next installment. No questions asked. They even asked me to pass along their thanks."

"For what?"

"Um, for boosting sales and putting them in the forefront of sought-after agencies, duh!"

Katharine gave a thin smile and picked at her blouse.

"Girl, you are one sad, pathetic puppy. When was the last time you talked to him?"

Without looking up, Katharine mumbled, "The party."

"You haven't spoken to him since Saturday? Why not? I know from Justin Mitch has tried to talk to *you*. So why are you ignoring him?"

Katharine's shoulders went up, then drooped down again.

Tori made a 'tsk' sound and rolled her eyes. Then she took Katharine's chin in her hand and forced her to look up.

"What's wrong with you, hmm? You're crazy about him. He's crazy about you. The whole world sees it. So: What. Is. The. Problem?"

"It doesn't matter."

From the doorway, a rich baritone.

"It matters to me."

Katharine's heart cartwheeled. Mitch.

"Hey, Mitch. I'll leave you two to talk," said Tori.

Tori patted Mitch's arm as she passed him in the doorway and he gave her a short smile. But his eyes were on Katharine. She looked straight ahead but could see it all in peripheral.

"Can I come in?"

"Sure." Katharine tried to sound nonchalant, but the break in her voice gave her away. Mitch walked in slowly. Since she wouldn't look at him, he moved between her and the dresser mirror. Unless she swiveled the chair around, she *had* to look at him. Even Katharine realized how childish it would be to spin her chair away, so she looked up into his careworn face. It said he meant business, and he wasn't leaving until he got answers.

"Why have you been avoiding me, Katharine?"

"I haven't. I've been—"

"Don't. Please don't insult my intelligence. Something is going on between us. You know it, I know it. Hell, it's like Tori said—the whole world seems to know it. I'm not afraid to see where it goes. But it seems you are."

Katharine opened her mouth to speak.

"Let me finish what I came in here to say." He leaned in close, placing his hands on the armrests of her chair. "I'm a grown man, Katharine. I know what I want, and it's you. You're a grown woman, stop hiding like a child. Meet me halfway."

She wanted to, she really did. But...

"Miss Ev— oh, Mr. Ford. Ah, we are about ready to have Miss Evans come out. Then you, sir."

Mitch took his eyes off Katharine and turned his head toward the young man in the doorway. She closed hers for a moment and breathed in his scent deeply. The man walked away, and Mitch returned his attention to Katharine. He waited, saying nothing more. She was frozen, her stare fixed firmly on the shoulder seam of his shirt. The words were locked behind the wall she'd spent a lifetime building around herself. This was the moment, her chance to say she was crazy about him. That she was scared and unsure. That she'd never loved anyone before. She remained silent. Mitch dropped his head down and shook it with a sniff.

"Alright then. I guess I've got my answer."

He walked out of the small dressing room. The word '*wait*' remained caught in Katharine's throat. She tried to tell herself it was for the best. He'd be gone soon enough and on to his next great adventure. *It wouldn't have worked anyhow.*

"Miss Evans? We're ready for you."

For the first time in her writing career, Katharine was getting national exposure. Excitement and joy were what she was supposed to be feeling, and yet sadness blanketed her. It even outweighed her nervousness. Despite it all, she managed to get through the interview with a semblance of poise. Her prepared 'impromptu anecdote' went smoothly—as smoothly as anyone could've expected, at least. The host of the show, comedian Jackson Day, was everything they all said he would be. Kind, funny, encouraging, and best of all, able to navigate through any awkwardness on her part. Before she knew it, he broke for commercial.

"You're doing great, Katharine. I love your books, by the way. Now, when Mitch comes out, we'll have you slide down. All you have to do is roll with it."

"Okay, sure. Wait—roll with it? With what?"

"We're going to have fun, don't worry."

He'd already turned away and begun prepping for the next segment.

Mitch. In moments they'd be sharing the same stage once again, but now with even more tension between them. How would he act? How would *she* act? A live studio audience would be watching their every move, gesture, and hanging on every word.

Later that night, it would be televised for the rest of the world to see.

I'm not freaking out. I'm not freaking out. The mantra had the opposite effect on Katharine. She wiped her damp hands on her lap, then took slow breaths to calm her wildly palpitating heart. The audience was a sea of indiscernible faces that she scanned with deer-in-headlight wide eyes. The first recognizable person they fell upon was Tori. She waved, then gave Katharine a 'thumbs up' and a reassuring nod.

Okay, well, at least someone is feeling confident about this.

The cue to begin again came from the edge of the stage and before she knew it, Jackson Day was telling the audience about the next guest. He stopped and restarted twice, deciding to add a joke, then change the delivery. Each pause sent Katharine further on edge. The anticipation was torture that everyone around her was oblivious to. She internally rehearsed calm, neutral greetings for when Mitch walked out. She'd extend her hand. No, she should probably go for a cheek kiss. It's what he was most likely to do. Would he go to the left or the right, though? She began cursing him in her head. Meanwhile, Jackson Day called Mitch out onto the set, and the audience applauded and cheered. Suddenly, his shadow fell over her. Katharine blinked up at Mitch. His eyes bore into hers, his face stony. What was he just standing there for?

"Oh!" Suddenly remembering what she was supposed to do, Katharine stood abruptly to move down on the couch, misjudging his closeness. Mitch, instead of stepping back and giving her room, reached out to put a gentlemanly hand on her elbow to help her up. Katharine was turning at the same moment, so his hand pushed her further off-balance, and she sat down hard on the cushion. Instinct caused her to grab *his* arm, and she pulled him with her. He pivoted quickly, but not quite fast enough. Instead of entirely landing on top of Katharine, he only half fell on her. The studio audience roared with laughter. The Mitch that Katharine could see was not amused. The face he turned to the audience was all amiable Mitch Ford charm and self-deprecation.

"Now, that's how to make an entrance, Mitch," said Jackson. Then to the audience, "That was not rehearsed, ladies and gentlemen! How about a hand for these two?"

They whooped and cheered as if they'd witnessed an academy award worthy performance, rather than an embarrassing display of extreme awkwardness.

"Feel free to edit that out, Jackson," laughed Mitch.

"Oh, man, no way! That was gold, right there. You two are like a—a modern day Ricky and Lucy. So, tell me, buddy—is she always trying to kill you like that?"

Mitch turned his smile over to Katharine, then back to Jackson, "No, I think I'm relatively safe from Miss Evans."

"Are you sure about that, Mitch?"

"Why, yes, I'm pretty sure," he chuckled.

"Really?" Jackson Day looked out at the crowd and tapped his finger against his chin before continuing. "That's interesting you say that because I've heard differently. In fact, I have proof."

Katharine froze, the blood draining from her face.

"Proof? I— wait—" stammered Mitch.

"Let's roll that special montage your production crew sent us, hmm?"

The lights dimmed. A large screen dropped down, and the theme music for The Rebuilder began. The same intro that played for the Connecticut Today Show played as well. Only this time, after Mitch said, 'Let's take a look, shall we?' a different clip played. It was Katharine throwing the soccer ball at Mitch. Then, a grainy, phone-camera video of Katharine dumping a drink over Mitch's head, followed by her attacking him with an oar. Last but not least, another phone video of Katharine splashing her wine on Mitch's shirt.

While the audience alternately gasped and guffawed, Mitch used the moment to lean in close to Katharine. He put a hand on her shoulder and said, "Katharine, I swear on my life, I did not mean for this to be aired. I screwed up, and I'm sorry."

She bucked her shoulder away, refusing to even acknowledge his words. Katharine gripped the chair cushions tightly, her knuckles white. Her gaze was locked straight ahead. In a moment, the cameras and lights would be back on them. There was a new mantra on repeat in her head: *I will never let Mitch Ford get the best of me again*. Katharine knew the camera would be on her any moment, so she let go of the cushion, rested her hands in her lap, and unclenched her jaw. A placid smile replaced the hard line of her lips, and she sat up straight. She would take the impending onslaught with grace. Then, when it was all over, she'd cancel all her appearances and fade into anonymity, where it was safe.

"Well, how about that? Katharine Evans, I must say, you are a ball of fire!" Jackson Day turned to the viewers, "Am I right guys?" Raucous shouts and boisterous clapping. They didn't hate her, they loved it. Katharine blinked, and her gaze swept across the audience. A small, genuine smile pulled at the corners of her mouth. A woman shouted,

"You get him, honey!"

Another followed,

"He probably deserved it, the dog!"

Katharine, still in disbelief, laughed along with everyone. The only one *not* laughing, was Mitch. The tension left Katharine's shoulders. She sat back in her seat and did precisely what Jackson Day had told her to do. For the first time in her life, Katharine Evans *rolled with it*. In fact, she did one better. Katharine came out of her shell.

When the laughter subsided, Katharine angled herself to face Mitch and said, "You know what, Mitch? Move over. Jackson and I need to discuss this a little bit more."

The audience erupted. Mitch heaved a sigh and pasted a good-natured smile on his lips as he stood and proffered his vacated seat to Katharine. She strode past him with an arched brow and sly smirk and took her place beside the amused host again.

"Now Katharine," Jackson began, "tell us, what on earth did that big brute over there do to upset such a sweet, tiny thing like yourself? I mean—look at her, guys—is she not the cutest thing? You're like an adorable, gentle—"

"Alright, alright," interjected Mitch, "now, let me say that I—"

"Oh, Mitch. Don't be such a bully. I can speak for myself."

Laughter and more cheers filled the room.

"Okay, you two. Before this becomes, oh, I don't know… a boxing match, what do you say we settle this the old-fashioned way with a—wait for it—a *boxing match*!"

Wild cheers, applause. Katharine and Mitch blinked at Jackson. He cut to a commercial break, then addressed the pair.

"Ah, you guys are great sports! This is going to be so much fun! Thanks so much for agreeing to all this."

Mitch and Katharine spoke at the same time.

"Wait, I never—"

"Agree to what?"

They looked at each other in confusion, then out into the audience, where Tori and now Justin sat. They wore matching 'oops' expressions and apologetic smiles. Neither had informed their client as to what their appearance on the Up All-Night Show entailed. Katharine glared at Tori and Mitch buried his head in his hand. Before they could say another word, several Up All-Night Show staffers were ushering them from the interview seats to the stage area. The curtain opened to reveal an

American Gladiator-style jousting ring. They shoved sparring helmets on them both and pushed them into the ring. Then they helped them onto opposing pedestals and thrust the pugil sticks in each of their hands. Everything happened so fast that by the time Katharine could find words to protest, they were signaling to start taping again.

Thank God, I wore pants. Please tell me he looks more ridiculous than I do. I'm going to kill Tori.

She couldn't know what Mitch was thinking, but the look on his face said his thoughts probably mirrored her own. Katharine looked down at the padded baton, then back up at Mitch. He did the same. She broadened her stance and tilted her chin down to her chest. His eyed sprung wide, then narrowed.

***

Oh, is she for real? She wants to do this, huh? Okay then. It's on.

Mitch watched the shift in Katharine's posturing and realized she intended on knocking him off the pedestal. Jackson Day began his segment introduction, but Mitch barely registered him. He was too busy preparing for battle.

"Alright, you two. Are you ready?" asked Jackson.

They both gave him a curt nod.

"Uh oh, guys, this looks like it's going to be epic! Okay, wait for the bell—and fight!"

As present as Mitch was for the insanity that was currently taking place, it was like he was having an out-of-body experience, watching the whole scene from above. This was *not* the direction he anticipated his career going. Yet there he was, on a nationally broadcast show, about to have a-a *jousting match* with a petite, angry woman who he may or may not be slightly or very in love with.

He was well aware he could knock Katharine clear off the pedestal with one swipe, but the maniacal look on her face told him *she* was not mindful of such an undeniable fact. Part of him was almost inclined to let her win, but there was also part of Mitch that was ticked off at her for ignoring his attempts to talk. It would feel kind of satisfying to take *her* down a peg or two, instead of continually being on the receiving end of her abuse.

Mitch jabbed his pugil stick at Katharine's arm, she dodged it. Katharine swung hers and connected with Mitch's hip. It barely phased him. "Ha! Is that all you've got, Evans?"

She swung again, aiming for his head. He ducked and laughed again.

Aiming for the head again, are we? Two can play that game. Mitch had enough sense to not swing at Katharine's head. He intended to give her helmet-covered forehead a good boop and knock her off her wobbly pedestal and end the silly farce. However, Katharine Evans was once again full of surprises.

***

Katharine watched Mitch with a feline slyness. She may have failed to mention she had every Billy

Blanks Tae-Bo DVD ever made and had been practicing with them for quite some time. She had quick reflexes, excellent core strength, and lean muscles. Her size made her easy to underestimate, and that was about to work to her advantage.

She knew what Mitch Ford was going to attempt even before his stick came up, so when it did, Katharine was ready. Like a scene from the Matrix, Katharine arched backward, then grabbed the pugil stick that was thrust at her and pulled it toward her. Mitch, caught surprised by the sudden pull, lost his balance and tottered forward, arms flailing. Katharine took the opportunity to whop him on the shoulder. It was enough to finish him off.

In what looked like slow motion, Mitch fell inelegantly onto the padded mat. Jackson Day entered the ring to the wild applause of the audience and handed Katharine down from her pedestal. He took her hand in his and raised it high.

"Ladies and Gentlemen, your champion! Alright, we're going to take a break, and when we come back, we'll have young Robert Irwin here to show us some cool animals."

A flood of staffers rushed the stage area and began disassembling the ring, removing their protective gear from their heads, and escorted Katharine and a disgruntled Mitch out of it.

"Hey, I can't thank you two enough. Great job, really great job. Katharine, so nice meeting you, hope to have you back again."

Jackson Day shook Katharine's hand and kissed her cheek, then turned to Mitch. "Mitch, buddy!

Awesome seeing you again. See you at the golf tourney next month?"

"Yeah, sure, Jack. Sure thing. So, whose idea was this again? Just so I know whose head to put on a platter."

"Not me, pal," Jackson put his hands up, "ask your boy Justin. I think they're all in the green room with the kid and his animals. Okay, well, gotta get ready for the next round of madness. Take care!"

Jackson Day dashed back over to his desk and Katharine and Mitch were ushered to the green room, where Tori and Justin were no doubt coordinating their stories. Or maybe playing 'rock, paper, scissors' to see which one of them would be the fall guy for the inevitable wrath of their clients. Together Mitch and Katharine marched down the cloistered hall to the green room, united in their mission to kill their publicists. However, Katharine couldn't stop herself from throwing a verbal shot at Mitch.

"You went for a headshot? Nice."

"Oh, excuse me, Miss I'm a Secret Ninja. Oh, no. *You* don't get to be the angry one, here. *I* do. *I'm* the one who got blown off. Not to mention ambushed."

"Um, no. We *both* got ambushed, Mr. Ford. I just happened to win, is all."

"Well, at least you don't deny blowing me off. And let's be clear—I let you—"

"Don't you even say it! You did not *let* me win, I won fair and square, thank you," said Katharine.

"Cheater," said Mitch.

"Poor sport."

They walked into the green room bickering.

"I am not a poor—"

Katharine ignored him. Her jaw dropped, and she blinked hard at the sight before her.

"Is that—oh, my God. Is that a sloth? *That* is a sloth. I'm dying."

She swatted Mitch in the gut, he oofed. Then she grabbed his arm and shook it in barely contained excitement. All her anger dissipated, at least for that moment. Tori, followed by Justin, approached them like two wary lion tamers.

"That's right, honey," cajoled Tori, "it *is* a sloth. And this nice boy said you can hold it if you want." She glanced over her shoulder at the peaches and cream complexioned boy. "Isn't that what you said, Richard?"

"Ah, right. It's Robert, by the way. Here you go, Miss Evans. This is Valentino, and he's a real sweetheart."

"I can touch him?"

"You can do better than that. Here, put your arms out." Katharine did as she was told. "There you go. He's a love, isn't he? That's why we call him Valentino."

Katharine was in heaven. If someone had told her a year ago she'd be in the green room of a late-night television show, holding a sloth, she'd have never believed it. But here she was. Mitch came up behind her, equally awed by the furry, slow-moving creature.

"Hey there, fella."

Mitch's hand was on Katharine's shoulder, his face close to her cheek. Her breath caught in her throat and she found herself not wanting to move. She was also hyper-aware of everyone else in the room staring at them, so she made what she hoped was a great show of nonchalance. The more she tried to act normal, the more her face flushed. Then, an unbidden and slightly ridiculous image came to mind with startling clarity.

It was of them, standing as they were at that moment—Mitch slightly behind her, his hand on her shoulder, smiling down. But in the vision, it wasn't a sloth. It was a baby. *Their* baby on her hip as he gazed at his little family. She pictured someone taking their photograph, calling them to look up at the camera.

"Miss? Miss—" said the sloth handler.

"Um, Katharine? You have to give him back now," said Mitch.

He said it softly. His deep voice vibrated against her skin, and his breath tickled her ear. She looked around the room, realizing where she was. Her eyes welled, and she quickly blinked the tears back. When Katharine's eyes met Tori's, it was with an unspoken plea. Tori nodded once, then brusquely took charge of the room.

"Alright, then. That was fun! Thanks, kid." She helped remove the sloth from Katharine's reluctant hands and put an arm around her. "Let's get you on your way, hmm? Mitch, great seeing you. Justin, send me your pics, and I'll send you mine. Bye, all!"

In a flash, they were out of the green room and walking briskly down the hall, leaving a trail of Tori's floral perfume in their wake. Technically,

Tori walked briskly while Katharine shuffled alongside her, dazed. She barely registered Tori handing over her purse or being shuttled to the waiting car or even the one-sided conversation Tori carried. Tori's eyes were on her. Katharine's stare stayed locked on the slowly passing scenery. Taxis and tall buildings. Hotdog carts and street artists. A homeless man shouting toothlessly at a fire hydrant. A skinny chestnut mare harnessed to a carriage. The car stopped, and Katharine watched as the horse impatiently hoofed the ground and shook her silky-maned head as the driver tried to entice a young couple for a ride. At last, she spoke.

"I'm fine, Tori."

Tori tilted her head and pursed her lips.

"Really. It's just—" Katharine began.

"That you're in love with the guy and you refuse to act on it?"

"It's not that simple. It'll never work. We're too different."

"You're kidding, right? You two are like peas in a pod, Katharine. You're a lot more alike than you think, you know."

"Well, we have totally different lifestyles. He travels the country, I stay home. He loves the limelight, I hate it. I mean, there is no chance of a conventional life. He—"

Tori raised a graceful, brown-skinned hand to her eyes and threw her head back. Katharine went to say something more, but Tori held up one long, manicured finger and dropped her head back down to look at Katharine.

"Uh-uh. Nope. Do you even hear yourself? Girl, this is the twenty-first century. There's no such thing as *conventional*." Tori shook her head and muttered the word conventional again as if it tasted terrible in her mouth. Then she sighed loudly. "Katharine, I get it. But you'd have to be out of your mind not to give this man a chance. Give *yourself* a chance, honey."

Katharine dropped her gaze to her lap. Tori was right, she supposed. She'd had the same argument with herself for days. Every time she resolved to talk to Mitch about her feelings for him, the old Katharine voice snuck up and whispered in her ear. 'You'll get hurt,' it said. 'It'll never work,' it insisted. Time and again, it stopped her in her tracks.

"I know," Katharine sighed. "I—it's like, whenever he's around I turn into—"

"A lunatic?"

"Okay, wow. I was going to go with a hot mess, but thanks."

Tori and Katharine laughed good-naturedly. These were things friends could say to each other, Katharine discovered.

"Lunatic, hot mess, lovestruck puppy—they all fit. Promise me, you'll talk to him?"

"Yes. I will. I'm going to march next door tomorrow and," Katharine took a deep breath, "tell him how I feel."

"You're not going to yell it at him, though. Right?"

Tori gave Katharine's knee a gentle shove when she said this, and they both laughed again. Then

Katharine gave Tori the death stare. "Now, how about you tell me whose bright idea was the jousting thing? And why was I not consulted *beforehand*?"

Tori put her hands up and said, "Okay, okay. Easy, now. For the record, it was Justin. Sorry. When that boy comes up with an idea...I don't know. It sounded like great press, and..." she trailed off at Katharine's unamused scowl.

Katharine let her squirm for a moment longer, then said, "Fine, but don't do it again. Remember what they say about payback, right?" She pushed Tori's knee and smiled, and Tori visibly relaxed again.

Once Katharine had finished scolding Tori for her role in blindsiding her with that ludicrous jousting nonsense, she was able to see the humor in it all. As long as it wasn't going to be repeated, that is. The rest of the ride was spent discussing the hilarity of their appearance on the Up All-Night Show. As they did, Tori posted, commented and shared across Katharine's social media accounts. She was 'striking while the iron was hot.'

SIXTEEN

AVOIDANCE

The next morning, Mitch—as per his habit—entered a quaint coffee şhop named ECO in the center of town. The rich aroma of freshly brewed coffee mingled with warm bread and bacon, and he breathed it all in deeply as the door closed behind him. Then he ordered his coffee from a black-aproned barista behind an immaculate counter. Soft music—Norah Jones, he recognized—drifted out of a speaker. The whir of an espresso machine was the only break in the tranquil quiet of an early morning. Mitch loved this time of day. It was the calm before the craziness.

Soon, the regular customers—the work crowd—would be bustling in. After that, the mommies pushing strollers and dressed for jogging or the gym. But, for that brief time before it all began, the place was his alone. He didn't care so much if it boasted an organic menu—Mitch was a coffee, regular kind of guy—nor did he pay much attention to the variety of items for sale artfully displayed here and there, impressive though they were. No, for Mitch, it was all about atmosphere, and the charming little coffee shop had plenty of it.

The young woman behind the counter treated him like he was a beloved regular customer, not someone relatively famous. In fact, the first morning he walked into the shop, he was greeted with a warm, 'Hey, Mitch. What can I get ya?' It made him smile and chuckle a bit. She smiled guilelessly back at him, and when he said—after reading her nametag— "Mornin' Lisa. How about a regular coffee," she only asked if it was 'for here' or 'to go.' He intended on taking it to go, but when he looked around, he spotted a cozy looking leather sofa facing the window. It gave a people-watchers view of the street, which was quiet but for occasional jogger, dog walker, and a few cars at that time of day. Since then, it had become his routine.

On this morning, just as it was on the several before it, the morning sun was beginning to brighten the day. The town was still in a sleepy hush and the shop in a soft glow. This time—after handing him his coffee—Lisa the Barista pushed a white plate across the counter toward him. On it was a flaky, warm chocolate croissant. When he looked up at her, she shrugged.

"You look like you could use some comfort food."

"Hmm," he tilted his head and squinted at her, "let me guess, you saw the show?"

Lisa blushed a little and raised her shoulders again, then admitted, "Yeah, I kinda saw part of it. Okay, well, all of it. Is that stuff—I mean, was it, like, scripted, or something?"

"I can assure you, it was not."

Lisa winced in sympathetic pain.

At least one person was taking pity on me. Mitch thanked her as he paid. He tipped the bill of his cap at the barista, and Mitch took his steaming mug, along with the local paper, to the sofa and made himself at home. The moment he sat down, he sighed with contentment. He needed this quiet kind of start. Catching the sunrise, greeting the day peacefully. No urgent phone calls, no social media, no noise or chaos. That would all begin soon enough. But for that first hour of post-dawn, the morning was his alone. He looked down at the paper folded neatly in his lap. The headlines were of the usual sort—doom, gloom, tragedy, and turmoil—and with more than a little disgust, he tossed it aside. His slight grin returned as he brought the mug of heavenly smelling java to his lips. It hovered there, little tendrils of steam dancing beneath his nostrils, as a familiar figure passed by the long window.

No, say it isn't her. It was Katharine, jogging. Or rather, stopping her jog directly in front of the window of the coffee shop. Mitch watched her as she curled her lean body forward and placed her palms on her knees. He could see, by the rise and fall of her back, that she was breathing heavily. Her long hair was in a pony-tail, and when she'd bent over, it swooped over her shoulder and blocked her face from his view. Katharine stayed like that for only a few moments. When she stood upright again, she flicked her hair back, giving him her profile. She smiled and put her hand on her hips as she spoke to someone out of sight. The sun had risen enough to cast a golden hue across her face, and the highlights in her hair shone with the same shade of gold as the sun.

Mitch was frozen in place—his mug still poised against his lower lip, the steam curling beneath his nose, and his eyes transfixed on the perplexing beauty outside the coffeehouse window. His heart was doing that—that *thing* it did whenever she was around. It was squeezing and bursting all at the same time. It was terrible and wonderful all at once. The first time he'd ever experienced a sensation like that was when he was sixteen, and Rebecca Lynn Hollister walked into his second period social studies class for the first time.

She was the new girl, shy and delicate—until you got to know her, that was. She had long blonde hair, swept up into a ponytail, and when she leaned forward to hand the teacher her pass, it fell over her shoulder. She straightened, and with a quick flip of her head, the ponytail swung back. She glanced around the room, and their eyes met, then lingered. There was a mischievous glint in those grey eyes of hers and the small smirk that pulled at the corner of her bow-shaped mouth. As it turned out, she was as wild as the day was long. Her father was the new chief of police in town, and she was determined to rebel against him.

From that day on, Mitch followed her around like a lovesick puppy. Thanks to her, he found himself in a heck of a lot of hot water that year. They got into the kind of antics that would've landed him in a juvenile detention home, had the instigator not been the daughter of the chief of police.

Mitch never forgot the dressing down he'd gotten from Chief Ned Hollister after what would be their last act of foolishness. They'd driven out to the new home construction site off RT 9 because Mitch hoped to see the latest developments. His Dad had been a builder before his accident, and Mitch had always loved visiting the construction sites. Somehow, Rebecca had convinced him to *borrow* a skid-steer loader.

"It's just *sitting* there, Mitch. C'mon. I want to drive it. No one will ever know," she said.

Well, all she had to do was give him that pout some girls are born knowing how to do, and he was putty. The next thing he knew, she'd driven it into a steep ditch. As Mitch was helping Rebecca out of the cab, a patrol unit pulled up alongside them.

"What the h—oh. Rebecca? Is that you?"

"Hi, Jerry. Are you gonna tell my Dad?" Rebecca started to plead her case and throw herself on his mercy, but the officer already had dispatch on the two-way radio.

"Yeah, it's Jerry. Send the Chief on over to the Andover property on RT 9."

"Is it—" began a staticky female voice.

"Uh-huh," he threw a side glance in Mitch's direction, "with an—*additional* situation."

A pause.

"Roger that, Jerry. Chief is en route."

At that point, Mitch hung his head in defeat.

"Run, Mitch. I was driving, I'll take the blame. He won't do anything to me," Rebecca hissed in his ear.

Despite being smack in the middle of doing something wrong—criminal, even—Mitch was a good kid, raised by great parents. His true nature showed him to be responsible, earnest, and kind. Therefore, he would not let Rebecca take the fall. A voice in his head—one that sounded suspiciously like his father's—said running away wasn't the way a man would handle it. A real man would own up, no matter what the consequence.

When the chief arrived—driving an unmarked, thunder cloud-grey car with his blue and red lights flashing but silent—he rolled down his window to speak to Jerry. He didn't look at Rebecca or Mitch until the cruiser had pulled out of the lot and onto Route 9. He turned off the ignition and climbed slowly out of the car. The chief came around the back of the cruiser, hiking up the pants of his dark blue uniform and his duty belt. His cuffs, two shiny rings of cold steel, clanked together when he did that. Mitch gulped, his eyes golf ball wide as they took in the handcuffs, baton, and most of all, the gun holster.

The chief wasn't imposing in size—Mitch already had several inches on the man—he was probably no more than 5'9" or 5'10", but he had a *presence*. His skin was ruddy, there were creases at the corners of his blue eyes, and he was mostly bald but for a closely shaved ring around his head. Ned Hollister had the beginnings of a belly paunch, but his back was board straight and his shoulders broad. In that moment—even though everything about his attire screamed Chief of Police—he just looked like a dad as he stared down at his daughter. Chief Hollister didn't seem angry. He looked tired. Defeated. Rebecca stared past him, over his right shoulder, and crossed her arms over her chest. She flipped her long golden ponytail off her shoulder, and it swung back, hitting Mitch in the arm. Her pointy jaw was thrust out defiantly as if he were yelling at her, or about to. But Mitch could see he wasn't going to do that—*yell*.

"Bec, sweetheart, get in the car. I'd like to talk to your friend a moment."

Mitch half expected Rebecca was going to defy her father, but she surprised them all. Her only act of defiance was when she turned on her heel, grabbed Mitch's arm, and pulled him down sideways so she could kiss his cheek. She'd done it so fast Mitch hadn't time to react or stop her. Surely, that was the chief's boiling point? But no, he merely looked down at the ground by Mitch's feet, his hands on his hips. He stayed like that as Rebecca brushed past him, climbed into the passenger seat of the cruiser, and slammed the door behind her. Then Chief Hollister ambled to where young Mitch stood nervously.

"Relax, son. I ain't gonna bite."

"It's not a bite I'm afraid of, sir." Mitch glanced down at the gun holster as he spoke.

The chief gave a short laugh. "You've been watching too much television, kid. Settle down. How about you tell me what you kids were doing out here, hmm?"

"It was my idea, sir. Rebecca had no idea what I was going to do. She's innocent."

At this, the chief laughed longer and harder, even slapping his knee, as if Mitch had told him a funny joke. Mitch did not laugh with him.

"Son, you think this is my first rodeo? You think it's *her* first rodeo?" He jerked his thumb in Rebecca's direction, who was staring straight ahead and not looking at either of them.

"Sir, I take full responsibility for—"

"I know you do, son. You're a good kid. Listen to me, now. Rebecca—she's a handful. Has been since her mother left us. She's rebelling, I know. They say it'll get easier, but—anyhow." The chief cleared his throat, then his eyes locked on Mitch. "I've already checked you out—did it the first week you two started spending time together—you come from good stock. Your dad was a builder before his accident, right? Hear you're a natural talent, too. Is that right?" The chief looked around the site and nodded his head, answering his own questions. "You've got a chance at decent future. *If* you stay out of trouble."

"Sir, I—"

"No. I talk, you listen. Here's what you're going to do. Tomorrow morning, before school, you're gonna come back here and ask for Bobby Andover.

You're gonna say to him that Ned Hollister sent you over. Then, you're gonna work off your part of the damages to the skid-steer."

Mitch looked around him, over at Rebecca's stoic figure, and opened his mouth again.

"Don't worry about her. She's gonna take responsibility, too. Kid, I'm gonna give you some advice. Stay in school, keep your grades up, and you stick with Bobby. He'll teach you everything you need to know, get you on the right track, set you up for an honest living doing man's work."

Chief Hollister scratched the back of his neck, looked back at his defiant daughter, and then back at Mitch. He waited for him to say, 'And stay away from my daughter,' but the chief surprised him once again that night.

"If I tell you to stay away from my daughter, it's only gonna make her chase you around more. So, I'm gonna tell you this, son. She's vulnerable. That tough act she's got going? That's all it is, an *act*. Now, I'm gonna ask you to be a man of integrity. Of *honor*. You hear me, son?"

Mitch understood him loud and clear. "Yes, sir. I promise you, I will."

He did as the chief told him to do. The next morning, before school, he went back to the construction site and found Bobby Andover. It wasn't hard. He was the short, stocky man in a faded denim work shirt, standing over a skid-steer that was half in a ditch and swearing. Mitch approached, his stomach in knots, his palms sweating. He wiped one of them off on his jeans and extended it to Bobby.

"Mr. Andover? Chief Hollister said you're the man I need to speak to, sir? My name's Mitch Ford, and I'm responsible for this. If you let me, I'd like to work off all of the damages."

Bobby Andover grunted and looked Mitch up and down. Mitch could almost hear what he was thinking by the way he appraised him. Tall kid. A little lanky. Big, sturdy looking hands. He grunted again. Mitch figured Ned Hollister had already told him about his and his daughter's antics and that Mitch was only responsible for *half* the damages. Despite what the chief had said, he still chose to own it all. Years later, Bobby would tell Mitch that he'd liked Mitch on sight, but he wasn't about to let *him* know that. The kid needed to squirm a bit.

"That so? How you propose to do that?"

"Well, sir, I'll do whatever work you need to be done. Errands. Clean-up. You name it."

Bobby grunted again and briskly rubbed his black beard-stubbled cheeks with both hands.

"Alright," he huffed, "get back here after school. I got plenty you can do. Don't be late."

Mitch did as he was told, and came back after school that day, and every day after that. Once Mitch had proven himself to be reliable and responsible, Bobby took him on as an apprentice and did exactly what the chief had said he'd do—he taught Mitch everything about building and construction there was to know. Bobby was a Master craftsman, and by the time Mitch was twenty-four, so was he.

As for Rebecca, she grew frustrated with Mitch and his newly found drive and dedication. She needed a playmate and a partner in mischief. Still, they stayed together for the whole school year and well into the summer. Mitch loved her in the way young men fall in love—hard and fast, and full of machismo. Rebecca loved *him* in the way girls fall in love—madly and deeply, and with a hurricane of emotions. They fought and made up, then repeated the cycle many times over. It was inevitable it would end, but when it did, it took him by surprise. It was early senior year.

"Mitch, we need to talk," Rebecca said one day.

They'd had a pretty nice afternoon. No fighting, but not much talking either. A surprisingly warm October day everyone was taking advantage of, including them. They'd gone to the park for a picnic. Rebecca began telling Mitch about her college applications. All along, Mitch had assumed she would stay close by to be near both him and her father. He was wrong.

"I've decided to go to Washington State. If they accept me, of course." she said.

"Washington? But that's practically on the other side of the country. What happened to staying local?"

Rebecca shrugged, then began twisting her class ring. She wouldn't look at him. In that moment, Mitch knew. She was breaking up with him. He didn't feel anything at first, nothing other than a numb sort of detachment. Like he was watching the scene from above, this young couple sitting on a blanket in the park. Instead of a cliched romantic picnic, they were breaking up. The rest was a blur. He recalled standing abruptly, shooing her off the blanket, swooping everything up into the checkered flannel sheet and stomping to his rusty old truck with her in tow.

Her calls of, 'just listen to me, Mitch,' and 'can't we at least talk,' were ignored. He drove her home in silence, turning up the radio every time she opened her mouth to speak. It wasn't until the day before she left for her tour of Washington State that he came around. Mitch stood at her front door, hands thrust deep in his pockets. Chief Hollister answered the door and grinned out at him.

"Atta boy. She'll be right out, son."

A few minutes later, Rebecca came out onto the porch. They were both hesitant and awkward, standing on opposite sides of the long front porch. Neither quite knowing what to say. Then Rebecca did something that was so *Rebecca* of her—a silly thing, really. There was a row of tiny potted cacti on the wide railing, and she carefully picked one up, studied it, then threw it at him. Mitch dodged it easily, and it sailed out into the yard, smashing on the neighbor's driveway. He pulled his hands from his pockets and put his arms wide. Rebecca ran to him then and buried her face in his shirt. She cried quietly. Mitch did, too.

They reacquainted once, several years ago at a build. Time had been kind to Rebecca. Sure, there were faint lines at the corners of her eyes, her figure was softer, fuller—but she had a calm confidence about her now. The hard edge was gone, and in its place, a woman content with herself and her life. She'd stayed in Washington, married a guy she met in college. Rebecca had discovered the show was taping there, so she took the ride over to see him. On a whim, she said. She had two kids, a boy, and a girl. The girl, she told him with a smile, was as wild as the day was long. Mitch smiled too when she'd said that. Serves you right, he told her with a chuckle. They talked about her dad, long since retired and moved nearby. He was a doting grandfather. They talked about old times, how crazy she'd been.

At the end, Rebecca said, "You know, Mitch. You were my first love. Thanks for setting the bar so high."

"Aww, stop. I'm happy for you, Bec. I mean it. It's been good seeing you."

He kissed her forehead, she squeezed him tightly around his waist, and they said goodbye. Mitch smiled softly at the memory. His eyes refocused on the woman outside the coffee shop window. It was easy to see why he was reminded of Rebecca. Sure, the hair flip *triggered* the memory, but it was more than that. Katharine had that same willfulness and fire, that air of intrigue and imminent excitement that called out to him. He was an adventurer, after all.

Mitch felt like a voyeur, watching Katharine in an unguarded state. Her mannerisms and demeanor were so different from the watchful, suspicious Katharine he'd seen so much of. The person she'd been speaking with came into view. Mitch recognized her to be Katharine's neighbor, Janie. Mitch could tell by their gesturing they were discussing their route. Katharine was shorter than her friend and looked up at her as Janie spoke, nodding and smiling, though still breathing heavy.

She was mid-nod when she froze. Mitch didn't know if she had a feeling or if it was her peripheral vision, but Katharine seemed to sense Mitch's stare, and she slowly turned her head to look inside the shop. Mitch, for lack of a better idea, quickly set down his mug and grabbed the newspaper. He held it up in front of his face, hiding from her and not caring how childish he was behaving. He realized too late that the paper was upside down.

***

Katharine watched in amusement as the work boot and faded denim-clad man inside ECO slowly righted the newspaper in front of his face. She could see the well-worn baseball cap over the top. There was no mistaking who it was.

"Do you see what I'm seeing?"

Janie turned her gaze to where Katharine's was and burst out laughing. "Does he think you don't see him? Is he—does he think he's *hiding* from you?"

Katharine shook her head and laughed, too. *Fine, you big baby, be that way.* To Janie, she said, "Come on, I'll deal with him later. Right now, I want to run!"

The duo ran off, shaking their heads and laughing as they did. Mitch Ford was not going to ruin her good mood. Like Katharine, Janie was a jogger, so when they learned this about each other, they decided to run together. Actually, Janie came up with the idea, and Katharine—after a brief hesitation—agreed. After doing practically everything solo for so long, it was strange to have a companion, but not at all unpleasant.

After a long talk with Tori the night before, and then another with Janie that morning, Katharine decided to renew her oft-broken resolve to change her self-destructive habits. She went down her short list of new skills—she'd made friends, thrown a party, and survived not one but two television shows. Now all that was left was telling the man of her dreams she loved him. Or maybe she should start with *likes* him. Love was such an intense word. What if he didn't feel as strongly? Then she'd be making a fool of herself.

"Janie," huffed Katharine, "I can't do it."

"Oh, c'mon. We only have one more mile to go. You can do it!"

"No, not the run. I mean I can't tell Mitch how I feel about him."

"Oh, my God. Stop it! I thought this was settled," Janie said in between strides. "New day, new Katharine, remember? Quit talking yourself out of it, silly. No more overthinking, okay?"

"Okay, fine. You're right. Today. I'll do it today."

"Good. Now let's sprint the last stretch."

Two hours later, a freshly showered and changed Katharine paced her living room. She'd rehearsed what she would say to Mitch at least a dozen times. There was to be no turning back, no chickening out. Whatever happened, happened. And no matter *what* happened, at least she'd be able to say she told him.

These were Janie's parting mantras to Katharine after their run, and Katharine kept them on repeat in her head. *You can do this*

SEVENTEEN

BLAST FROM THE PAST

Mitch arrived at the Genoma build site promptly at eight o'clock. Sam was waiting for him, without his camera on his shoulder. Mitch stopped in his tracks, pulled his cap down low, and put his hands on his hips. He braced himself. If Sam didn't have that thing sitting on his shoulder like a parrot, it meant one thing. Something was up.

"Hey, boss. We've got a situation."

"What'd she do now?" Mitch asked.

"Huh? Oh, not her. Remember the Atlanta build from last month?"

"Yes, Samuel. I'm not senile yet. I can remember events from a month ago. What's the problem?"

"Well," Sam squeezed one eye closed and held his breath a moment before letting the words rush out, "they need you—us, actually— to go back. They want more filler for the segment and the big boss wants it asap."

Mitch pulled his cap off and scratched his head. He glanced over at the bushes separating the Genoma property from Katharine's. *Forget her, old man. She made it clear at the Up All-Night appearance. She doesn't want to see you.* "When do we leave?" Mitch asked.

"Now, buddy. We have barely enough time to pack a bag and get to the airport."

"How long will it take? And what are we doing with the Genoma build in the meantime?"

"Not sure, Mitch. A week? Two weeks? They, uh, tied in some interviews and appearances, too. Genoma's is getting pushed back until we return. Sorry, man."

Mitch nodded and pat Sam on the shoulder. He gave one last glance in the direction of Katharine's house, then followed Sam to the SUV. Perhaps the unexpected trip was for the best. The past few weeks had been a whirlwind of bizarre events, and at the center of it all, a woman who somehow managed to turn him inside out. Him, a guy who prided himself on being level-headed, and a realist. He wasn't the kind of guy who spouted phrases like '*it was love at first sight.*' He didn't swoon or get mushy. Mitch Ford was a man's man. Plenty of women loved that about him. He didn't want for lack of female attention. So why was he so twisted up over this woman?

Enough already. Why are you doing this to yourself? The answer was simple. Deep down, he *knew* Katharine felt something for him. Mitch had also gleaned enough from Nate, her book, and her bio to have his suspicions as to why her walls were built up so high. It kind of made him feel a bit protective of her. Not that she *needed* protecting. She'd certainly proven *that* time and again. Mitch could hear the echo of his kid sister, Lizbeth, in his ear.

"Mitch," she'd said, "you're a fixer. Just like Dad, you fix things. But you can't fix *people*, Mitchie. They have to fix themselves, you know."

"How'd you get to be so smart, Lizzie?" He'd chuckled at her.

"I learned from the best, brother dear."

Lizbeth was two years younger than Mitch, but always behaved lightyears older. She became a psychologist, which was no surprise to anyone. After their parents passed away, Lizbeth and Mitch decided to keep the old farmhouse in Virginia that they'd been raised in. Lizzy lived and had her practice from there, and Mitch always had a place to call home. They spoke nearly every day, and she was well aware of the goings on with Katharine Evans. In fact, she was the only one who knew how affected Mitch was by *that woman*.

After much cajoling from Mitch, Lizzy had ventured an opinion, filled with professional disclaimers like, 'I can't diagnose a person I've never met,' and 'this isn't an analysis, but I'd *guess* that *maybe*, she *possibly…*' and so on. Eventually, she'd reluctantly confirmed Mitch's own, nonprofessional opinion—the woman had some serious trust issues. When he'd confronted Katharine before the Up All-Night taping, Mitch had been following Lizzy's suggestion to tell Katharine how he felt. Well, he *sort of* followed her suggestion.

He recalled what he'd said to her in the dressing room of the late-night show. He'd intended on being soft-spoken and gentle, he really did. He'd gone so far as to rehearse what'd he say: 'Katharine, I have very strong, undeniable feelings for you. I would like to see where this can go, but I don't want to pressure you or scare you away, so take your time and let me know.' Instead, he'd charged in there like a bull and demanded she declare her feelings immediately, and then stormed out when she couldn't.

That wasn't Mitch, not the *real* Mitch Ford. He was a sensitive guy, thoughtful. He wasn't a bull or—what had Jackson called him—a *brute*. Yet, somehow, whenever Katharine Evans was around, he lost his cool. She made him want to kiss her one minute, then pull his hair out the next. It was all up and down with her, no middle ground. Was that always how she was? If so, Mitch couldn't be on board for that. He'd already been with one crazy woman. *Leanne*. He groaned internally, mindful of Sam beside him. How he had ever let himself get sucked into her vortex, was beyond him. Hard to believe it had been just about two years since she'd packed her backs and moved to Italy. Or was it Spain? No matter, as long as it was far, far away and she took her crazy with her.

They'd met in Aspen. The Rebuilder Show had reached an all-time high in ratings, and as a reward, Mitch was on his first vacation in years—and he was having a terrible time of it. The elite crowd wasn't his scene, but he hadn't the heart to tell his boss—who'd generously footed the bill—so he brought his laptop and a book to read by the fire. Every time he'd settled in for the rest and relaxation he'd envisioned, Allen Wakefield—aka the boss—interrupted with 'someone he just had to meet.'

On day four Mitch had found himself caught in the middle of a group of real estate investors who had *great ideas* for his next build. They'd found him tucked into one of the lobby nooks, before a roaring fire with his book held high in front of his face. They took this as an invitation to join him. Someone had pressed a cognac in his hand. That's when Leanne Pearson walked through the ornate doors of the Le Regent. He was taking a sip of the strong amber liquid when Leanne's eyes met his. She leaned casually against the check-in desk, one hand on her fur coat covered hip, and watched him. There was a small smirk on her lips as she gave a sweeping glance at the men surrounding Mitch. Her perfectly sculpted eyebrow raised, and she tilted her head ever so slightly at him.

Mitch gave a small shrug, tipped his drink towards her, then sighed and took a sip. She took this as an invitation. He watched as Leanne sauntered over to where Mitch and the raucous back-clapping and blustering investors yammered loudly. They all stopped and gaped when the tall, lithe blonde reached them. Her playful sapphire eyes remained on Mitch.

"There you are, darling. You naughty boy, I've been looking all over for you."

She spoke in a haughty, aristocratic English accent. Mitch Ford was instantly enchanted.

"Ah—yes. Right. So sorry… sweetheart."

"Very well. Shall we?"

She extended her hand, palm down as if waiting for it to be kissed. Mitch stood and excused himself. One of the men brayed, "You sly dog, you."

Another, "Don't keep a lady like that waiting, boy!"

The blonde goddess took Mitch's big hand in her slender one and led him away without a backward glance. When the pair rounded the corner, she pulled him to her with surprising strength. She had a wicked grin on her pouty lips and declared,

"You owe me, Mitch Ford."

There was no trace of an English accent. In fact, it was entirely American. She wouldn't tell him her name until he'd bought her a drink in the hotel bar. By the time they'd said goodnight, Mitch was thoroughly infatuated with Leanne Pearson. Sure, she was eccentric. Yes, she was definitely wild. But she was so impossibly beautiful, Mitch overlooked the warning flags. He was having too much fun.

Lizbeth met her once and deemed her certifiable on sight.

"Is that your professional opinion, Lizzy?" Mitch had asked with a laugh.

"No, that's my *personal* opinion, Mitchell," she'd hissed. "There is something off about her. She has crazy eyes."

Mitch knew Leanne was, well, a bit much, but he'd been taken aback by Lizzy's harsh assessment. It was unlike her to be so critical and blunt. Mitch cleared the rose-tinted glasses after that exchange and began to see a side to Leanne he'd missed. Or ignored. For one, she tried on accents as if they were shoes she could slip on and off at will. Her temper was quick and often burst out over inconsequential or trivial matters. She never stayed in one place for long. Leanne Pearson was what some would call the 'idle rich.' Living off a trust, Leanne had never worked a day in her life, and it showed.

After six months—and with his sister's comments stuck in his mind—her once charming eccentricities began to wear on Mitch. He was a work hard, live clean, blue-collar man. Leanne expected formal dinners and jaunts to Paris. They were incompatible, simple as that. However, Leanne did not accept rejection well. Meaning, she didn't accept rejection, *period*. Mitch had tried to end the relationship with as much kindness as he could. He got twelve stitches in his temple as a thank you. Leanne expressed her displeasure in a most familiar way—she was yet another thrower of things. In Leanne's case, it involved tantrums, shoes… and one heavy, sharp crystal vase. *Women do love to throw things at you, old man.*

She apologized, which was very nice of her. She drove him to the emergency room. Also, very nice of her. However, when he came out of the emergency room, she was nowhere to be found. He had to take a taxi back to her place, where his keys and phone still were. Once there, he found both items, but she was gone. A scribbled note sat on the dining room table. The pen had rolled to the floor.

"Mitch——
By the time you read this, I'll be gone.
Don't come after me, it'll only make things
Harder for us both.
All my love,
-L."

Perhaps it was the concussion, but Mitch had the distinct impression she was breaking up with him... after *he'd* already broken up with *her*. She called twice after that, a month or so later. Both times, she'd left rambling messages. He'd never returned the calls. A slight guilt knotted Mitch's gut each time, but the fear of welcoming her back into his life validated his decision. Occasionally he caught sight of her in some magazine or other. She'd taken up with a wealthy French businessman and spent her time doing what she loved—spending money, traveling the world, and likely wreaking havoc everywhere she went.

"Okay, well. We're uh, about ready to board," said Sam.

"What? Yeah, okay. Great." Mitch glanced at Sam, then grimaced. He had the sour expression of someone unwilling to hide their annoyance. "What, Samuel? Say it. Whatever it is, go ahead and say it."

Sam opened and closed his mouth, then clasped his hands together and steepled them under his chin.

He seemed to be weighing his words carefully. "Mitch," he began, "I love ya like a brother, man. You know that. But you're driving me crazy. One minute, I can't get you to shut up about her. Then next, we're together for almost two hours, and you haven't said more than one sentence. Just *call* her. Or text her. Let her know you're out of town for a bit and you want to talk when you get back."

Mitch blanched. Sam was right. They'd gone from the build site to the inn, and then to the airport. They'd passed through the security checkpoint and strode through the terminal, and Mitch couldn't recall one word having been spoken. He clapped a hand on Sam's shoulder and looked him in the eye. "I'm sorry, pal. I know—I've been out of sorts. From now on, laser focus. I'll deal with… things when we come back."

If Sam had doubts, he kept them to himself and shrugged, "Whatever you say, boss. Here's your ticket."

Mitch looked at the ticket, then laughed. "First class, huh? The honchos are sparing no expense these days, I see."

"Yeah, well, the whole, uh, *thing* that's been going on lately has given the show a boost in ratings. A couple new sponsors, too. I guess they want to keep the star of the show happy."

Mitch rolled his eyes. Though he was grateful for it, the quasi-fame status had always baffled him. As far as Mitch could see, he was a craggily guy remodeling houses for people who'd had a tough break. Sure, he could understand the emotional connection the rebuilds created—people getting a second chance or being rewarded for being good humans—but why *he* got so much attention was beyond him. If he were *forced* to say so, Mitch considered himself a decent enough looking guy. He'd add—because calling one's self decent looking seemed vain—he looked little weather-beaten. The mirror and the camera told him he had some of those crow's feet lines around his eyes. His nose, once broken, had a slightly crooked notch at the bridge. You'd notice it if you stared long enough, but maybe not right off the bat. It gave his face character, or so he was told. Mitch had also been deemed—by others—to have a strong jaw, and eyes that were a particularly appealing shade of blue. That's certainly not something *he'd* say. His height, all six feet, two inches of it, was apparently attractive as well. His body, well, it was the body of a man who did manual labor all his life. Sinewy muscles and a mostly lean frame—heck, he was also a man who enjoyed a good beer here and there. These attributes were all well and good, he determined, but he was no male model. Not by a long shot. Mitch was more like the Marlboro man, except healthy. He was, in a word, rugged. Not that *he'd* use the word. Leanne summed him up once, calling him the quintessential Man Americana. She also called him the Ford truck commercial guy. She was disappointed when he said he was no relation to the famed Ford family.

"Excuse me, sir? Mr. Ford?"

Mitch had just settled in his seat. He looked up to see a kid who couldn't have been older than twenty-one looming above him. He was dressed in his Alphas—or Marine base uniform.

"Hey, son. What can I do for you?"

"I want to thank you, sir. You know, for what you're doing for that Marine and his family? It's a great thing."

The young man put his hand out to Mitch, and Mitch stood and shook it.

"You're a Marine, too I see."

"Yes, sir. I finished my second tour two weeks ago. On my way home to see my folks. Sorry to disturb you, but I wanted to say my thanks."

"Where you sitting, son?"

The Marine squinted at his ticket, then said, "Um, seat 32B. Economy."

"No, son, you're not. Take my seat. Thank you for your service." Mitch shook his hand once more and clapped him on the shoulder. The young man stammered his thanks, but Mitch shook his head, smiled and traded tickets with him.

"See ya when we land, Sam," he said with a tip of his hat.

Mitch settled into his new seat. It was between an elderly woman and a very pregnant woman. He tried to fold himself in as much as possible, but it was a tight squeeze. Fortunately, the flight was short, and before long, Mitch was once again walking through an airport terminal with Sam by his side. This time around, Sam repeatedly shoved his cell phone under Mitch's nose with a self-satisfied laugh each time.

"Look at this. One thousand," Sam exclaimed.

"What am I looking at?"

Mitch may or may not have needed reading glasses for the better part of a year. He wouldn't know because he declined an eye exam. Several times.

"The video. You know, of you giving up your seat for that Marine on the plane."

Mitch stopped midstride. "The what? Video? Who on earth took a—oh, *you* did. Geez, Sam. That wasn't for the show."

"Relax, Mitch. Besides, I wasn't the only one. Half the plane was recording it. *I* had the best angle, though. And held my phone properly for shooting video." He grimaced at his phone screen and shook his head, "Amateurs."

"Can I do anything in private these days?"

"Come on, now. Don't be like that. It's all a means to an end, right? Publicity equals ratings. *Ratings* equal more shows. More *shows* equal more people—like the Marine, for example—that you can help. It all works out in the end, buddy."

"Hmm," said Mitch.

Yes, it was all fine and good, as long as he got to do what he'd set out to do all those years ago. Immediately, he thought of his Dad. A Marine himself, a war veteran, too. After the war, Mitch Senior began working construction. He was a talented carpenter and quickly made a name for himself as a reliable, honest builder. Somewhere along the line, Senior had met and then married Mitch's mother, Deanna, and they had him and his sister. They lived a good, stable, middle-class life. Deanne was a homemaker; Mitch Sr. was the breadwinner. Then, when Mitch was fourteen, Sr.

had an accident on the job. He fell thirty feet from some scaffolding and broke his back. It was a year before he could walk again, but he was never able to work again. Not doing what he loved, at least.

The meager government assistance checks were barely enough to pay the mortgage, let alone anything extra. His mother did whatever she could to make money. She sold Avon and Tupperware and even tried her hand at retail. Mitch got his first job at fifteen—bussing tables, then of course, eventually working for Mr. Andover's construction company. Lizzy babysat the neighborhood kids. They all did their part, without complaint or bitterness. Throughout it all, the Ford's held their heads high and remained thankful for all they had. They believed no matter how tough *they* had it, someone else was suffering more.

Mitch admired his parents tremendously. That appreciation had inspired him to develop and pitch the Rebuilder Show concept to an old high school friend of his, who happened to be a top guy at a new cable network called GoodDeed TV, or simply GDTV. Their plan was innovative and impressive— create original series, all with inspiring and uplifting themes. It was a perfect match, and thanks in large part to Mitch's show, the network was thriving.

"Oh, stop grumbling, Mitch. Enjoy the fame, man. Speaking of that, we've got to get you to your first appearance."

"Can't we go to the hotel first?"

"No time, they're expecting you."

Mitch sighed and let Sam take the lead. "Wonderful. Let's keep them on task this time, hmm? Tell them I'm only talking about the Atlanta build and nothing else."

Sam's bushy eyebrow lifted, but he nodded. He tapped out a text—presumably to Justin—to give the forewarning. Mitch had no interest in playing the role of demanding celebrity, but he had even less interest in discussing the non-existent KatMitch thing. He was determined to think of only business on this trip, and nothing else.

EIGHTEEN

CARY GRANT CURE ALL

Katharine glanced at the clock on the microwave. 11:07. It was the perfect time to pay Mitch a visit next door. Past the morning bustle, but before lunch. An odd time which seemed spontaneous and nonchalant, like she'd *just happened* to think of seeing him on a whim and *not* like the hours and hours of planning she'd put into it. She texted Tori:

OK. I'M GOING TO TALK TO HIM.
WISH ME LUCK.

A minute later, Tori responded:

YOU GOT THIS, GIRL.
TELL HIM HOW YOU FEEL.

Katharine smiled, then sucked in a great big breath. She let it out slowly, then walked to the back door. Everything tingled, her palms were sweaty, and her insides trembled as if she'd drank a whole pot of black coffee. She wiped her shaky hand on her pants and opened the door. It was bright and hot outside—too hot, too bright—and Katharine squinted across the yard at the tree line that separated the two properties. Her senses were heightened and yet she felt foggy, her nervous system had gone haywire. Katharine Evans was about to talk about feelings. *Her* feelings. There was a first for everything.

Katharine passed through the now well-beaten path between the yards and carefully made her way across the beleaguered lawn. The crew had yet to tackle the front and had in fact added to the mess with their building remnants and debris. They'd begun working on the house itself—the siding was stripped, shutters removed, and battered gutters torn away. Blue and white house wrap protected the bare wood from the elements and a bright blue tarp covered one half of the roof. A long, industrial size dumpster took up most of the cracked driveway. There was a man on the uncovered part of the roof, clad only in faded jeans and work boots. He was tossing sections of roofing into the bins. He nodded at Katharine but continued his work.

"Excuse me? Could you tell me where Mitch is?"

She had to shield her eyes from the glaring sun as she looked up at him.

"Mitch? He ain't here."

"Oh. Well, do you know when he'll be back?"

The man shrugged, pulled a bandana from his back pocket and wiped the sweat from his forehead.

"Dunno. He's gone. Got on a plane this morning for Atlanta. Sorry, lady, but I gotta get this done."

He'd already started back to work before Katharine could ask him anything more. She turned and blindly made her way back through the bushes. Once again in the safe confines of her kitchen, she sank into the nearest chair and put her hand to her throat. *Gone. He left without a word. No goodbye. Nothing.*

Katharine couldn't decide if she was numb, or if every nerve in her body was on fire. This was not the scene she'd envisioned. She imagined finding him out in the backyard, calm and commanding as he directed his crew. He'd sense her presence, then turn to face her. A mega-watt smile would shine on his suntanned face, and he'd slowly pull his faded cap off his head. He'd gaze at her, his blue eyes questioning, and Katharine would nod her head, '*Yes, Mitch. I'm here because I'm in love with you,*' that nod would say. Mitch would then drop whatever he had in his hands—blueprints, or a hammer, or something—and he'd spread his arms wide for Katharine to run to.

It was going to look like an old, black and white movie, with Katharine ending up wrapped in his strong arms, looking dainty and perfect. She'd throw her head back to look into his adoring eyes, and he'd have kissed her the way Cary Grant kissed Deborah Kerr in An Affair to Remember. It was a perfectly scripted happily ever after ending. Or beginning, really. Only, Mitch was gone. There was no classic, golden age of cinema, romantic scene. There was only Katharine, sitting alone at her kitchen table with only the muted hum of her dryer tumbling her bedsheets down the hall.

Katharine stared at her phone. It was silent, but an incessant blue notification light flashed repeatedly. Someone had left a message. Her heart lurched, perhaps it was Mitch. Katharine grabbed it, almost knocking it to the floor in her haste. The screen illuminated, showing two messages. One was from Tori, the other from Janie. They both wanted to know how it had gone with Mitch. She wasn't ready to talk to them, or anyone for that matter.

She stood and wandered throughout the house. First, the kitchen. Was she hungry? No. But she could clean out the refrigerator. That would keep her busy for a while. So, she set about her task, discarding two-week-old hummus and the curry chicken she'd had every intention of reheating, but never did. A rock-hard lime had gotten wedged in a far back corner of the fruit bin, and a half-empty bag of grapes had begun to grow whiskers. Katharine discarded all the definites and most of the questionables, all the while repeating the mantra in her head, 'don't think about him.'

Maybe he— she shook her head.

Don't think about him.

How could he— she slammed the lime into the garbage can.

Don't think about him.

On and on like this she went until the refrigerator was gleaming, but near bare. The garden was overflowing with vegetables and herbs, so out she went with a basket slung over her arm. One task led to the next, and by four o'clock she'd run out of energy to find more things to do. Katharine considered going up to her office to write, but this was about the time she usually *finished* writing, not began it. She was usually an 8 a.m. to 4 p.m. writer—treating it as if she were going into an office job—rather than traipsing through her house in her pajamas. Mitch—or the lack of him—had disrupted her workflow, and now she was unmoored and drifting listlessly. She glanced up at her reflection in the foyer mirror.

"Oh, my God. Stop being such a—a *girl*. Go find something else to do."

She took her mirror image's admonishment and grabbed her water shoes. A late day paddle around the lake would be perfect. Only, when she stepped out onto her back deck, she found the sky had begun to swell with ominous clouds. Low and dense, they curled and billowed above the lake. The muttering rumble of distant thunder trembled the air. The scent of impending rain filled her nostrils, and Katharine groaned.

"Really?" she called up to the sky.

She spun on her heel and stomped back inside. As she closed the back door, her doorbell rang. Despite herself, she hoped, and half expected it to be him. Instead, it was Janie. In one hand she held up a large bottle of wine, in the other, a packet of microwave popcorn.

"Hi, honey! I figured maybe you could use a girl's night. What do you say—you, me, this bottle of wine, some popcorn and a Cary Grant movie marathon."

Katharine looked from the bottle to the popcorn, to Janie, then grinned. "I love you. Get in here."

Katharine opened the wine and poured them each a glass, then tossed the popcorn in the microwave. After she hit the 'start' button, she gave Janie a suspicious stare.

"Okay, spill it. How'd you know I'd be needing this," she waved her hand at the offerings, "and how'd you know I was a Cary Grant fan? Oh, and where is your gaggle of menfolk?"

"Let's see. Last question first—Jim took the boys to see the latest Transformers movie, so I'm free for the next three hours. Next, you have three framed movie posters in your living room— all with Cary Grant, and you mentioned it in the interview you did for that magazine—I forget which one now—so, it was pretty easy. As far as your first question—don't you *ever* look at your social media?"

Katharine shrugged. No answer necessary.

"Well, Mitch was all over it today," Janie continued. "Or videos of him were, I mean. Here, look."

Janie tapped her phone screen a few times, found what she was looking for, and turned it to Katharine. It was a shaky phone-camera video of Mitch on an airplane, talking to a tall man in the aisle. The phone's owner zoomed in and out a couple times, causing the image to blur then sharpen once he finally got the right perspective.

Katharine knew it was a man holding the phone because he gave commentary.

"Okay, so that's Mitch Ford—the guy from the Rebuilder Show—and the guy he's talking to is a Marine. I think he's giving him his seat." Slightly muffled, he says "Dude, that's awesome, right?" Then back into the phone's built-in microphone, "This guy is the best, man. Mitch Ford is giving up his first-class seat to a Marine." Again, muffled, "Yeah, yeah, I'm getting it, relax, man."

He zoomed in and out again, then the video ended right after Mitch walked by him. Without saying a word, Janie scrolled to yet another video of the same incident. This one was clearer and closer, taken from behind Mitch. Katharine knew even without seeing him, it was Sam holding the phone. Mitch's voice came through clear as day.

"Thank you for your service."

Katharine had an urge to see more videos, from any and every angle, but she pushed the phone back to Janie.

"He's amazing, isn't he? Don't answer. I know he *is* amazing. I pushed away the most remarkable guy I'll ever meet, and now he's gone. Over before we've begun."

"Oh, honey, now don't say that. You don't know that. Not for sure, at least. He'll be back soon enough, and you can talk to him then."

As much as Katharine wanted to believe Janie, she had her doubts. "Maybe it's for the best, Janie. I mean, every time—and I mean *every* time—we get close to, you know, getting close, something happens to ruin it. Maybe we're not meant to be,

ELSA KURT

and like, the universe is trying to tell us that. I think it's time to… move on."

Janie opened her mouth to say something, then gave Katharine a new, appraising look. "Well, I'm not so sure about any of that. I do know that your…*experience* is, well, on the minimal side of the spectrum. I happen to have the perfect practice date for you."

"A…practice date?" Katharine eyed her with skepticism.

"Yes, you know, a date with a guy that you can practice your social skill on. Now, before you say no, hear me out. Jimmy works with a guy in Troop F, he's a sweetheart. His name is Ryan. He's divorced, no kids, and he says he's ready to start dating again, but he's *so* not over his wife. He's perfect practice material. Why don't I set it up?"

"Ugh. I don't think so, Janie. You've seen what a disaster I am. Besides, I'm not anywhere close to being—"

"Over Mitch. I know, silly. That's why he's the perfect guy. You'll both dip your toes in the water, build up your confidence. There'll be no one-sided love connection, so no worries. Let your hair down. Like, literally—wear your hair down when you go out. It makes you look more…approachable."

Janie blinked and smiled sweetly at Katharine. Katharine grabbed a bowl from the cabinet by the sink and then filled it with the popcorn.

"Bringing Up Baby or The Bachelor and the Bobbysoxer?"

"Ah, avoiding the question, are we? Fine, be that way. Bringing Up Baby, please. I'll grab the wine. Hey, looks like that storm fizzled out."

They talked through most of the movie, stopping for Katharine's favorite parts, then resuming whatever meandering conversation they fell upon. They avoided talking about anything to do with Mitch, and they both left their phones in the kitchen. Temptation avoided. After Janie went home, Katharine had no more excuses to not look at her phone. So, she did what any slightly drunk, lovesick, and desperate woman would do—she cyber-stalked Mitch Ford like a teenager with a crush.

She skipped over social media, went straight to her search bar, and typed in his name. A laundry list of articles, interviews, and YouTube links of his show dominated the page. But it was the first one that caught her eye. It was dated that day and had a still shot of a beautiful blonde hanging on Mitch's arm and smiling for the camera. Mitch's mouth was open as if they'd caught him in the middle of speaking, and one hand was extended toward the camera. He was trying to block the photographer's shot.

Katharine's brows knit together, and her jaw clenched as she studied the blonde. She looked like a movie star, lithe and perfectly made up. Her hair was cut in a tidy bob that barely grazed her tan, narrow shoulders. Her arms were wrapped possessively around Mitch's arm—the one not extended out. No, this hand was wedged into the pocket of his jeans. She looked again at his face. He seemed neither pleased nor displeased. If anything, Katharine would say he looked surprised.

Yeah, surprised to be caught with another woman. Guess he moves on quickly. Katharine was hurt and feeling hurt made her angry. Without clicking on the article, she closed out her browser and opened her text messages.

Two can play that game. She tapped the screen's keyboard harder than necessary:

SET UP THE DATE

WITH THE TROOPER.

I'M READY TO GET OUT

THERE AND PRACTICE.

She hit send and stormed upstairs with the remainder of her wine and started a bath. If he could move on like that, then so could she. KatMitch was no more. Not that it ever really was *a thing*. She spent an hour arguing with herself and having imaginary fights with Mitch. In each scenario, she won the argument, and he slinked away like a kicked puppy. In most, she threw something at him, and in some, she punched him right in the gut.

None of it actually made her feel any better, though. What *did* make her feel slightly better, was the realization that she hadn't reverted to the old Katharine the moment someone hurt her. The old Katharine would've shut down and sworn off people. This new and improved Katharine jumped in an entirely different direction. She was going to go out on a *date*. With a complete stranger, no less. She wished she could feel more excited about it all.

NINETEEN

ONCE A TROUBLEMAKER

"What is it, exactly, that you're doing here, Leanne?"

Mitch's teeth gritted as he spoke. Leanne had ambushed him, and someone had helped her do it. By the guilty look on Sam's face, he was able to guess easily. He'd have to deal with him later. For now, he had to get Leanne's claws off him— literally—and make his escape.

"Mitch, darling, I thought you'd be *happy* to see me. After all its been at least a year. Come on now, give your Le-Le a proper kiss hello."

"Leanne, I have never once called you...Le-Le. And it's been two years. Now, what—" Mitch took a deep breath and willed himself to calm down. He softened his tone and forced a small smile. "What brings you to Atlanta, Leanne."

Leanne pouted and finally released Mitch's arm. They were in a park across the street from the last rebuild. It was late afternoon, and they'd just finished taping a filler segment for the upcoming broadcast. She strolled casually toward the pond in the center of the park and looked over her shoulder at him as if she were a runway model. He'd never noticed before how calculated her every move was. Now it was clear as day. The way she walked, the way she stood—all put upon, like her many accents. She was acting out a role, performing a show. How Mitch ever found her enchanting was beyond him.

"Oh, Mitchell, if you must know...I *missed* you. I miss *us*. Say you've missed me, too. Come on, just a little bit?"

"I find that a little hard to believe, Leanne. What happened, did your French businessman get tired of your antics?"

"Jon Paul? No, silly. He's in Tokyo. Or is it India? No matter, it's over. Leaving you put a permanent scar on my heart."

Mitch scoffed, "Scar on your heart? Really? Let's talk about the twelve stitches I had to get on my forehead. That left a *real* scar, Leanne."

"You were supposed to have ducked. How could I have known you wouldn't duck, for goodness sakes?"

Mitch blinked at her. Now that he didn't see her through those rose-tinted glasses anymore, it was evident Leanne was intentionally goading him. There was no possible way she was as obtuse as she acted. She had the terminal illness that most idle-rich people were afflicted with—boredom. Leanne loved a good fight, it gave her an excuse to throw things and yell. Once upon a time, she was very good at baiting Mitch, but no more. Mitch was not going to fall into her trap ever again. He bit back the retort on his tongue and instead repeated his question.

"What are you doing in Atlanta?"

"I told you, I—"

"Leanne."

"Oh, fine. I'm in Atlanta because Daddy is opening another hotel. And a little birdie told me you'd be here, so—"

"Who is the 'little birdie' Leanne?"

"I-well, it was Sam. But don't get all mad at him. I tricked him into thinking I was from corporate, He's still the most gullible man on earth, I see."

She laughed in the girlish giggly way she always did in public. It was affected, not her real laugh. Mitch knew both. Her *other* laugh had a mean, Cruella Deville cackle, and burst out of her when no one was around. It was the laughter of a bully.

"Anyhow," she continued, "I decided it would be fun to have a little visit with my Mitchie. You know, for old time's sake, hmm?" Leanne's gaze on Mitch was steady. One perfect eyebrow lifted, and a smirk tugged at the corner of her pink lips as she added, "Your little bookworm girlfriend doesn't have to find out."

Now Mitch knew what Leanne's game was. She'd seen the tabloids, and she was jealous. Not because she wanted Mitch back, but because he was in the limelight which she craved. It was time to end her charade.

"Thanks, but no thanks, Leanne. It was…nice to see you. You take care now." Mitch turned to leave, but Leanne called out and took his arm.

"Mitch, don't leave like that! Come, give me a proper goodbye."

"Leanne, I—"

"Hey, Mitch! Over here!" Mitch looked to the sound of the voice. *A photographer, great.*

Mitch began to say, "No pictures, please," but it was too late. The rapid shutter clicks were audible, and the man took off before Mitch could stop him. The moment he left, Leanne released her grip on his arm with a Cheshire cat grin. Mitch was disgusted. Not only with her and her antics, but with himself for ever desiring her.

"Happy now? Enjoy your fifteen minutes of fame. It's the last you'll ever get with me. Goodbye Leanne. Don't come around again." Mitch strode away, leaving Leanne pouting by the pond. But as typical of her, Leanne had to get the last word. She called out to his retreating back, "Have fun with your boring little book girl. Hope she won't be too mad about our photograph. My, we do look cozy in it!"

He wouldn't give her the satisfaction of seeing his surprise and dismay. Could their picture already be hitting the internet? Mitch waited until he was safely ensconced in the confines of the courtesy limo before pulling his phone from his pocket and checking the web. Sure enough, the first thing that came up in his search was the picture of him and Leanne. Her arms were linked around one of his, and she wore a coy smile for the camera. Mitch was caught between two expressions—startled and dismayed. His hand was out, trying to block the photographer's shot. It gave the impression of a man getting caught in a clandestine meeting. He tossed his phone onto the seat beside him and slumped down, causing the smooth leather to make an unpleasant sound. The driver shot a glance at Mitch though the rearview mirror.

"I didn't—it was the leather."

The driver averted his eyes and said nothing.

Great, that'll end up a tabloid story, too. Agitated, Mitch picked up his phone again and called Sam. The moment he answered, Mitch laid into him. "Sam, what the—"

"I know, I know. Sorry, man. I don't know how she—well, anyhow, I'm gonna call Justin and we'll get him to do damage control."

"Really? How's that, Sam? You know what, don't tell me. This isn't what I signed on for, buddy. You realize that, right? My dream was to rebuild houses for people on hard times, not be a-a *celebrity*. I mean, I'm a builder, for Christ sakes. Not an *actor*."

"I know, Mitch. I know," said Sam.

"Stop trying to pacify me, Samuel. I am not a child."

"No, Mitch. You are not a child. I understand completely."

Mitch yanked the phone from his ear and rattled it in front of his face. The driver gave another furtive glance in the rearview mirror. Remembering that he was not only being watched but listened to as well, Mitch composed himself.

"I'm hanging up now, Samuel. I hope the next time I look at my phone—which will not be until after I've showered and slept—it won't be plastered with images of Leanne and me. Goodbye."

Sam managed to squeeze in, "I'll pick you up at eight a.m. for the reshoot of—" before Mitch disconnected.

To the driver, Mitch leaned forward announced, "I'm not usually this…tense. Long week, you know?"

"Uh, yes Mr. Ford." Several nervous glances from the mirror to the road followed, then "Um, Mr. Ford? It's only Tuesday."

Mitch rubbed his eyes with the tips of his callused fingers, flopped back into his seat again and said, "So it is, son. So it is."

For the life of him, Mitch couldn't figure out how everything got so out of hand. One minute he was just a guy on a relatively popular reality-based television show, doing what he loved—building things and helping good people. He'd even been able to start his highly successful Mitch Ford Future Tradesman Scholarship fund, thanks to that show. When people recognized him and asked for the occasional autograph, he was both honored and happy to oblige. Now, suddenly, he was Mitch Ford the television *personality*. For the first time in his career, Mitch wondered if it was all worth it—living his life under a microscope, losing some of his anonymity for—

The buzz from his phone halted his ruminations. He didn't recognize the number on the caller ID but answered it anyway. "Hello?"

"Is this, uh, Mr. Ford?"

"That depends, pal. Who's this?"

"Uh, yes sir, this is Vinny Genoma? You're doing the rebuild on my grandpa's house? In Connecticut, sir?"

Mitch chuckled to himself. "In that case, yes. This is Mitch. Good to hear from you, son. How're things?"

"Very well, sir. Thank you for asking. I, uh, got your number from Sam? He said it was okay to call you? I called to say thank you again, Mr. Ford. Me and Emily—that's my wife, you remember—we saw the pictures of all the demo work you and your crew have been doing, and it's incredible already. I can already imagine little Vin and our baby girl—we named her Kayleigh Ford Genoma, in honor of you, Mr. Ford—I can already picture 'em running around the yard and swimming in the lake. I can't believe we're gonna get to call my grandpa's house home."

The young man's voice quavered and broke on the last sentence, and Mitch was humbled. He knew full well Sam was behind this call, and he was grateful. Hearing from the earnest man bolstered him and reminded Mitch of exactly why he did the show.

"Well, that is quite an honor, son. I appreciate that. Don't know if your little girl will when she gets older, but it means a lot to me. No thanks are necessary, either. We're all glad to do this for you. I'll let you get back to your family now, but we'll see you in a few weeks for the show. Take care, son."

"Thank you, sir. You too."

The call ended as the limousine arrived at the hotel. Mitch thanked the driver and climbed out. He was about to pass through the doors when the man behind the wheel called out through his open window.

"Hey, Mr. Ford?"

Mitch turned back, "Yes?"

"I'd like to add my thanks, Mr. Ford. My sister is in the Air Force—stationed in Germany right now—and she says they all love your show. You're doing great things for them, you know."

Mitch bowed his head a moment, smiling. "What's your sister's name?"

"It's Tracy. Why?"

"Are you my driver tomorrow?"

"The whole week."

"Alright then. You get me Tracy's address tomorrow, and we'll get something out to her. See you in the morning."

Mitch went up to his room feeling considerably lighter than he had been all afternoon. He made a vow to himself to not let the madness—meaning the tabloids and media— get to him. Not for the first time, he wondered how Katharine was faring. Had she seen the picture yet? Did she even care? He was tempted to send her a message. But what would he say? '*Hey, Katharine. I know you rejected me and we're not even vaguely a couple—other than in the media—but hey, nothing is going on with Leanne and me.*' He was too old for romance dramas—real or imagined. Katharine had his number. She could call and ask him herself.

Mitch planned to spend the remainder of his night reading outlines and show proposals...and checking his phone for texts every ten minutes like a jilted teenage girl. There were none from Katharine, but plenty from Justin and Sam. He gave them both perfunctory responses and tried to stay focused on his work. In the back of his mind, a mantra: *Katharine. Katharine. Katharine.*

He quickly realized the meager distractions in his hotel suite weren't going to be enough. How could he divert himself? The hotel had a pool, a fitness room. And a bar, of course. *No, old man. Go for a swim. It's a much better choice.* Mitch heaved himself off the bed, changed into shorts and grabbed a towel. *Healthy choice it is...*

TWENTY

TWO TO TANGO

"Katharine? Hi, I'm Ryan. It's nice to meet you."
Katharine looked up from her phone into a pair of warm brown eyes. "Hi, Ryan." She stood and reached her hand out. He came in for a polite hug. It was awkward, but they both laughed. "I already ordered a glass of wine. Hope you don't mind."

They were on the outdoor patio of Angelico's Lake House, a neutral and casual location that seemed ideal for a first date.

"Not at all…as long as *you* don't mind if I order something stronger. As you can probably see, I'm kinda nervous."

Ryan flashed a boyish grin. No dimples. *Good.* This had been her stipulation—that he bore no resemblance or reminder of Mitch Ford. After seeing yesterday's media storm surrounding him and his heiress girlfriend, she wanted nothing whatsoever to do with him. *Ex*-girlfriend, Tori had said. They looked awfully cozy for exes, Katharine had retorted. She willed her attention back to the handsome, no resemblance to you-know-who man seated across from her.

"I—wait, *you're* nervous? A man who arrests bad people for a living is nervous to go out on a blind date? Interesting."

Katharine was feeling both the effects of her wine and an insatiable need for revenge. If Mitch was going to be out with other women, then she would go out with other men. And if anyone happened to catch it on their cell phones and take pictures to post to social media, so be it. *You're doing it again. Pay attention to the cute trooper, he's talking. And remember, it's a practice date.*

"Ah, don't be fooled by the hype. It's mostly traffic stops and construction details."

Modest. Cute. Non-Mitch.

"Oh, I'm sure it's much more than that. How long have you been a state trooper?"

"About seven years now. My wife—sorry, *ex*-wife, couldn't stand the job. The hours, the overtime. Not to mention the—sorry. I think I broke a major first date rule."

"Oh? What's that?" Katharine asked. *Does he not know this is merely for practice?*

"I mentioned my ex. Not cool, right?"

Katharine shrugged. She really didn't mind. They were making conversation, something she'd been afraid there'd be a lack of. The more he talked, the less she had to. "Don't be silly. Janie kind of filled me in, so I had the heads up."

Ryan visibly relaxed. They ordered dinner and conversation flowed more easily than she'd expected. He did talk quite a lot about his divorce, but Katharine was sympathetic. It was a relief he truly was nowhere near being over his wife. It suited her perfectly because she, of course, was nowhere near being over Mitch Ford.

"…Mitch Ford?"

"What? I'm sorry, did you—"

"I know your story, too, Katharine," Ryan smiled kindly. "I've known Jim and Janie for eight years, we went to high school together, and Jim and I went to the academy together. Plus, I have internet access, so…"

"So, you got all the intel, hmm?"

Ryan laughed, "What kind of trooper would I be if I didn't?"

Katharine shook her head, laughing too. "Well, cheers to us and our complicated lives!" They raised their glasses and clinked them together. When they did, a bright burst of light suddenly illuminated them. It was a camera flash. Its owner—a stout woman with frizzy blonde hair held back by over-sized black sunglasses— leaned her ample torso over her table to get the picture. Realizing her subjects were looking at her, she hurried back into her chair, knocking her water glass over in the process. Her dinner companion—likely her husband, based on their matching orange t-shirts and round bodies—hissed something at her and waved his hands around. She hissed something back at him, and they both cut their eyes to Katharine and Ryan several times.

Bemused, Ryan asked, "Does…that happen a lot?"

"It didn't before Mitch Ford. It's fairly regular now, but not too bad. They must be out of towners. The locals were over it after the first week. Funny what you get used to, isn't it?"

Ryan agreed, adding that his job made him virtually impossible to surprise. He'd seen enough head shaking, mind-numbing events for a lifetime. They exchanged stories and laughed comfortably with one another. Knowing it wasn't going to be a love connection for them made it easier to have a fun, pressure-free night. The camera happy woman had left, but not before 'sneaking' a few more photographs. Katharine encouraged Ryan to ignore her when he chivalrously offered to reprimand her.

"It'll make her vindictive if you do. This way, she'll hopefully either keep the pictures to herself, or—if she does share them on social media— she'll say something nice."

"Well, you sure know how to handle it all with class."

Katharine laughed hard enough to snort. "Oh, you may be just about the only person to think *that!*" She went on to tell him about the past incidents with Mitch and photographers and video cameras. If he'd seen them—which he probably had—he was gentlemanly enough not to say so.

After a pause, Ryan said, "Katharine, do you realize your face lights up when you talk about Mitch Ford? I know you said nothing is going on between you two, and I also know it's peculiar to be saying this on a date, but—I think you should tell him how you feel."

"You're right…that was really weird, Ryan." Katharine's expression was serious, then she grinned and gently tossed a small piece of bread at his face. "I'm teasing. I know, and you're right. I think it might be too late. Anyhow, are we getting dessert, or has this night strayed too far into Bizzaro-Land?"

"Please, I'm sitting across from a beautiful, famous writer, who snorts when she laughs and only has eyes for another man. How could I turn down dessert with you?"

"Ah, says the man still in love with his ex-wife."

"Touché, madam writer, touché."

Later that night, not long after she'd said goodbye to Ryan in the parking lot of Angelico's, she texted Tori and Janie—they were now in a group chat—and told them about the date. Tori sent several emojis, which seemed to mean she was laughing and crying in equal measures. Janie texted a happy face, then called her.

"So, perfect practice date then, huh?"

"Yep, thank you Janie. By the way, he really was as cute as you said. Hang on, unlocking my door." Katharine wedged the phone between her ear and shoulder, unlocked the door and threw her keys and purse on the ledge. "Okay, so anyhow—Operation Practice Date, success. Good looking guy, bonus."

"I know, right? That black shirt made him look super-hot. Don't tell Jim I said that, though."

"Wait, how did you know he was wearing a black shirt?"

"Social media, duh. Someone named CATLADYFOREVA posted it, and it was shared, like, I don't know, seven thousand times or something. That was over an hour ago, so it's probably more by now. Hang on—" There was rustling, then a muffled, "Jeremy Michael McNamara, if I tell you one more time, I swear to God. We do *not* wear underwear on our heads. Joseph James, stop burping the alphabet. Get to bed. Now!" The rustling stopped, and with an exasperated tone, she was back to Katharine. "Anyhow. What were we saying? I remember, Ryan's super hotness not being enough to distract you from—"

"Do you think Mitch has seen it?" Katharine's stomach clenched, then she reminded herself of *his* most recent picture on social media. "Not that I care, or anything."

"Oh, *no*. Of course. I'd say—since you are following each other on all the sites—yes, he's seen it. So, why don't you—I don't know—*call* him, and tell him... How. You. Feel?"

"Following each other? But I never—oh, Tori and Justin." Katharine plopped down on her sofa. "I can't tell him how I feel, Janie. Not *now*. It's too late. He's with the tall, blonde goddess. Did you know they were a thing? They met at some fancy lodge in Aspen."

"You don't follow the tabloids, though, right?" There was a definite sound of amusement in Janie's voice.

"I don't. I mean, not like, on a regular basis. It so happens I was researching some location stuff for the book, and I kind of—I don't know—stumbled on it." Even to her own ears, Katharine sounded petulant and full of it.

"Mhmm. Okay. So, how is the book coming along, anyway? I know things have been hectic with all the whole, you know—"

"KatMitch nonsense. You can say it, it's true. I haven't been as focused as I'd like to be. The publisher gave me an extension when the appearances and interviews started, but honestly? I'm *so* ready to get back to work. In fact, now that there's a little break in the... activity next door, I think I'm going to take advantage of it and power through until the book is finished."

"Wow, no kidding, huh? Well, good for you. Does that mean no wine and gossip hour tomorrow?"

"I'm afraid so. I'm going old-school—complete electronics shutdown, self-imposed isolation, the works. You know, when I bought this house, that was the exact vision I had. I totally went for the cliché 'writer's cabin on the lake' thing. Like, I was excited about being so secluded from everyone and everything. It's funny that now, it's almost like a punishment. I think I kind of *like* being a part of things."

"Aww, well, I think I'll go ahead and take credit for that, then." Janie laughed into the receiver.

"Rightfully so. I'm glad you're my friend, Janie. Thanks for putting up with me."

"Aww, look at you—talking about feelings and stuff. See, you didn't spontaneously combust or anything!" Janie laughed, then added in a softer tone, "And hey, you're not so bad. I'm glad we're friends, too. Hurry up and write your book so we can drink and be merry."

"I will work tirelessly. Right after I call Nate, text Tori, and get a good night's sleep. See ya on the other side!"

"Alright, lady. Talk soon. I'll keep the locals updated and at bay."

Katharine stuck to her word, calling Nate for one of their marathon chats. Nate told her that the foundation had received an anonymous donation for ten-thousand dollars and that they were creating a video to promote Nate's Great Cause. "You have to be in it, too, Katharine. Now that you're famous. And you can ask Mitch to be in it, right?"

Katharine didn't have the heart to tell him what was really going on, so she said, "Sure, buddy. I'm sure we can arrange that."

He saved his most exciting news for last—not only was he still seeing Alyssa, she had told him she loved him, and he'd said it back. Katharine was overjoyed for Nate. At least *one* of them had a love life. As they were about to say their goodbyes, Nate surprised her.

"Katharine, don't worry about the blonde lady. He doesn't like her."

"Oh? How do you know that, Nate the Great?"

"I can tell. Trust me, Kit-Kat."

Katharine smiled against the receiver. "Okay, Nate. Goodnight and I love you."

After they'd said their goodbyes, Katharine closed up the downstairs, shutting off lights and locking doors, then went upstairs and started a bath. As the tub filled, she sat on the edge and texted Tori:

HEY, STRANGER. HOPE YOUR
WEEKEND GETAWAY WENT WELL.
AS OF EIGHT A.M. TOMORROW,
I'M OFF THE GRID. POWER
PUSH WRITING MARATHON TILL
THE BOOK IS DONE! EMERGENCIES
ONLY, PLZ!!

A few minutes later, she responded:

GETAWAY WAS GREAT, THX!
GOOD FOR YOU, GIRL. GET HER DONE!
YOU OK?

Katharine started to respond, but another text from Tori came through:

WAIT! OFF THE GRID? YOU CAN'T GO OFF THE
GRID!! YOU-

She winced and considered how to respond. She answered the part about being okay and ignored the 'can't go off the grid' part. She was—basically—okay. Sad, more hurt than she dared to admit, and disappointed... but okay. She'd had long internal conversations in which she volleyed feelings versus facts like a tennis match. She'd rationalized and then justified, gotten mad... the whole gamut. In the end, it came down to reality. Mitch had moved on. He'd left without a word to her—not that he had any reason to do otherwise, thanks to her behavior—and they were never actually *a thing*. It was time for Katharine to stop languishing like a jilted school girl and get on with life. She tapped the phone's virtual keyboard.

ALL GOOD.
NO WORRIES, THX.
JUST READY TO GET BACK
TO WORK. TALK IN A WEEK.
SOONER IF I REALLY KICK INTO
HIGH GEAR!

Katharine hit send and set the phone on the sink counter. She turned off the tub faucet, then glanced once more at it before undressing. When her eyes slid back to the phone yet again, she snatched it from the counter and marched it into the bedroom. Katharine powered it off and set it face down on the nightstand as if it were in time out. Then she threw a tank top over it. *Out of sight, out of mind*. With a satisfied nod and a *hmpf* sound, she turned on her heel and went back to her bath. *Forget eight a.m. I am off the grid starting now.*

TWENTY-ONE

REGRETS, I'VE GOT A FEW

Mitch squinted at the sharp sliver of harsh light stabbing through the vertical blinds. His head—still on his pillow—was thick and fuzzy, like it was stuffed with cotton. Until he lifted it, that is. Then it was like a herd of tiny elephants stampeding against his skull. He dropped it back onto the soft pillow and slowly turned it away from the bright light. His bloodshot eyes landed on the near-empty bottle of bourbon and the glass tipped over beside it. A low groan eked from Mitch's dry mouth as the night before came back to him.

He'd said goodnight to the limousine driver, entered the plush hotel lobby and went straight up to his room with every intention of calling it an early night. He promptly became bored, changed for a swim, went to the pool area to find it under maintenance. He stopped at the Concierge to ask when the pool would reopen, then bee-lined for the elevators. As he pressed the round, UP arrow button, a hearty bellow from the doorway of the hotel bar halted him.

"Mitch Ford? You old son of a gun, I see you trying to sneak off. Git on over here and have a drink with us."

Mitch recognized the voice immediately. Chet Carney, old college roommate, a good ole southern boy from Atlanta, and successful voice-over actor. Mitch hadn't seen him in years. However he always recognized his voice when it rumbled through his television speakers. It gave him a good chuckle every time, too. Time and rich living had given him a big round belly and a far receded hairline, but Chet's rich baritone could still roll through a crowd like thunder.

Unlike Chet, Mitch elected to not yell across the hotel lobby, but waited until they were an arm's length before exclaiming, "Chet, you wily old goat! Had no idea you were staying here. How the hell are you, buddy?"

"Not as good as you, you sly dog, you." He turned to his two companions—a couple of shiny suit-wearers with gelled back hair and slick smiles—and introduced Mitch as, "My good buddy from back in the day." To Mitch, he said, "Old buddy, this here is Eduardo and Emilio Ramirez. They own a big chain of car dealerships, and they want me to do their commercials. What do you think of that, huh?"

He refrained from laughing out loud at Chet's pronunciation of the brothers' names—Ed-do-ardo and Uh-mel-ayo—and merely gave a noncommittal, "Very interesting. Nice to meet you both." Frankly, Mitch was a bit surprised. There was a time when Chet was doing voice work for big motion pictures and even had a steady gig narrating a highly popular nature series. A car dealership seemed to be a bit of a step down in Mitch's opinion. And where was his agent? He opted to not voice his concerns, though.

The brothers shook Mitch's hand, made polite conversation for a few more minutes, then said their goodbyes. "It was a pleasure to meet you, Mr. Ford. Mr. Carney, we hope to hear from you very soon, yes?"

"Yeah, yeah. Sure thing, boys. I'll let ya know asap. Take care, now." Once the Ramirez brothers were out of earshot, Chet leaned in conspiratorially and said, "I thought they'd never leave. C'mon. Let's you and I have a drink."

One drink had turned into four, and four had turned into shots, and shots had rolled into bourbon. It was then that Chet told him what was going on. "Trina left me, Mitch. Just up and left. I swear, I didn't see it coming. She must've been planning it for a while, though. She cleaned out the accounts, maxed all the cards, and cleared out the condo. Left me only my clothes and the DVR. What do I need that thing for, when she took all the televisions?"

Poor old Chet was in quite a state, and Mitch had felt awful for his old friend. The memories of their conversations—Mitch suddenly recalled spilling *his* guts, as well—flooded back. He even had a hazy recollection of telling Chet he'd get him a job on the Rebuilder Show. Mitch groaned as he tried to sit upright. He dropped his gaze down at himself—he was still in swim trunks. At least he'd managed to kick his sandals off. A knock at the door sent a fresh wave of stampeding elephants through his skull.

"Hang on, hang on," he grumbled. Mitch stumbled to the door, slid the deadbolt and cracked it enough to see Sam's bug-eyed face peering through. "Ugh, it's you."

"Yeah, it's me," Sam said pushing the door wider and hurrying both himself and his ever-present video camera through. This time, he brought a much smaller, hand-held version. Instead of having it pressed to his eye, it was held out low in front of him. He kept glancing up and down from the small screen to Mitch. "I have been calling you all morning. I thought—wait. You're in shorts? You've got to be kidding me." He snapped the camera closed and looked Mitch up and down, then added, "Geez, you look like sh—"

"Thank you very much, Samuel. Gimme ten. I'll—get me aspirin and coffee please—I'll hop in the shower and be ready before you know it."

Sam's lips pressed together in a tiny, hard white line and his breath whistled through his nose a few times. He bunched his fists on his hips, kind of looking like the little teapot that tipped when it got all steamed up. Mitch gave him his trademark boyish grin and waited for Sam to give in.

"C'mon, buddy, help a dyin' man out, here, will ya?"

Sam let out a big puff of air through his mouth, dropped his fists and stomped over to the hotel telephone on the nightstand. "Hello, yes, this is Room 217. Could you please send up coffee, orange juice, and aspirin? That's right. Thank you." He put the receiver back down with more force that Mitch thought necessary and turned to him with his arms spread wide. "There, Mr. Ford, sir. Is there anything else, I, Samuel the Servant, can do for his Majesty?"

"Oh, stop that, now. I had a rough night, got a little carried away. Cut a guy some slack. Geesh." Mitch shuffled to the bathroom, closed the door, and started the shower.

Sam, from outside the door called out a muffled, "Oh, don't worry, I know. Half the world knows, too."

Mitch—in the shower at this point—cocked his head and frowned. *Now, what's that supposed to mean?* He knew he'd find out soon enough. With as quick a movement as a hung-over man in his forties could, he washed up and then dried off. He half opened the bathroom door and called out, "Hey, Servant, toss me my clothes on the bed, there, will ya?" Sam whipped them at his head. *Nice, yet another person throwing things at me.*

Twenty minutes later, they were in the idling limousine. Mitch waited for the aspirin to kick in, and Sam waited for an explanation. Mitch knew this by the way Sam was doing his whole tight mouth, nostril flair breathing thing again and tapping his closed camera. He tried to recall the last time he'd seen Sam this agitated. It had to have been during the Leanne phase. He'd gotten *plenty* mad at him then. Rightfully so, as it happened—Mitch had been a tad bit off the deep end—but what was he so fired up about now?

"Mitch, how long have you and I been friends, hmm?"

I guess I'm about to get my answer.

"Um, about eight years, I think?"

"Mhm. Mhm. And how long we been working together? About the same, right?"

"Yeah, that—"

"And in all those years, how many times have I had your back?" When Mitch opened his mouth to answer, Sam held up a finger and continued. "I'll tell you. Countless. Count-*less*. That's how many. You know how I'm able to do that, Mitch? Because *you keep me in the loop*, Mitch. You give me *a heads up*, Mitch. Did you give me a heads up you were going on a bender last night—an *in public* bender, mind you?"

"Well, I—"

"No, you didn't. Did you keep me in the loop when you were offering a job to Chet Carney last night? Nope, you didn't. So, now, because you decided to go off the deep end over Katharine's little romantic dinner picture on social media, I— the guy who somewhere along the line became your personal assistant without the added pay—am answering to corporate, doing damage control, *and* being your babysit—"

"Wait. What picture of Katharine's little romantic dinner on social media? And what damage control?"

For a second, Mitch could see the entire whites of Sam's eyes. Then he slapped his hand over them and threw his head back. "Look at your phone, Mitch," he groaned.

So, Mitch pulled out his phone and began scrolling. It wasn't long before photos of him sloppy drunk at the hotel bar—a bottle of bourbon in hand, no less—and him being carry-dragged through the hotel lobby between the hotel manager and bartender popped up. They had captions like, "Star of Hit Show Hits Rock Bottom" and "Looks Like the Rebuilder Needs Rebuilding!" Then, "Is KatMitch No More?" and "Despondent Star Turns To Blonde, then Booze After Break-Up." That one had a split picture of Mitch and Leanne on one side, and his drunken stupor on the other. As the pièce de résistance, there was even a grainy video of him standing on his bar stool, raising a shot glass, and shouting, "Drinks are on me" to the mostly empty bar.

After the chagrin of *those* photos came the next blow. Several pictures of Katharine and a dark-haired, clean-cut, muscular looking man having dinner. They were gazing at each other, not the camera, and smiling. In the next, they were caught in the act of clinking glasses together, and the last, looking in the direction of the camera, blinded by the flash. These captions were no less snarky: "Looks Like the Writer Has Begun A New Chapter!" and "Life After KatMitch...You Go Girl!".

Most, if not all, of the accompanying stories revolved around speculations—who dumped who, which unnamed companion was the cause of the break-up or the rebound, and so on. Mitch reread the last one and rolled his eyes. Then he enlarged the photo of Katharine smiling. She looked radiant. Happy. The guy was alright, sure. Not the "Hunk-O-Rama" one of the captions proclaimed. Mitch scoffed out loud, then became aware of Sam's eyes on him.

"So, you didn't know about her date?" Sam asked warily.

"No, Samuel. I did not. I ran into an old college buddy, we got a little...out of hand. End of story. She—Katharine—that's, uh, good for her. That's, you know, great. Great for her."

Sam's eyebrow climbed up his forehead so far that it risked disappearing into his hair, but he said nothing.

Mitch added, "I'm serious, Sam. She's a free woman. The whole KatMitch nonsense was a media creation. It wasn't real." Then, under his breath, he muttered, "Obviously not to her, it wasn't."

Sam, for some reason, decided to cut Mitch some slack and back off. He spent the rest of the car ride making phone calls—strategizing with Justin, giving a mea culpa on Mitch's behalf for offering a job to someone, and rescheduling the appearance they were already an hour late for. Mitch had been staring out the window as Sam did all of this, but he turned back in surprise at the last call.

"You rescheduled? Won't that add more time to our stay in Atlanta?"

"You in a hurry to get back to Connecticut, or something?" The eyebrow rose again.

"No—well, yes, actually. We've got a build to finish. The family is counting on us. Besides, the sooner we're done there, the sooner we move on."

"Sure thing, boss. I'll get right on that." There was a not-so-subtle snarkiness to his tone until he added, "Oh, and good news. They're going to consider your friend for the voiceover work for the show."

Before Mitch could respond, Sam was back on the phone. In the end, he'd not only rescheduled the reschedule but moved two more interviews up. Mitch appraised his friend with a new, more appreciative eye. "Personal Assistant, huh? Not a bad idea, you know."

"*Paid* Personal Assistant, you mean," scoffed Sam. "And I still run the camera crew."

Mitch chuckled as he nodded. "I will make the request."

"Yeah, well, do it quickly while you're still the network darling." Sam tried to keep a straight face, but soon he was laughing alongside Mitch.

Relieved to have everything settled, Mitch sat back and closed his eyes. It was going to be a long, busy day, but it was just the thing he needed. Distraction was to be his friend until he could get his head straight again, and not scrambled by images of Katharine Evans. On a *date*.

TWENTY-TWO

THAT'S WHAT FRIENDS ARE FOR

Nine days had gone by since Mitch had left for Atlanta. A skeleton crew milled around the Genoma property—clearing debris, filling the dumpster, and any other odds and ends they could busy themselves with until their boss returned. Katharine knew all of this because she'd been regularly spying on them, under the guise of trimming her already well-maintained shrubs and bushes. On day ten, Brandon—aka Shaggy—caught her.

"Uh, Miss Evans?"

Katharine jumped back, letting the whip-like forsythia branches snap back in her face. "What—

I'm not doing anything. I mean, I'm not looking next door if that's what you're implying."

"I—no, you want me to trim those back? You said last month to let them grow, but—"

"That would be fine, Brandon." She strode away, trying to appear composed.

"Excuse me, Miss Evans," stammered her landscaper, "can I, um, have the trimmers?"

Katharine looked down at the hedge trimmers still in her hand, then up at Brandon. He looked as if he expected a beating. She surprised them both by laughing. "Sorry, Brandon. I'm a little out of sorts lately."

Brandon accepted the tool gingerly, perhaps fearing this nice version of his employer was a ruse. "It's okay, Brandon, I'm not going to bite. I'm sorry for being such a jerk since the first day you came to work for me. I'm not good at people-ing."

Brandon stuttered and blushed. "Aw, it's all good, Miss Evans. And so you know—anytime someone called you the dragon lady, I stuck up for you. I told them, 'Miss Evans is just a lonely, friendless person, and she always pays me on time."

Katharine blinked rapidly, then said, "Ah. Yes Right, then. Well, um, thank...you, Brandon. For...that. So, okay back to it, shall we?" She turned away and walked back to the house, her head cocked slightly. When Brandon called out to her again, she only half-turned.

"Hey, Miss Evans? I heard Mr. Ford got back into town last night. They're probably gonna start work again next door."

Katharine's heart knocked hard against her chest, but she merely nodded and continued to the back porch. Mitch was back. Would he avoid her or seek her out? Never mind him, how was *she* going to handle it? After nine days of mostly uninterrupted work, her self-imposed media and electronics semi-blackout—and those numerous pesky trips across the backyard to the tree line—Katharine had managed to complete book three of the Chelsea Marin Chronicles. It had gone off to the editor that very morning. All she could do now was wait for the first round of draft edits to come back. Usually, she dreaded the wait, but this time around, she would be kept busy by all the book signings and appearances Tori had rescheduled for her.

Tori's response to Katharine's 'off the grid' text was filled with capital letters and exclamation points. Katharine stayed firm, though, citing her need to finish the next installment of the series before momentum and interest were lost. In the end, Tori caved, but with a caveat—Katharine was to do whatever appearance she was scheduled for without complaint. So, it was with great trepidation that Katharine went into the house and picked up her phone to call Tori. She picked up on the first ring.

"Girl, it is about time you got back into the real world. You know how busy I've been, dealing with your drama?"

"Hello to you, too. And what drama? I've been holed up for over a week. I've been living on Thai, pizza, and Chinese deliveries. I could not possibly have any current drama to speak of."

"Mhm. Hang on." The was some rustling and clicks and taps on Tori's side of the phone line. Then, "Okay, put me on speaker and open your email."

Katharine did as Tori ordered. She'd sent several links and Katharine warily clicked on the first one, holding her breath. Once the images filled the small screen and she skimmed the story, she released the trapped air in her lungs with a rush. "Oh, is that all? We knew that lady was taking pictures. Love the 'You Go Girl' part."

"Now click the next one."

Katharine did. Her mouth pulled down and her eyebrow lifted. "Well, that's not very nice. A *Jezebel*? Really? Are there really t-shirts out there that say, 'Team Mitch' and 'Team Katharine?'"

"One more."

For a third time, Katharine clicked on a link. This one took her to a series of photographs of what appeared to be Mitch in a most unflattering state of being. His hair was disheveled, he appeared to be waring swim trunks, and in his hand, a bottle— undoubtedly alcohol— hung from his slack grip. He was supported by two, less than amused looking men. Katharine enlarged the picture. Even overly pixelated, she knew it was him. She scrolled through the captions, reading each aloud to Tori as if she hadn't been the one to send them to her.

"Star of Hit Show Hits Rock Bottom. Is KatMitch No—"

"Yes, I know. I've read them all. Twice. Here's the gist, Miss I-Was-Off-The-Grid. While you were playing in your little Chelsea Marin world, Justin and I have been playing the roles of Mitch Ford and Katharine Evans in the social media world."

Katharine pressed her palm against her forehead and groaned as she listened to Tori give a catalog of 'heated banter' she and Mitch had been exchanging on Twitter. Apparently, they were making veiled, passive-aggressive, yet somehow cute snipes at each other and the fans loved it. They were taking sides—hence the team shirts— and the hashtags #teamMitch and #teamKatharine had been trending since Wednesday.

"So, I use hashtags now," Katharine laughed.

"Really? I tell you all this and all you want to know is if you use hashtags? Yes, you use hashtags. Are you happy?"

"Yes, thank you," replied Katharine.

"Good, and now you are mostly up to date."

"Mostly?" Katharine braced herself. This was Tori's style—drop little bombs, let the dust settle for a moment, then drop a nuclear bomb. "What else?"

"The W.T. Taylor Gala for Literacy. It's in four days and... you're a guest speaker."

Katharine plopped down in the nearest chair. Well, at least it couldn't get worse.

"There's more, Katharine. Mitch has been added as a guest speaker, too."

Katharine made several, unintelligible sounds, then through clenched teeth asked, "Is there anything else you'd like to ruin my day with?"

"Alright, sunshine. I don't know what is going on with the two of you, but if you don't communicate before the gala, it's only going to be that much worse. I mean, the whole media thing is great publicity and all, but I'm telling you as your friend, and not your publicist—talk to the man."

"I can't. You saw the pictures of him with the Amazon blonde. He's moved on."

"Mhm. And you don't think he missed those photos of you and the hunky cop? Please."

"That's different, mine was totally innocent. They blew it all out of proportion. By the way— Ryan is a Trooper, not a cop. They get touchy about that, apparently."

"Does that really matter in this conversation? I swear, girl, you make my head spin. And *by the way*—what makes you think his pictures with the blonde aren't innocent? Or at least, not his fault. That chick has some beady eyes if you ask me."

Katharine laughed a little at that. She'd had the same uncharitable opinion when she first examined the photos. Then she straightened up. "Did you say four days? I don't have anything to wear. Oh, my God, I haven't had a haircut in nearly a year. And my nails…oh, Tori, I'm a hot mess!"

"Yeah, you probably look like a miniature Sasquatch after your little isolation stint. Relax, I'll be coming to charming East Hampton to help my wayward friend. Can't leave you to your own devices, you'll show up looking like an eighties Duran Duran groupie."

"Well first, the term 'miniature Sasquatch' might be an oxymoron, second Duran Duran was awesome and third… you are the greatest. When will you be here?"

"Tomorrow, mid-morning. Why don't you get Janie on board, too? I think this is going to require a team effort."

Katharine took no offense—it was all true. But then another wave of anxiety rolled through her. "What if Mitch brings a date? What if he brings *her*?"

"Let's not worry about that right now, okay? I can put in a call to Justin and see what he knows—*after* I find us a day spa for some pampering. I'll see you tomorrow."

They said their goodbyes and Katharine ended the call with a sigh. Interviews, appearances, a fake romance drama, and now—a gala. Her life had officially moved so far into the realm of the surreal, that nothing could surprise her anymore. Was it good or bad? She had no idea. However, if there was good to be had, Katharine was out of her shell. While she wasn't excited about the gala—all the people, the dressing up...Mitch Ford and the possibility of him with a date—she also wasn't terrified by the prospect of it all.

Over the course of one summer, twenty-plus years of anti-social behavior, a chip on her shoulder, and a giant wall had all been systematically reversed, knocked off, and torn down. If someone had told her this would happen, she'd have laughed in their face. But there she was, sitting at her kitchen table anticipating the arrival of her friend. And for a spa day, nonetheless. *Well, look at me.*

With a grin, Katharine grabbed her phone again and texted Janie.

I'M BACK ON THE GRID!

WANNA SPA DAY?

ONE CATCH—IT'S TOMORROW.

Five minutes later, there was a knock at her front door. As she walked the short distance from the kitchen to the foyer, Katharine found herself hoping it would be Mitch on the other side of the door. She smoothed her hair and checked her shirt for wrinkles or stains. She put on her most aloof, haughty expression and swung the door open, not bothering with the peephole. It wasn't Mitch.

"Janie! Hey, hi." Katharine deflated.

"Great to see you, too. Geez. Let me guess, you were hoping for—"

"Don't say it. Come on in, there's still coffee left if you want any."

Janie followed Katharine to the kitchen and chirped, "Sure, love some!" She clearly knew Katharine well enough to not push her on the topic. "So, anything...*new*? With you, I mean. Not anything—you know, with...anyone." She was also distinctly lousy at subtly.

"He's back in town. But I'll bet you already knew that, didn't you?"

"What? I—okay, yes. I went to the gym earlier and passed him on the road. He waved, I waved. So, have you—"

"Nope, don't want to talk about him. What's new with you since I saw you last?" Katharine's voice was an octave higher than her usually low tone—she could hear it herself—so, halfway through the question, she tried to make it sound more normal.

Janie blinked rapidly at her for a moment, then answered. "Oh, well, you know. The usual—boys are driving me nuts. It's that end of summer antsy-ness. They're totally ready to go back to school, but they would never admit—"

"I'm sorry, did you say you passed him this morning? On our street? Like, as in he was driving to Genoma's house?"

More rapid blinking from Janie's big blue eyes, then a hesitant, "Um, well, yes. I mean, I didn't see him turn onto—"

"And how long ago was that?" Katharine asked through what was meant to be a casual smile but resembled something slightly more...scowl-ly.

"Katharine, maybe you should go over there and—oh, I don't know—*talk to him* once and for—"

"Janie, I told you, I do not want to talk about Mitch Ford. I could not *possibly* care less about whatever it is he's doing. It's, like, physically *impossible* for me to care, so now what were you saying about the boys and school?" Katharine nodded a few times for encouragement.

"Boys are crazy. I'm going nuts, and Jimmy's studying for the sergeant's exam."

This brought Katharine out of her Mitch spiral. Janie had mentioned on one of their runs that Jim was considering applying for a sergeant's position and they were cautiously excited by the prospect. With a huge grin she said, "Janie, that is great! When is the exam?"

"Not for a couple months. In the meantime, it's study, study, study, every possible minute. Keep your fingers crossed and don't tell anyone. Jim wants to keep it on the down low in case he doesn't pass."

"Understood. Hey, did you get my text about tomorrow?"

"Sure did. That's why I rushed over. I came to say heck yes—I would just about sell an organ for a spa day, thank you—in person."

Katharine's phone chimed, and she smiled as she read the text. She waved it at Janie and said, "Well, no need to sell off any body parts. It's all set, Tori has us in at the Norwich Inn and Spa for ten a.m. tomorrow. Oh, but what about the boys? If Jim is studying—"

"Already taken care of. My dad is coming in from upstate New York to twin-sit. He was a Marine, a high school varsity football coach, and father of four boys—basically, he's the only one who can handle them."

"Wow, so you're the only girl out of five kids?" Katharine shook her head in amazement.

"Yup, and I was the baby. Imagine trying to get a date with all that testosterone? It wasn't pretty. Jimmy was the first one they sort of, kind of liked."

"Yikes. Must've been fun though. Growing up in a big family like that." Katharine was wistful. She'd sometimes wondered how different her life would've been had she grown up in a family like that. It seemed impossible to be reserved and closed off in such a large group.

As if she were using telepathy, Janie said, "Oh, yeah. Lots of fun—no privacy, no quiet time, no peaceful introspection. Just lots of yelling, a bunch of throwing things, a handful of fistfights. Oh, and tons of food. My mom was forever cooking food for us all."

Though she sounded as if she were complaining, there was a big smile on her face. Katharine smiled, too. Janie's upbringing explained a lot about her big, open personality and it made Katharine like her more.

"Speaking of food, do you want to stay for some lunch?"

Janie looked at her watch, grimaced, and stood sluggishly. "Love to, but I have to get back to the brood. If I let them feed themselves, it'll be junk food and Gatorade. I'll see you in the morning, though." They walked to the front door. Janie turned back and said, "Oh, and Katharine? Go *talk* to him, will ya?"

It was just about the push she'd needed, but as she walked out the back door onto the deck, her stomach growled at her. She couldn't talk to Mitch on an empty stomach, she rationalized. The vegetable garden still had an over-abundance of small, round, ripe sunburst tomatoes, crisp green lettuce, and plump cucumbers, so Katharine grabbed a basket and made her way over to the fenced-in garden. As she unlatched the gate, she glanced over at the forsythia bushes, noting both Brandon's absence and the newly trimmed back branches. He'd done his work, cleaned up after himself, and left quietly, like he'd been told to do back when Katharine was...*the mean neighbor lady*.

Unconsciously, every time Katharine picked a few vegetables, her eyes slid back to the line of shrubs. A dozen or so little orange tomatoes—glance. A deep green cucumber—look. Romaine, buttercrisp, red leaf—peek. When she realized what she was doing, she sighed loudly. Then Katharine got the idea in her head that maybe, just maybe, Mitch was peeking through the thick green leafed branches at her. So, she did what any woman would do. She studiously ignored that side of the yard and moved in graceful, smooth steps. She angled her face, so it would be in profile, deftly flicking her long hair over her shoulder and making her expression soft. In short, she was putting on a show.

In her mind's eye, she pictured Mitch staring at her with longing, forgetting himself and pushing his way through the bushes to get to her, ignoring the stinging whip of a long branch as it cut his cheek. Katharine was so engrossed—the scene in her mind was so vivid—that she turned expectantly to where she pictured Mitch standing, and…nothing. There was no Mitch. Only her trees and bushes, her flowers and bird feeders. Katharine swore under her breath at herself.

Ridiculous fool. He doesn't care. He's probably over there having a good laugh at your expense.

She pursed her lips and snugged her full basket against her hip, then stomped inside the house. Her lunch was made with lots of overly-hard chopping and aggressive tossing and even eaten with some unnecessary fork stabbing. By the time she'd washed and dried her bowl and utensils, Katharine had decided there was absolutely no way she would be the one to make the first move. If anyone were going to break the ice, it would have to be him.

TWENTY-THREE

ANOTHER MISSED OPPORTUNITY

Mitch turned his baseball cap backward and rested his arm against the sun-warm hood of a truck in Genoma's torn up driveway. He and Sam—along with his top construction guys—had their eyes trained on the large rectangular sheet of the blueprint. There were notes and arrows, and one bold red question mark over the section representing the kitchen. Sam's camera was propped on his shoulder and Mitch could feel it's hooded glass eye on him. He looked up, stared directly into the lens, and gave it a 'this ain't good' expression—head cocked, one raised eyebrow, half-smile/half-grimace.

"Alright, Teddy," sighed Mitch, "what you're telling me, is we can't take down this wall?" He poked a finger at the red question mark. Sam's camera zoomed in on it, then panned back to the group until he found Teddy and zoomed in again. This time on the large, round-faced man.

In a strong Polish accent, Teddy confirmed, "Tak, this is what I tell you. This support wall, no come down."

"Teddy, come on now. Where there's a will, there's a way. Vincent Genoma said his wife is a gourmet cook. She needs a gourmet sized kitchen, and *we* are not going to let her down. Posts. That's your answer. Make them look stylish but useful. Maybe even build one of them out and give her a spice cabinet."

Teddy and the others leaned in close over the blueprints, while Mitch stepped back with a small smile. It was silent but for the clanks and clatters from inside the house as the rest of the crew gutted the interior. After few moments, Teddy stated, "This will work. I start now."

Mitch clapped him on his broad back and said, "I knew you could do it. Never doubted you for a moment."

When Teddy and his crew walked away, Mitch turned to the camera and spoke. "Without fail, every build has moments like these—when something looks impossible—yet these guys figure out a way to *make* it possible. They give everything they have to these builds because they know a family is waiting, *depending* on us to do a good job. Let's take a look at how far we've come."

Sam gave Mitch the thumbs up signal to let him know he'd stopped taping. He bumped the camera off his shoulder and said, "Nice. We'll edit the segments either tomorrow or Thursday, once we get some more demo shots."

"Sounds good, Sammy. Work your magic, my friend."

Mitch's words were for Sam, but his eyes were on the tree line. Katharine was likely on the other side of that line. What was she doing? Working on her next book? Maybe she was reading, or gardening or—

"I said, are you just going to stare over at the trees, or are you gonna go over there?"

Mitch slowly turned back to Sam, who wore a knowing smirk. "What? No, I—we have a lot of catching up to do around here if we want to stick to the deadline."

"Mitch, I hate to be the one to tell you this, but there's *no way* we are going to be done that fast. We're a solid week behind. You know we always give ourselves plenty of cushion, why the rush?"

"I just want it done, okay?" Hearing the harshness in his tone, he added, "For the family."

"Sure, sure. I get it. I guessed maybe you were—oh, I don't know—trying to avoid dealing with a certain…situation."

"No, Samuel. I am *not* avoiding anyone. Any*thing*. Can we get back to work, please?"

Sam didn't push any further and followed him around back. They were shooting filler spots to introduce each new segment of the build. He also said nothing when Mitch lost his place repeatedly and needed to start over. Whenever he caught Mitch peering through the bushes, he merely cleared his throat loudly and feigned ignorance. Mitch bought none of it, of course, but they both played their respective games and acknowledged nothing.

Somehow, Mitch made it through an eight-hour day without losing his mind. Or storming through the bushes and demanding that Katharine speak to him. Later, over dinner at Angelico's, he tried to continue his noncommittal attitude, but a call from Justin opened the floodgates.

"Hey, Justin. What's up?"

"Mitch, bro, how's my favorite hombre? Um, if you have Sam the Man with you, put me on speaker."

Mitch pulled the phone from his ear and rolled his eyes at Sam as he mouthed 'Justin'. Once he tapped the speaker icon, he said, "Alright, Justin. You've got both of us. Now, what's up?"

With the phone on the table between them, Mitch reached for his beer bottle and took a swig. Justin— after a few 'bro's and 'hombre's—said, "Okay, so that gala on Sunday?"

He paused, so Mitch and Sam both said, "Yeah?"

"Right. So, Mitch, dude, you are gonna, like, present Katharine with her award, and Sam, you are gonna film it. Cool, right?"

Mitch stared at the phone as if it had grown arms and legs and was doing the cha-cha. Sam filled the silence. "Uh, award? What, uh, is the award for?"

"Oh, right. It's for, like, her work raising awareness and advocating for Down's Syndrome through her books and her charity."

Mitch finally found his voice. "Why would they have me do it? Why not her brother?"

"Oh, right, yeah. So, like, her brother is getting the award, too. It's all supposed to be a surprise for her, so don't, like, spill the beans, or anything, dude."

"Okay, Justin," said Sam quickly, "got it. We'll check in with you later." Then he ended the call before Mitch could add anything.

"This is a bad idea, Sam. For one—I can guarantee Katharine would not like to be surprised. Second, I'm not the guy she wants handing her an award. Tell him to get the guy she was cozied up with in those pictures."

"Mitch, you don't know if she's seeing that guy, or—"

"I know she's not seeing *me*. I also know this whole thing is a bad idea. I made a mistake letting the media create the KatMitch nonsense. If I'd put a stop to it in the beginning, we wouldn't be dealing with any of this."

Sam picked at the label on his beer bottle and said nothing for a long moment. Mitch was too busy stewing to notice. At last, Sam spoke. "Listen, Mitch. The media stuff—you can't control that. It is what it is. Once they get a hold of a story they like, they beat it to death. But like it or not, this time it wasn't some made up thing. It was based on a very real—I don't know—chemistry thing between you two. Everyone sees it. The *camera* sees it, man. Now, you know, I'm no romance guy. Heck, I'm basically a beer and football guy, so, this ain't easy. But, I'm telling you—you let this woman walk away, you'll regret it for the rest of your life."

Mitch opened his mouth, then closed it and nodded instead. Sam was right. It was more than a fleeting attraction. It was—well, whatever it was, it was driving him crazy. One more try. That's what he'd give it. Tomorrow, he was going to march over to her house and ask her again. Only this time, he wasn't going to act like a bull and demand her answer. He would be gentle and patient with her. Decided, he raised his bottle to Sam's and clinked them together.

Later that night, Mitch sat at the desk in his room at the bed and breakfast. He opened his laptop with every intention of working, but his fingers had a mind of their own, it seemed. In the search bar, the name Katharine Evans appeared, and within seconds, the arrow hovered over the most recent images of her. Mitch clicked on the first one—her and the dark-haired guy at Angelico's. He gripped the edge of the desk and tapped the mousepad a little harder than necessary.

After looking through nearly a dozen pictures, Mitch became annoyed with himself. *You look like a stalker, old man. Go to bed.* So, he did. It took some time before he could fall asleep, and when he finally did, his dreams were a jumbled mess of replayed conversations and bad endings. The next morning, he awoke unrested and irritable. Coffee at ECO would hopefully restore a semblance of his good-natured amiability and fortify him for his planned conversation with Katharine. Only, his plan was foiled by unforeseen circumstances. Katharine wasn't home.

TWENTY-FOUR

READ ME

"Ah, now this—*this* is what we all needed. Am I right, girls?"

Katharine sighed her answer, "Totally right."

Janie mumbled something that sounded like an affirmation. They were drinking mimosas and relaxing in a hot tub. When Tori arrived at Katharine's in the morning, she told her and Janie to pack an overnight bag. Not only had she secured a full day of pampering, but she'd also booked them a deluxe room at the Inn.

"I take it you both enjoyed your massages?" Tori laughed. "And that's only the beginning. Next up is facials, then lunch, followed by manicures and pedicures. Oh, and for something different—tarot card readings. Doesn't that sound fun?"

Katharine lifted her head from the edge of the hot tub and studied Tori from under her half-closed lids. Janie tilted her head and opened one eye. They were trying to decide if Tori was pulling their leg.

"I'm serious, you two. We are getting our futures read."

"Ugh, I already know mine—twenty loads of laundry and a weeks-worth of chaos to clean up," groaned Janie.

"A week? We're only going to be gone overnight," said Katharine.

"Says the woman with no kids. One day, one week—it's all the same when you're raising boys. Jim and my dad are great, but they're still no better than the kids when it comes to cleaning. They're probably eating pizza for breakfast, too. But you know what?"

Katharine and Tori spoke together, "What?"

"I. Don't. Care. At least, not today I don't." She drained her champagne flute to prove her point.

"Well," said Tori as she refilled Janie's glass, "make that tomorrow, too, if you can. We still need to go dress shopping for little miss Katharine over here."

Katharine lifted her head again and paid new attention to Tori. It struck her how exceptionally generous and outright coddling she'd been lately. Suspicion narrowed her gaze. "Hmm, an expensive spa getaway. Dress shopping. No muttering under your breath about what a pain I am. Something is up. Spill it, Tori."

"Oh, my Lord, girl. Look at you, all suspicious and what not. Why does anything have to be 'up'? Can't one friend do something nice for her other two friends without being treated like a—"

"Okay, now I know something's up. Let's get it over with."

"Yes," chimed in Janie, "tell her whatever it is so we can get back to indulging in the sound of silence."

Tori huffed and grabbed the champagne bottle. She filled Katharine's glass to practically overflowing, then topped off her own drink. "I'm not supposed to tell you."

Katharine raised her eyebrows and stared hard at Tori until she caved.

"Okay, fine. But you're ruining a great surprise." After a dramatic pause, Tori announced, "You're getting an award for your advocacy for Down's Syndrome."

"Oh. But—I—no, it should go to Nate! He's done all the hard work, not me."

"Oh, Katharine, you really know how to ruin a good surprise. Nate is going to be there, too. And of course, they're giving him an award. You're presenting it to him, but don't panic. I can write a speech for you. You happy now?"

She was ecstatic for Nate. He, more than anyone she knew, deserved recognition for his accomplishments. Katharine couldn't decide whether she was happy or mortified. It was certainly humbling. In all her imaginings about what it meant to be a successful writer, fame and accolades were never given consideration. All

Katharine had ever really dreamed of, was to write books that made people feel good. All she'd hoped, was to make enough money to keep writing. Now, here she was, like a diva at a spa preparing for a gala event at which she'd be receiving an award. She had friends. Oh, and she was in a pseudo-romance with a cable network reality television star—with whom she had genuine feelings for.

"Oh, that's one thing I *can* do with ease. Thank you, though. Wow, I feel like I'm living in an alternate universe. This is the absolute antithesis of everything my life was a few months ago. It's—"

"Surreal. I know," said Tori. "You gotta learn to kick back a little and let things go where they go. This is all *very* big for your career, Katharine. It's opportunity knocking at your door. But if you don't open it, the opportunity isn't going to just stand there and wait for you to want it. There are thousands of struggling writers out there that would kill for what's happening to you. So, don't curl back up into your little cocoon, you hear? This is the chance of a lifetime."

"Yeah, what she said," called Janie from the opposite side of the hot tub. Then she hiccupped.

"Okay, I think it's time to get ready for our next treatment. Come on, before party pants over there passes out."

Katharine laughed, and she and Tori helped Janie out of the steaming water. As they walked along the winding sidewalk, Katharine reached out and squeezed Tori's arm. When Tori's dark eyes met hers, she smiled and nodded. The pep talk had worked, Katharine as ready to embrace the next phase of her career and her life. Unbidden, the image of Mitch sprang to mind. There was no use denying it to herself, how she wished he would've been a part of it. But wishing wouldn't make it so, unfortunately. Katharine shook her head quickly, trying to clear the melancholy mindset and stay focused on the fun day ahead. There would be none of those heavy ruminations in such a setting as the Norwich Inn and Spa, not if she could help it.

It was as if an unspoken pact was made, and no one mentioned a word of anything Mitch Ford related. Janie regaled them with one hysterical— and terrifying—stories of marriage and motherhood. Tori spilled the enviable details of living in SoHo. When she went down the long list of celebrities she knew, Katharine and Janie practically fell out of their chairs. Tori's life was full of excitement, beautiful peoples, and action, yet Katharine found herself envying Janie's life more. A house that was a home, a husband and children... all things Katharine hadn't even known she'd desired until Mitch Ford came along. She could virtually hear her biological clock saying—

"Tick-tock, Katharine. What's your preference?"

"Hmm, I—oh, um... George Clooney." Katharine had only half heard the debate over who was hotter, Clooney or Pitt.

"Clooney, huh? I'm sticking with Pitt. He's pretty," Tori pronounced it 'purty,' and they all laughed.

"Nah, I like em rough and rugged. You two can have both of those pretty boys. I'll take a Harrison

Ford or a Hugh Jackman any day over them," declared Janie.

"Met them both. Nice guys. Hugh is even hotter in person. Just sayin'." Tori shrugged nonchalantly as Janie and Katharine gaped at her. "Life of a publicist, what can I say?"

The day went on much like that—jokes and easy banter in between spa treatments and over lunch. In all, Katharine was having a perfect day. Of course, she couldn't entirely shut her brain off from Mitch, but she was able to keep them tucked away. Her tarot card reading changed that, though.

'I am Amara. Please sit," said the dark-haired, older woman in a husky voice.

"Hi, I'm Katharine. Nice to meet you. I've, uh, never had a tarot card reading before." Katharine tucked her hair behind her ear and crossed her arms in front of her. "I'm actually a little nervous," she said.

"Yes, that is very common. There is nothing to be nervous about. Relax your body and your mind. Think of a question or a problem you would like to resolve."

"Oh, okay. Well, I'd like to know—"

"No need to tell me," Amara smiled, "the cards will know. First, choose one card from this deck. It is the Major Arcana, and it represents you. "

Katharine did as she was told, and drew one of the ornately decorated cards, flipping it as she did. It showed a woman in elaborate garb, below it, in gold script it read 'The High Priestess.' For Katharine, the card was upside down, so she had to crane her neck to read it. Amara made no move to turn it.

"Now. Take the cards and shuffle eight times. Please."

Once Katharine had shuffled them thoroughly, Amara separated the deck into three stacks. Her hand hovered over the first stack, and she asked Katharine, "Focus now only on what you want the cards to tell you."

Katharine took a deep, slow breath and exhaled. "Okay, I'm ready."

"This card represents the physical realm. It is your current circumstance." Amara swept the card off the stack with a flourish and turned it over with an audible flick. They both leaned forward and studied the card. It was a figure holding two swords. "Mhmm," nodded Amara.

"What? Is that bad?"

"This card," Amara's hand hovered over the middle stack, "represents your Mental Realm."

Like she'd done with the first, Amara flipped the card with a theatric flip. It showed the 'Page of Cups.' She nodded again and glanced up at Katharine with a small smile.

"Is that good? What—"

"The last card represents the Spiritual Realm." One more dramatic turn of the card, one last reveal. It read, 'Queen of Pentacles.'

Katharine gripped the armrests of her chair and inched closer to the table, her eyes darting from the cards to Amara and back again. The tarot card reader studied each card, nodding here, shrugging there. At last, she spoke. "You're not married, yes?"

"Yes—well, I mean, no—I'm not married. How did you know? Did the cards tell you that?"

Amara blinked at her for a moment then laughed gently. "This isn't fortune telling, dear. Tarot cards, they...well, they tell a story. *Your* story. They are for clarity and direction. You decide your future, love. Oh, and," Amara gave a pointed glance at Katharine's left hand, "no ring."

"Oh," said Katharine, her cheeks flushing pink. "So, I'm sorry, but how exactly does this work?"

"I tell you what the cards symbolize, then we figure out what they mean all together for you. In tarot, two people can be shown the same cards, in the same order, yet they can mean very different things. But never mind all that. Let us focus on you, yes?"

"Okay, I'm game."

Amara explained the meaning behind the first card she drew—the 'High Priestess.'

"The High Priestess represents your intuition, your inner voice, and your subconscious—"

"That sounds good, right?"

Amara raised her eyes from the cards and held up one finger. "The card is reversed. This changes the meaning somewhat. Perhaps you have lost your inner voice? Or maybe you are repressing feelings, hmm? This is maybe her way to get your attention again. Okay, yes? Does this sound right to you?"

Grudgingly, Katharine nodded. Amara continued. "Now, here we have the II of Swords in the physical realm. You are...hmm. Yes, you are at a crossroads, I think? You are undecided about a significant decision. Maybe more than one, I don't know." She didn't wait for a response from Katharine. "Here is the Page of Cups—your mental realm. The Page of Cups—when it is reversed, like this is—represents your inner child. It is all about feelings, emotions, and relationships." Amara *tsked*, then said, "You are a ball of conflict, aren't you? Don't answer. Based on these cards, I would say you are having some relationship issues. Perhaps you have been a bit...temperamental? Impulsive? Stubborn, even?"

"Well, I—not just *me*. Him, too."

"Mhmm. Moving on. This is the third and final card. The Queen of Pentacles. She is Earthly and represents the comforts of domesticity, family, and home. This, I think, is promising. The spirit realm sees what you long for, your heart's desire. She is telling you, it is yours for the choosing, love."

Katharine's eyes unexpectedly filled with tears. In embarrassment, she turned her head and tried to blink them away, but Amara reached over the table and grasped her wrist. "Don't be embarrassed. Your tears are confirmation that the cards have both spoken to and for you. Like I said before, this is not fortune telling. You decide your future, my dear."

Katharine, her head still down, nodded. Amara waved a tissue under her nose, and she looked up. "Thank you, Amara. That was...incredible. I feel—I don't know—lighter? I don't know how to explain it, but—"

"Good, I am glad. The tarot can be a great tool for enlightenment. Come back anytime. You may send in your friend on your way out, dear."

Katharine thanked her again and walked out onto the well-manicured grounds to find Tori and Janie lying on lounge chairs in the late day sun. As soon as she approached, Tori asked, "Well, how was it? Did she tell you that you have a tall, dark, handsome stranger in your future, or what?"

"It doesn't work like that, silly. But it was pretty amazing. Go on, you'll see."

"Hurry up, added Janie, "I want to know my future, too!"

"Didn't you hear what I said? No future telling." Katharine laughed and shook her head.

Janie shrugged, "Oh, well. I already know my future anyhow. A house full of dirty dishes, a mountain of laundry, and a bare refrigerator."

"You love it, though, don't you?" Katharine asked softly.

"Didn't you hear *me*? Dirty dishes. Laundry. Bare fridge. Blech."

Katharine gave Janie's knee a playful shove. "You know what I mean. Your life. You love it, right?"

Janie lifted her head from the chair back and looked Katharine in the eye, smiling. "I wouldn't trade it for all the money in the world. Not even for Harrison Ford. Well, maybe…kidding. Just kidding. I *do* love it, Katharine. Even when everything is insane, I love it. You know what else? I can picture you having that kind of life, too." Then, with a wicked smirk, she added, "You know, now that you're not all mean and crazy anymore."

"Janie!" They both laughed, and Katharine took Tori's vacated chair with a contented sigh.

After a short silence, Janie spoke again, the teasing gone. "You seem—I don't know—lighter, or something. Good reading, I take it?"

"Yeah, you know, it really was. Funny—that's the same word I used to describe how I felt at the end. Lighter. I think I know what I want now. Or, I guess, more importantly, I'm not afraid of it anymore. I'm ready for what's next, no matter what."

"Good for you, kid. Whatever happens, I've got your back."

"Thank you. I know you do. Now, before we get all mushy again, should we go inside and wait for Tori to come out from Madam Amara's lair?"

"Oh, my God, is she really called Madam Amara?"

"Ha, no, I made that part up. It's just Amara. You'll love her."

They'd stepped back inside when Tori walked out of the reading room. "Huh. Maybe *you* got nothin' but love for Madam Amara, but not me."

Tori crossed her arms over her chest and scowled. Janie and Katharine looked from her to each other. Katharine mouthed, "What do I do?"

Janie shrugged, and said, "Okay, let's—you hold that thought, Tori. Don't say a word about it until I come back out. Katharine, get her over to the wine tasting thing. Remember, no discussing anything until I get back." Janie burst through Amara's door and called out, "Okay Madam Amara, let's get this show on the road!"

Despite her scowl, Tori chuckled. "That girl is crazy, but she's right. I need a drink. Let's go."

The pair managed to talk about nothing of relevance, determined to wait for Janie. Otherwise, Tori would have to repeat the whole thing all over again. Less than twenty minutes into the tasting, Janie quick-stepped into the long, narrow tasting room. As she passed the Sommelier, she grabbed the glass from her hand, loud whispered, "Thanks, hon," and dropped into the chair across from them with a self-satisfied grin.

"How did you get done so fast," Katharine whispered.

"Never mind me. What's with the pout on this one?"

"I am not pouting, thank you very much," Tori replied, also whispering.

"She's right, Tor, you're definitely pouting. What gives?"

"Okay, fine. Can you believe that crazy woman said I have the hots for Justin? *Justin*? Uh-uh, no way."

Janie and Katharine widened their eyes and smirked.

"Shut up. Both of you."

"Wait," said Katharine, "Amara said you have...the hots for Justin? Like, those were her exact words?"

"Well, no. I mean, not exactly. But it was close enough." Tori folded her arms in front of her again and cut her eyes away from her two incredulous friends.

Janie took over the questioning. "Okay, honey. So, what exactly *did* she say?"

Tori rolled her eyes and shook her head, then, in a most petulant tone said, "She said I have a...*love interest*, or whatever, and it's in my workplace."

Katharine frowned and tilted her head. Janie put her hand to her mouth to hide her grin. After a moment, Katharine asked, "Okay, so...why—what makes you say it's Justin? I mean you work with lots of people so...oh. Ohhh. I see." Katharine began smiling, too.

"No. *No*, you do not *see* anything. What? Why are you two smiling? It's not funny. I don't like him. *Please*. Do you know he called me 'dudette' the other day? What kind of grown man talks like that. Actin' like we're at the beach in SoCal, or whatever. Ridiculous."

By the end of her rant, she'd trailed off and was muttering under her breath and shaking her head. Janie leaned in close, and with a deadpan delivery said, "Oh, you got it *bad*."

A loud burst of laughter erupted from Katharine. She clapped her hand over her mouth, but it was too late. The Sommelier had finally had enough of them. "Excuse me, ladies? Perhaps you might enjoy the lounge area better?"

"Are we getting kicked out of the tasting," Janie loud whispered. Tori and Katharine nodded, and the three women slowly stood up and inched their way through the other women as they stared. Janie plucked a bottle from the table on the way out and shouted, "Run, girls!" So, they did.

A few hours later, they lounged in their suite. They'd covered nearly every topic, including Katharine's vast and deep feelings for Mitch, and

Tori's for Justin. Or rather, her horror at realizing she had feelings for Justin.

"Hey, wait a minute. Janie, you never told us what Amara said to you. Spill it."

Janie picked at the hem of her thick terry robe and shrugged. "Oh, you know, the usual. I'm a domestic Goddess and whatnot. Um, let's see. Something about wanting another baby. Oh, and I have to resolve a conflict with my brother. It's no big deal though— he owes me money from when he started up his stupid home micro-brewery thing. It was a flop, just like—"

"Janie!" Both Tori and Katharine shouted.

"You want to have another baby? Why is this the first we're hearing of this? Does Jim know?" Katharine had a million questions.

"Well, it's something I just started thinking about lately. I don't know. Wait, that's not true. I do know. I really do want another baby, guys."

Katharine and Tori hugged Janie. Then they toasted her with their bottled waters, "To a future baby McNamara," said Tori.

"May this one be a girl," laughed Katharine.

"Slow down, you two. I haven't even told Jimmy yet," said Janie.

"Oh, please," scoffed Katharine, "I've seen how he is with you. You could ask him for a two-headed alligator, and he'd say, 'Whatever you want, babe.' Right, Tori? Tori?"

Tori was staring off, a small smile on her lips. She startled slightly at hearing her name. "Yes! Right, definitely."

Janie slanted her eyes to Katharine and Katharine narrowed hers at Tori. "Spill it, Tori. Something else happened at your reading, didn't it? You've had some other revelation besides your love for surfer-boy Justin."

"Eww. Don't say love. And yes, fine. There was something else, but I wasn't getting it until now. Amara said one of my cards represented, like, a crossroads or something, and based on the other cards, it looked work related. Basically, my whole reading revolved around work stuff. Which makes sense, because I have had something big on my mind—no, not Justin, before you even say it—it's something I've always dreamed of doing, since I was a little girl. But I—"

"Okay, so are you going to tell us, or are you going to keep being cryptic?" Janie threw a pillow at Tori.

"Okay, okay," sighed Tori, "I've always wanted to design clothes. And have my own boutique. I know, I know, it's ridiculous."

"Um, I'm sorry...*why* is that ridiculous? Didn't you tell me once that at least half of your clothes were handmade? And that you practically dress two of your clients? I mean, I don't think I've ever seen a more fashionable woman than you, Tori. Granted, I don't get out much..."

"But *I* do, Tori. And I read fashion magazines. You've got the magic touch. In fact, forget regular dress shopping tomorrow. You dress her in something of yours. I'll bet you have a whole closet full of stuff, don't you," asked Janie.

Tori shrugged then laughed, "Try a whole room full of them. Well, if you're okay with that, Katharine, then I am, too. Oh, and while we're there, you might want to pick out something, too, Janie."

"Me? Why? The fanciest place Jim and I go is Angelico's."

"For the gala, silly. I have tickets for you and Jim. Surprise!"

Janie's jaw dropped, and she looked to Katharine for confirmation. Katharine laughed and said, "Don't look at me, this is the first I'm hearing of it. Can you get a sitter on such short notice, though?"

Janie was already on the phone. "Daddy? Can you stay through the weekend?" A pause. She smiled, looked up at Tori and Katharine, and gave the thumbs up. "Thanks, Dad, you're the best. Love you. No, I'll call the boys before bed. Bye."

She ended the call, and all three squealed like schoolgirls in excitement. *So, this is what having girlfriends is like.* Katharine decided it was pretty awesome. In a few short months, Katharine had bonded with these two women who she, on the surface, had nothing in common with. Yet, their friendship had developed quickly and easily, without drama or mistrust. Sure, her circle was small, but at least she could say she finally *had* a circle to speak of.

They stayed up late into the night and rose surprisingly cheerfully the next morning. Tori had a driver bring them into the city, where they lunched and shopped in the comfort of Tori's beautifully decorated apartment. By early evening, they had dresses chosen, and Tori was able to do the minor alterations on the spot. They said their goodbyes-for-now and gave Tori copious thanks for everything she'd done and climbed back into the waiting car.

"Whew. I feel like Cinderella at the ball, don't you," sighed Janie as she settled back into the leather seat.

"Yes, and we haven't even gone to the ball yet," said Katharine.

They laughed weakly, exhaustion had set in. The ride home was comfortably quiet. Katharine's mind turned back to Mitch practically instantly, as if they'd been waiting for the first break in conversation. After her reading with Amara, she'd been so full of confidence and determination to tell him once and for all that she...had feelings for him. *You really need to come up with something better than that.* The doubts and insecurities began to creep in again. They'd had no contact in nearly two weeks. Unless she were to count the ongoing social media war they were engaging in via Tori and Justin. *Tori and Justin.* Now *that* was a curious pair. Katharine grinned, picturing the two together. Laid-back Justin, with his sun-bleached shoulder length, blond hair, his puka shell necklace and meditation bead bracelets. Tori, with her sharp, sleek New York style, dark skin, and elegant bearing. No question they'd *look* gorgeous together, but how would their personalities mesh?

How would she and Mitch mesh, for that matter? Assuming they'd even get a chance to find out, that is. For the nearly two-hour ride, Katharine had battling visions of best-case scenarios, and disaster scenes play out in her head, while Janie snored not-so-daintily beside her. By the time the car pulled into her long driveway, Katharine had committed to talking to Mitch. Hopefully before the gala.

TWENTY-FIVE

IT'S ABOUT TIME

"Stay still, will you? You're worse than a kid on a trampoline," Sam admonished.

"You're taking too long. Do you even know how to tie a bow-tie?" Mitch slapped Sam's hands away and turned to the mirror in the hotel's banquet foyer. He was no better at it, but he fiddled with the ends nonetheless. Belatedly, he realized he shouldn't have waited until the last minute to put it on.

"Well, somebody's cranky. Jeez. I take it you still haven't spoken to her?"

"No," Mitch scowled at Sam through the long mirror, "I haven't. I stopped by twice. She either wasn't home or wasn't answering."

"Did you try calling? Or texting?"

"No, I want to talk to her face to face. I'm old-fashioned like that."

"Or chicken," Sam muttered.

"What was that, Samuel? You know what, never mind. In thirty minutes, I'm giving a speech, and then I'm giving an award to a woman I'm not dating and haven't spoken to in two weeks, yet the media has us in some kind of lover's quarrel. Oh, and I just happen to be crazy about her—*for real*."

"So, this is probably a bad time to remind you that Katharine still doesn't know you're giving her the award?"

Mitch's head dropped. "Tell me you're kidding. Whose bright idea was that? No, don't tell me—Justin?" He looked to Sam for confirmation. "Is there anything else I need to know, Samuel? Any other surprises?"

"Ah, none that I'm aware—"

"Well, hello, handsome. Still can't tie a bow-tie, hmm?" Two slender hands reached around him and deftly began knotting the black satin ends. Warm breath tickled his ear. A pair of ice-blue eyes met him in the mirror. *Leanne.* She gave him a sly smile and added, "Close your mouth, darling. You'll catch flies."

Mitch ducked out from between her arms and pivoted away. Or at least, he tried to. She closed the gap he'd created and reached again for his half-done tie, *tsking* at him as she did. "Oh, Mitchie, don't be so jumpy. Aren't you happy to see me again?"

"Leanne, what are you doing here," he asked through clenched teeth.

"Well," she drawled, "Daddy and W.T. Taylor go *way* back. I told him I needed to go to the gala, and voila! Here I am."

Mitch closed his large hands around her wrists and gently but firmly moved them off his chest. She tried to step in closer, but he held her at bay. The doors to the banquet opened. Mitch, Sam, and Leanne all glanced over to see Katharine, Nate and his girlfriend Alyssa, Tori, Justin, Janie and Jim walk in. Though Mitch was frozen in place, his breath caught at the stunning sight of Katharine in her simple, elegant black Grecian-style gown. Her hair was in a loose, low bun. Stray locks of wavy, honey-colored hair brushed against her clavicle. A smooth ivory pearl nestled at her throat, born by a delicate white-gold chain. It was the only jewelry she wore. He was dumbstruck. And he was still holding Leanne's wrists.

He realized this in the same moment Katharine's gaze swept across the room and their eyes locked. He released Leanne's wrists, but it was too late, Katharine had seen the contact. Mitch could see her take in the visage of him and Leanne and could read her reactions as if he were inside her head. First, surprise, even a flicker of delight. Then—as her gaze fell from his face to his hands to Leanne— confusion, followed by the dawning of understanding—which was a *mis*understanding, of course. Lastly, a wall of cold disinterest fell across her features like a curtain and her eyes slid away from him and shifted straight ahead.

He made a move—even began to say her name—but Leanne cut him off with a loud, sickly sweet croon of, "My poor Mitch, what would you do without me," just as Katharine and her entourage passed them by. Only Justin spoke to him, calling out, "Hey bro, how's—" until Tori swatted him in the stomach and pulled him through the doors.

Mitch glared at Leanne, and Sam stepped forward quickly, "Leanne, sweetheart, how about I take you inside for a cocktail, okay? Please?"

"Oh, but I was starting to have fun, Sammy," she pouted.

Mitch's hands clenched at his sides, his jaw worked in fast pulses, and his face was an angry shade of red. Leanne took her cue at last. "Oh, fine. Take me to the bar, Sam. Mitchie isn't going to be any fun, I see."

They left Mitch in the grand foyer fuming and counting to ten. Then he counted to fifty. When he'd gotten himself under control, he went inside the ballroom, determined to find Katharine before the presentation began. However, he couldn't make it five feet without someone or other grabbing his arm or asking for a photograph or making an introduction. He'd made it only half-way through the room when W.T. Thomas himself took the stage and asked for everyone's attention.

"Ladies and Gentlemen. I'd like to thank you all for coming out tonight for the tenth annual W.T. Taylor Gala for Literacy."

Copious applause followed, and Mitch used the moment to push his way through the crowd of standees and waitstaff and weave around the round dinner tables. The lights had been dimmed, and a spotlight was trained on W.T., so Mitch had to offer up numerous apologies as he crushed toes and bumped shoulders. Still, he kept moving and searching.

The applause died, and W.T. continued. "As in years past, the W.T. Taylor Foundation has made generous donations to a variety of causes near and dear to us. Charities such as—"

Mitch was only partially listening; his attention was on scanning the dimly lit heads of the attendees. She couldn't have gone far. If only he knew where her table was. Meanwhile, W.T. droned on.

"Which brings us up to date. This year, we've chosen yet another invaluable organization to contribute tonight's proceeds to. But first, let me tell you a little about—"

Still no sight of Katharine. He had made it practically all the way up to the front of the room, with one table left unchecked. In the light cast off by the spotlight, he could make out Janie in her yellow dress. As his eyes adjusted, he checked off each of Katharine's table mates. One chair sat empty. Katharine was missing from the table. In frustration, he turned quickly and nearly knocked down the person behind him. Instinctively, he reached out and grasped the woman's arms, holding her upright.

"Geez, watch where you're going, will—" she hissed. She looked up into Mitch's face. It was Katharine. They both froze.

Then, suddenly, the spotlight was on them. Mitch squinted and hooded his eyes with his hand, and Katharine shook herself free of his grasp.

"Well, how about these two, huh," guffawed W.T. Thomas into the microphone. The crowd laughed and applauded. "Like a real-life Han Solo and Princess Leia, aren't they?"

Mitch grinned and waved to the audience affably, Katharine glared at him. He made a motion to her—cutting his eyes from her to the crowd and giving a quick nod—she straightened, brushed back the stray hairs from her shoulder and plastered a tight smile on her lips as she gave them all a curt wave. They seemed to love it—the spectacle of the adorably warring couple—and more laughter-mingled applause ensued.

"Well, Mr. Ford, Ms. Evans," boomed W.T. again, "this seems like the perfect time to move on to the award portion of the evening. Mitch, if you can let the woman be for a moment, why don't you come on up here?"

Katharine questioned Mitch with her eyes, then frowned a little and shook her head as pushed past him to take her seat. Mitch sighed and pulled out his neatly typed, polite, but generous speech. Once at the podium, he smoothed the folded sheet several times and looked out at the sea of tables. He could feel Katharine's eyes on him. Beads of sweat collected at his temples and he cleared his throat. Mitch looked down at the sheet of paper, where words like 'quiet and humble, humanitarian, loving sister,' swam up at him. It was the speech he'd give for an acquaintance. Not the one to give if he hoped to woo the woman he'd somehow fallen madly in love with, despite their unending series of miscommunications. He looked down at Katharine long enough to make her squirm in her seat and a ripple of feminine twitters to ripple through the crowd. He crumpled the paper and tossed it aside. Then, he took a deep breath.

TWENTY-SIX

ALL'S WELL THAT ENDS WELL

Tori had spared no expense—on W.T. Taylor's dime, of course—and hired a stylist to do their hair, and Katya the make-up artist from Connecticut Today to do their make-up. She, Katharine, Alyssa, and Janie were primped and prettied while drinking champagne. Meanwhile, Justin, Jim, and Nate drank beer in Tori's kitchen and complained about how long they were taking. At last, it was time to go. Tori had even hired a stretch limousine to travel the relatively short distance to the hotel.

The limo glided up to the hotel, and the driver assisted each of the women out of the car. Katharine was nervous, but she quickly became more and more swept up in the excitement and elegance of the event as they entered the lavish hotel and made their way to the ballroom. Massive, heavy doors separated the hotel side from the ballroom foyer. Justin and Jim pushed them open and Katharine, followed by the rest of their party, entered the anteroom.

With wide eyes, she took in the ornately framed large mirrors, the scrolled and etched molding, the marble pillars, and the crimson carpet. There was a small group of people beside the second set of doors—those that led into the ballroom itself—and Katharine's gaze fell directly on the tall man in the center. *Mitch.* Unable to help herself, she began to smile. Then, the rest of the scene registered. The woman beside him, their close stance, his hands holding hers. It was that Leanne woman. Katharine then spied Sam, he stood off to the side, looking apologetic.

I see. So, this is how it is, then. Katharine immediately switched off her emotions—a skill she'd mastered over a lifetime. She would not let this ruin her night, or anyone else's. They passed by without a word or acknowledgment, except for Justin's call out which was abruptly silenced by Tori. Once inside, the women leaned in close to comfort Katharine, but she would have none of it.

"Girls, I'm fine. Completely fine. Now I know for sure where everything stands. Time to move on. Let's find our table, shall we?"

She ignored their concerned glances and behind her back whispers and led the way through the crowd. They would not discuss him, look at him, think about him, or talk to him. Mitch Ford no longer existed in her world. That was that. Amara, the tarot card reader, was wrong. She was silly to entertain the notions in the first place. Different people, different lives, incompatible. Apparently, he was with the Amazon woman with the beady eyes, so whatever. This is what she told herself on repeat as they took the seats. Katharine ignored her friend's nervous glances, as well as the furious looking back-and-forth whispers between Tori and Justin. She didn't care. She would accept her award graciously, enjoy the rest of the evening, then go home.

"Katharine, I have to tell you something." Tori grabbed her arm and pulled her in.

"As long as it's not about you-know-who, then—"

"Justin told me Mitch is the one presenting you your award. I'm sorry, Katharine, I had no idea."

Katharine balled up the napkin on her lap and threw it down on the table as she stood. With as much calm as she could muster, she said, "I'm fine. I need to get a drink. I'll be back."

She pushed through the crowd unseeingly, her eyes on the bar. Being short worked to her advantage, she could duck and weave through everyone with relative ease. It wasn't until she arrived at the bar that her height worked against her. Katharine was blocked by a couple—a tall woman and a stout man. He seemed to be admonishing her, and she seemed to be ignoring him. They accepted their drinks, and the tall woman turned to the man beside her. *Leanne*. Lacking a better idea, Katharine quickly turned away and hurried back to her table. W.T. Taylor had begun his speech, so she justified her cowardly retreat by reminding herself that the awards portion would commence at any time.

One last show for the crowd, then I never have to speak to him again. I can do this. I'll do it for Nate, and the Foundation. Just put on a big, happy smile and look Mitch right in the eye as he—

Something akin to a brick wall slammed into her, nearly knocking her to the floor. "Geez Watch where you're going, will—"

Mitch. He had his warm, strong hands on her arms, saving her from falling. It was like déjà vu. How many times had they been in similar circumstances? Despite herself and her resolve, her heart softened. His expression was earnest and full of…something. He opened his mouth to speak. Suddenly, they were blasted with a beam of bright light. W.T.'s voice boomed over the room like the voice of God, encouraging a wave of laughter to erupt. Katharine couldn't hear what he'd said over the ringing in her ears. Mitch's hands were still on her arms. He gave a quick squeeze before letting go. She swayed slightly, then righted herself.

Another ripple of laughter and the spell was broken. Katharine remembered who he was there with, and it wasn't her. *Stop being a fool.* She couldn't keep doing this to herself. Katharine shook her head—more at herself than anything.

Mitch began to speak. "Katharine, I—"

"Let's get Mitch Ford up on stage now, shall we," asked W.T. of the audience.

Mitch looked up at the stage then out at the crowd, and back to Katharine.

"Just… go up and do what you do, Mitch." Katharine turned away and walked back to her table. She didn't look back, nor up at the stage as he took the podium. But she could hear the rustling of paper and his breath, the microphone picked up and magnified the sounds. He cleared his throat and made a small noise, like a chuckle almost. Then the distinct sound of paper being crumbled into a ball. At this, she looked up. Mitch had his eyes on her, squinting a bit at the glare from the spotlight. Her heart stuttered and kick-started hard against her chest as their gazes locked. The room—which had been awash in clinks and clatters, conversations, and laughter—was hushed in anticipation.

"Good evening, ladies and gentlemen. As you can see, I've gone and rather theatrically crumpled up the speech I was going to give you tonight. You're probably thinking, 'oh, here's the part where he makes a dramatic speech, declaring his feelings for a certain woman.' Well, you're correct. Please, if you would, indulge a man in love."

There was an audible, collective sigh throughout the room. Katharine's was the only breath being held.

"Several months ago, I met a woman. Not just any woman, mind you. She was—*is*—the most confounding, stubborn, infuriating, baffling…beautiful, incredible, smart, funny…awful, obnoxious creature I've ever met. She has thrown things at me, laughed at me, poured drinks over my head, yelled at me…I mean, by rights, I should have a restraining order against her."

Laughter blanketed the room. Katharine, she too, laughed through the surprise tears that had sprung to her eyes. Janie took her hand, and Tori handed her a tissue. She couldn't take her eyes off the man on stage. He looked down a moment, chuckling to himself. Then he gazed back at Katharine, wagging his finger at her.

"You. Lady. You are truly something." To the audience, he said, "We have had one misunderstanding after another. Miscommunications, no communications. Meanwhile, social media and the tabloids have created their own version of...us. What was the name you all gave it?"

Numerous voices called out from the room, "KatMitch!" More laughter followed.

"Well, anyhow, I hate to tell you this, but the majority of all that was made up. Or at least exaggerated. The only thing I can confirm for you all tonight, is this: I am unequivocally, madly, ridiculously and genuinely in love with Miss Katharine Evans."

The room erupted in applause and cheers. Katharine, beet red, buried her face in her hands. But she was smiling and laughing. She looked up at Mitch on the stage and viewed him with clear eyes for the first time. Brave and vulnerable, sweet and gentle. And best of all: in love with her. The applause died down, and Mitch continued.

"So, now that I have humiliated myself up here, and likely mortified Miss Evans, I'm going to conclude my impromptu speech with part of what I was supposed to say. Tonight, we honor Katharine

Evans with the W.T. Thomas Leader in Advocacy Award. Katharine, please come up and accept this award. And please…don't hit me over the head with it?"

Katharine took a deep breath, released it and made her way to the stage. She received the award from Mitch, shaking her head and smiling as she did. He stepped back and off to the side. When the polite applause died away, Katharine began. Her voice shook, then steadied.

"A few months ago, I was the woman they called, 'the mean neighbor lady,' among other things, I'm sure. They, uh, weren't wrong. I have spent most of my life avoiding…people. You could rightly say I had built a wall around myself, shutting out anyone and anything that might possibly hurt or disappoint me. I liked *safe*. Quiet. Alone. It wasn't until *that man*—back there, behind me—came along and turned my universe—my quiet, safe, one-woman universe—upside down." She turned to look at Mitch, took a deep and shaky breath, and said, "You see, I uh, I fell head-over-heels for Mitch Ford the moment I saw him," She turned back to the audience again, fighting past the tremble in her voice, "and that made me feel…angry. I didn't want to *fall* for anyone—especially not a guy who lives under a spotlight. I wanted to be left alone. But something weird happened, and alone began to feel…lonely. Then two amazing, persistent and patient women came into my life, and made me realize it wasn't so terrible letting people in." Katharine sighed and paused. "Anyhow, Mr. Ford is as equally confounding, infuriating as he claims me to be. And he is way more amazing and incredible, too."

The audience '*awwed*' and clapped. "Now that we've both taken a turn at public declarations, I'll move on to the planned part of *my* speech. There is only one other man I know who embodies those qualities. He has taught me—or tried to teach me—what it means to forgive, to be generous of heart and spirit, and to do unto others as you wish done to you. He is brave and smart, and incredibly kind... he's my big brother. Nate Evans, please come up and accept this award for your work with Nate's Great Cause!"

Everyone in the room stood and applauded Nate. Alyssa kissed his cheek and beamed. Katharine's heart was fuller than she'd ever dreamt possible as she watched Nate cross the stage. She handed him the award, hugged him tightly, and then stepped back to stand beside Mitch. Katharine gazed up at him, and he winked, then put his arm around her and placed a soft kiss into her hair. Together they watched as Nate gave a beautiful, eloquent acceptance speech. Katharine had to use the handkerchief Mitch subtly handed her to dab her eyes periodically.

Once offstage, Katharine and Mitch were pulled in different directions, it seemed everyone craved a piece of their time. They laughed and shrugged helplessly from across the room at one another. As much as she longed to be by Mitch's side, Katharine discovered a new confidence. A kind of inner calm settled inside her. They had nothing but time.

"Miss Evans! Over here, please," called yet another patron of the event. Katharine huffed good-naturedly and turned to greet yet another new face. As she did, she caught sight of Leanne the Amazon stomping toward the doors with Sam close on her heels. Her smile grew. *Good riddance.*

The rest of the evening went by in a blur, and suddenly they were being shuttled into the waiting limousine again. Katharine searched around in vain for Mitch, but she couldn't find him. "Wait," she called out as the attendant handed each of them into the car.

"Sorry, Miss, we have a long line of cars waiting. We have to keep everyone moving," he replied.

Katharine sank down next to Tori, feeling a little bit crestfallen. A short while ago, the man of her unrealized dreams had told her—and an entire audience—that he loved her. Now she was in a limo with her nearest and dearest, but Mitch was nowhere in sight. It was too surreal to believe.

"Um, Katharine? Your purse is buzzing," said Janie.

Katharine fumbled with the clasp, frowning slightly. Everyone she knew was right there in the car with her. Everyone except…

"Mitch," she breathed into the receiver. The downturned corners of her mouth reversed into a smile.

His voice, like warm honey, spoke softly, "Hello, you. Trying to sneak off on me, hmm?"

"No, I—"

"I'm teasing, Miss Evans. May I call on you tomorrow morning?"

"Why, yes, Mr. Ford, you may. Goodnight, Mitch."

A chuckle on his end, then, "Goodnight, Katharine. Sweet dreams."

Katharine sighed dreamily and fell back against the seat, phone pressed to her heart. She bit her bottom lip in an attempt to contain the fit of girlish giggles that threatened to burst from her chest and stared unseeing out the tinted window. A small cough suddenly reminded her she wasn't alone. Slowly, she turned her head. Six pairs of eyes, six stifled smirks greeted her.

"Oh, shut up, all of you!"

They all erupted into laughter, Janie, Tori, and even Alyssa climbed over the men to give Katharine hugs. The guys laughed, rolled their eyes and shook their heads as the women squealed and talked over each other.

"Oh, my God, Katharine that was so romantic—" sighed Janie. Then, "I hope you were taking notes, Jimmy."

"It's about time you two got on the same page," said Tori.

"Mitch Ford is really good looking in a tuxedo," giggled Alyssa.

"Hey, what about us," asked Nate.

"Yeah, yeah, you boys clean up pretty well, too," Tori pacified, then rolled her eyes. "Anyhow, girl, that man had every woman in the room swooning. You are one lucky lady, Miss Katharine Evans. Now, don't blow it."

"Gee, thanks for the vote of confidence. It was kind of swoon-worthy, wasn't it? I mean…is this real life?"

Katharine laughed and shook her head again. The smile hadn't left her face, though. It was there when they said goodbye to Tori and Justin at her apartment building. It remained on the drive back home with Jim, Janie, Nate, and Alyssa. And still, after they'd dropped her brother and his girlfriend off at his place. When she'd closed her own door behind her and leaned against it in happy exhaustion, she suddenly realized her cheeks hurt. Apparently, her face was unaccustomed to so much happiness.

Her eyes traveled the familiar terrain of the living room, the staircase, the kitchen. She looked down to see her award clutched against her chest and pushed it away a bit to read it. The gold etching glowed in the warm overhead light of the foyer—

"In Honor of your exemplary leadership in advocacy for Down's Syndrome Awareness and Education, the W.T. Thomas Foundation *grants you with the* Leader in Advocacy Award…"

Katharine's eyes swam with tears once again. She'd never done anything for the sake of awards, but she couldn't deny it was nice to receive one.

"Okay, you big sap. Back to earth," she said aloud. Katharine brushed the tears away, pushed off the door. Setting the plaque on the ledge and bracing herself, she kicked off her right high heel and then her left, not caring where they landed. She pulled the pearl crusted hair clip out, shook her hair free, and yawned. Once upstairs, she changed into her favorite pajamas—thin, baggy, bunny-face covered sleep pants and faded Frankie Says Relax t-shirt—washed her face and brushed her teeth. She climbed into bed and grabbed a book off the nightstand, knowing full well she'd never retain anything she read. She needed something to make her drowsy enough to sleep… or at least distract her from her happy ruminations and giddy anticipation of tomorrow. After a few minutes, she slapped the book shut and set it on the nightstand with a thud. Katharine next fluffed her pillow, slid down between the soft sheets and turned on her side. She squeezed her eyes shut, and tried to focus on her breathing—inhale slowly, count to five, exhale slowly, began again—but another part of her mind imagined Mitch's voice calling her name, like Romeo outside her bedroom window.

"Katharine!"

Suddenly, Katharine sat up. She cocked her head. She heard it again— "Katharine!"

She swung her legs out from under the covers and stood, then tip-toed to her bedroom balcony sliding door. The nearly full moon shone through the thin curtain. Hesitantly, Katharine pushed it aside and slid open the door. As always, her gazed was immediately pulled to the lake. The sight didn't disappoint—dark water rippled gently in the silvery-blue moonlight, causing Katharine to feel like she was at a ship's helm and sailing through the night.

She let her gaze drop, first to her small dock, then to her hydrangeas. Then, just like Romeo in the famed story, *him*. Mitch, standing in her backyard, still in his tuxedo, smiling up at her with a handful of daisies. He lifted them up toward her and called up, "I picked these for you. No bees, I checked. Also—full disclosure—I picked them from your yard. Sorry."

"Mitch? What on earth are you doing here now? At this time of night? Are you drunk?"

"Yes, Miss Evans, I am. I am drunk on love. And by my watch," he looked down at his watch, "it's now two a.m. Therefore, it is tomorrow morning."

Katharine laughed down at him, "You're crazy. You know that, right?"

Mitch shrugged and grinned, and said, "I couldn't wait any longer. But... I could leave and come back later if you—"

Katharine turned and went back inside, then rushed down the stairs, to the back door and out onto the deck. There, she paused, bit her lip and looked down at herself. She was in her ratty old pajama's, and the man of her dreams was standing in her yard in a tuxedo. She looked up again, and Mitch was standing in front of her.

"Ballgown, bunny pajamas...it doesn't make a difference, Katharine. To me, you are beautiful."

"Oh, Mitch. After everything I've said and—"

"None of it matters. I said it in front of a roomful of people, and I'll repeat it now. I am crazy about you. I admit I'm practically dying to know if *you* meant what you said on stage tonight. Because, if you were playing along for the whole KatMitch thing, I understand. And if you're not ready to tell me how you feel, that's okay, too. I won't pressure you this time. Oh, and—"

"Mitch, I—"

"No, nope, hear me out first, okay? Then, I'll leave. Katharine, the moment I saw you, I didn't just think it... I *knew* you were the one. Even though you were this furious little ball of fire, I remember thinking, 'by God, isn't she beautiful, though.' I tried to deny it, ignore it, excuse it...nothing worked. You have been on my mind twenty-four seven, woman."

He clasped his hands together, flowers and all, and continued. "But here's the thing I've finally gotten through my thick skull: I *know* you build a wall around yourself to protect you from all the lousy things people do. I get it that it's hard for you to trust. So, I *can* be a patient man, Katharine. I'm not going to try to force you to talk again. I will give you the time you need to figure out how you feel, and I'll wait for you to be able to say it in your own way." Mitch paused, taking a deep breath.

Katharine used the moment to break in. "Are you done yet?"

Mitch opened his mouth, but she quickly spoke again. "Good, because I have some things to say to you, too." She rushed on, afraid he'd start again. "I wasn't playing the...KatMitch role up there on the stage, Mitch. I meant what I said." She smiled watching the tension leave his shoulders. "The moment I saw *you*, my heart practically stopped. Then, yes, I threw a soccer ball at you. And yelled at you. *And* was really mean, for a really long time. I'm sorry for all of that. I'm sorry for all the misunderstandings, miscommunications... everything. They were my fault, every single one. If

I hadn't been so—I don't know—closed off from the world, maybe I'd have better social skills. But I don't. You were right when you said I'd built a wall around myself. It was a massive, towering barrier."

Katharine shook her head and looked away, then back at Mitch, "But not anymore. I'm not—I don't want to be that woman anymore." She stepped down off the deck, took Mitch's large hand between hers, and looked up into his eyes. "*You* changed all that. Suddenly, I have visions of a very different kind of life. One with friends and family... and love. I've made friends, Mitch. Now, I'm ready for love."

"So," Mitch began cautiously, "you do mean with me, right? Not that guy—"

"Mitch Ford, you idiot, I'm in love with *you*. Completely, ridiculously, totally. I... love... *you*. There, are you happy now?" Katharine blushed furiously, and her heart beat like a tom drum, but she kept her eyes locked on his.

Mitch tossed the daisies on the deck. He cupped Katharine's face, his gaze and smile so full of gentleness, and brought his lips close to hers. He whispered, "And I love you, Katharine Evans," then, under the moonlight and stars, he kissed her

EPILOGUE

ONE YEAR LATER

"Here, Mitch. *You* hold the baby for a bit."

"Wait, I—"

"Oh, don't be a chicken, Mitch. It'll be good practice for you," Katharine laughed and patted her growing bump.

"Alright, Janie, hand over that little football. I'll show you two smarty pants," said Mitch as he set down his red, white, and blue cup and reached out to take the swaddled bundle.

"Okay, see, now *that*," scolded Katharine with a playful laugh "that little football is a girl, first off. Second, her name is Juliette. If *we* have a girl—"

"I'm going to teach her how to throw a football, change a tire, and built a house from the ground up," finished Mitch with a smug grin.

"Good," replied Katharine, "I would expect no less. Wait until she's at least three before you do all that, hmm?"

They were on Katharine's—Katharine *and* Mitch's—back deck, soaking in the midsummer's sunshine. Their gatherings had become practically a weekly event over the summer, with some new additions to boot.

"Hey, look who I found at the front door," called Jim from the slider. "just in time to help me set up the fireworks for tonight."

"Surprise!" It was Nate and Alyssa, followed by their new neighbors, Vinnie and Caroline Genoma and their kids.

"The addition is coming along great, Mitch," said Vinnie.

"Thanks, buddy. It's coming along. My wife," Mitch wagged his thumb in Katharine's direction, "is finally starting to see my genius."

"You made it," called Katharine as she crossed the yard. "Unfortunately, you're right on time to hear Mitch brag. She shoved him with a laugh and added, "Fortunately, it's also time to eat, too."

"Well, *almost* time to eat," said Tori from beside the grill, "Justin here thinks he's the Barbeque King of Connecticut after living here for only four months."

Everyone laughed, including Justin. He pointed at Mitch, "Your fault bro. You turned us into a bunch of Stepford husband's over here in CT."

There was some truth to the statement. One year had brought a great deal of change to all their lives. Mitch and his crew finished the Genoma rebuild three weeks after the gala. Two months after that, he and Katharine got married at Angelico's under twinkling Christmas lights, in front of their families and friends. During the post-vow festivities, Janie announced that she and Jim were expecting, and Tori announced that she and Justin were officially together and that she would be leasing the storefront next to Po's Rice and Spice.

"But that's such a long commute," Katharine had fretted.

"Actually, it'll be a few steps away. We'll be renting an apartment on the second floor. Justin will keep his place in the city so he can commute when necessary." Then, as casually as if she were commenting on the weather, she'd added, "Oh, and since I have to keep an eye on my sole client—author of Number One Best-Seller in Young Adult, Miss Katharine Evans—we're house hunting in the area."

Janie and Katharine had stared at her with jaws dropped, then in a flurry of hugs and girlish squeals, they congratulated her. Three months later, over coffee at ECO, Katharine announced that she and Mitch were expecting.

Tori couldn't help but tease, "Is that your way of postponing book signing events again?"

Katharine pretended to think for a moment, then said, "I dunno. Would it work?"

Tori's raised eyebrow told her it would not. Turning to Janie, she said, "Alright now, on to you. Do me a favor and tell baby McNamara in there to come out in time for Katharine and Mitch's Fourth of July party, okay?"

Lo and behold, they were all there for the party. Janie had her baby with weeks to spare, Tori and Justin had signed the papers for the house at the end of the street, and Katharine was beginning to show. Katharine smiled—her eyes shining—at her new life. One year and her whole universe had changed. It had been inconceivable at one time, and yet here they were. Knowing her as he did, Mitch—her solid, very real, sweet husband—took her hand and whispered in her ear. "Yes, sweetheart, it's real." Then he kissed her temple and rested his hand on her belly. "This is our life now, and I wouldn't trade it for anything in the world."

Katharine wrapped her arms around his waist and nestled her head against his chest, sighing contentedly.

"Neither would I, Mitch. Neither would I."

ABOUT THE AUTHOR

Elsa Kurt is a multi-genre, indie & traditionally published author of six novels, including book one of her YA, modern-day fairy tale, Into the Everwood. Elsa began writing in 2012, releasing her first children's book in 2013. Since then she has made writing her full-time career. In 2018, she has several novellas published through Crave Publishing in their Craving: Country Anthology and Crave: Loyalty Anthologies. She has also penned several children's books under the name Melanie Cherniack. In addition to writing, Elsa began her igoodhuman brand—positive, inspiring & uplifting message apparel. She is a lifelong New England resident and married mother of two grown daughters. Elsa can be found across social media:
https://facebook.com/authorelsakurt/
https://instagram.com/authorelsakurt/
https://twitter.com/authorelsakurt
https://www.goodreads.com/author/show/15177316.Elsa_Kurt
https://allauthor.com/profile/elsakurt/
https://amazon.com/author/elsakurt
and her website, http://www.elsakurt.com